"I am now giving every lad that knocks on for my daughter the evil eyes, and I've nailed her bedroom window shut"

ANDY WILKINSON

"It's like 'Raining Stones' and 'Shameless' rolled into one"

SMUG ROBERTS

"Sex, violence and fractured relationships, a kitchen sink drama that needs to be told and a fresh voice to tell it"

TERRY CHRISTIAN

BROKEN

YOUTH

A novel by
KAREN WOODS

EMPIRE
PUBLICATIONS

First published in 2010

EMPIRE PUBLICATIONS
1 Newton Street, Manchester M1 1HW
© Karen Woods 2010

ISBN 1 901 746 63 1 - 9781901746631

Printed in Great Britain by the MPG Books Group, Bodmin and King's Lynn

In memory of my stillborn son Dale,
Peggy Price, Sydney Price,
Michael Reddington, Eunice woods,
John Woods & David Woods

They have all been
inspirational in my life.

'If you do what you have always done,
You will get what you have always got'

About the Author

M Y NAME IS Karen Woods and I live in New Moston, Manchester. I am 40 years of age. I grew up in Collyhurst and Harpurhey living on a council estate. Those days will stay with me forever and I will never forget my roots. I have four children Ashley, Blake, Declan and Darcy.

Acknowledgments

T HERE ARE SO many people who have inspired me to follow my dreams of writing this book – first and foremost Christine Ansell. She was my English Tutor and works at MANCAT college. Having left school at 14 with no qualifications, I always knew I wanted to write a book, so thanks to Christine for providing me with the skills to achieve my dream.

Once I had completed an adult literacy course it was like a fire burning inside my belly and I knew I had to follow my dreams. I have two brothers, Alan and Darren and we all grew up together on a council estate. My parents, Alan and Margaret, split when I was 13 years old. Both my parents are really proud of me and have supported me throughout.

I used to work as a nail technician, until I started my job at Manchester City Council five years ago where I now work as as senior supervisor. My life and the cards life has dealt me have given me the tools to write this book and I hope to inspire women worldwide.

I would also like to thank James, Julie, Denise, Ken and Sue. They have pushed me and made all this possible.

CHAPTER ONE

"GET OUT OF that bed. You lazy cow, otherwise I'll fuckin' drag you out of it." This was the sound which filled Misty's ears as she hid her head under the pillow, hoping it would drown out the sound of her mother's piercing voice. Her heavy eyes felt like two iron shutters had closed over them, as she lay lifeless in bed.

"Are you getting up?" her mother shouted.

"Yeah chill out will ya" she replied, as she dived into her wardrobe, pretending to look for her uniform as her mother hurried into her bedroom watching her every move.

"I'm up, so stop shouting and leave me to get ready in peace will ya," she shouted in a stressed voice. Her mother left the bedroom, muttering under her breath but Misty couldn't be bothered with the arguing, so she collapsed into her wardrobe, searching for her school uniform, a job she should have done last night but the call of her friends had been stronger.

Sunday was pub night for Misty and her friends. Misty was only fifteen but with the help of makeup and her mother's high heeled shoes, she could easily pass for eighteen. She wasn't naturally the prettiest of girls but there was something about her that was pleasing to the eye. She was a typical fifteen year-old girl from Manchester and full of teenage attitude.

Misty found her uniform and ironed it, she knew she

must hurry; otherwise she would miss the school bus. Her head was banging and her legs were unsteady as she stood ironing. This job usually took only five minutes but today it seemed like it was taking forever. She considered pretending to be ill but her mother was like Juliet Bravo and would have seen right through her efforts to fake an illness.

Swaying into the bathroom, she held the door frame to steady herself. Once inside she began to brush her teeth. Looking down at the toothbrush she examined it closely, it had well and truly seen its day. The bristles were flat and looked like an elephant had sat on them, but needs must she thought, as she squeezed on the toothpaste. Her mouth felt raw after brushing her teeth and the taste of the toothpaste made her heave into the sink. As she looked into the mirror, she could see how bad she really looked. Taking a facecloth she rubbed her eyes trying to remove any signs of the night before, up and down she rubbed and side to side, until most of the makeup had disappeared. She knew if her mother found the remains of it on her face, she would be in deep shit. As she brought her face closer to the mirror, she focused on her eyes and pulled down her eye-lids with her fingers. The veins on her eyeballs reminded her of the cartoon characters from when she was a little girl. This was going to be a tough day.

Every inch of her body felt like bricks had been tied round it and any movement was painful. Finding her knickers she finally started to get ready. The knickers were old and grey and one wash from the bin, her mother had bought her days of the week knickers and by the state of them they should have been called months of the year knickers because she'd had them far too long now. As she examined them closer, she noticed that all the elastic had frayed off the legs. So pulling hard she removed all elastic and repaired them making them look half decent. Looking at the bra she held it up to the light and she could see that was also grey from over washing. "Oh fuck it, who's going to see it", she thought as she placed them onto her aching body.

Misty hurried to get ready and started to brush her long dark hair. Her hair was quite unique. It was only when you looked at it closely, you could see it consisted of mahogany sprinkles throughout and dark red highlights. Many people had made comments about it and it was Misty's crowning glory. Combing her long hair, she reached for the elastic she had rescued from her knickers and laughed to herself, "needs must" she thought as she connected both ends of the knicker elastic and placed into her hair, making an excellent ponytail from it. She checked herself one last time in the mirror and knew she was ready for inspection. So with a jump in her step she headed down stairs to meet her mother and the rest of the family.

Her mother had a face like thunder as she started to speak. "I'm fuckin' sick to death of you Misty" she shouted. "You need to get all your stuff for school ready the night before and then you won't be rushing each morning. You go to bed early enough, so there is no reason why you should be tired each morning". Misty agreed but unknown to her mother she had sneaked out of her bedroom window and joined her friends for a night in the local pub. This was routine for Misty. Every Sunday night she would wait for her mum to go to bed and once she knew she was asleep, she would climb out of her window and join her friends in the local, knowing that her Mum was dead to the world till the following morning. By the time Misty returned nobody would be any the wiser.

Everybody left the family home at the same time each morning. Misty's mother Lisa had to be in work early, so for that reason, she ran a tight ship so that everything ran like clockwork. Lisa loved the routine of daily life. Things were hard for her at the moment, as she was a single parent and her job in the supermarket kept the family afloat in more ways than one.

"Your bus is here" she shouted. She kissed her two eldest children on the head and watched them safely board the bus before she continued on her mission to get the smaller children to school on time. Lisa's children were her world. Max was sixteen and Misty fifteen and the two younger boys, Jonathan and Lee, were ten and five respectively. Lisa was like a corporal with her children and since she had been flying solo, it was her way or the highway.

Misty and Max boarded the bus that travelled down Rochdale Road collecting all the school kids. Once they had boarded they ran up the stairs to sit at the back of the bus. Max then pulled out his prize cigarette that he had stolen from his mother's bag earlier that morning. Reaching down into his sock, he pulled out several matches, ready to light the cigarette. Misty watched eagerly as she knew he would share it with her as he usually did each morning. He lit the cigarette and she watched as he took a deep drag, it seemed forever before he finally exhaled. She waited patiently and knew he would soon pass it to her. Max had become the head of the house since their father had left them. Nobody had officially given him the job but he took it on himself to be the man of the household. Max was quite a loner and he found it hard to laugh and have fun with his siblings, as this could be seen as a weakness, so he liked to keep himself apart from them whenever possible. He passed Misty her share of the cigarette and watched as she smoked it, making her feel quite uncomfortable.

"You better not fuckin' grass, nobhead" he said in his deep voice.

"I won't, how can I grass on you when I'm smoking too ya muppet?"

"Just checking," he snarled as he went to join some of his mates, who had just boarded the bus.

Behind his friends appeared Francesca, who was Misty's best mate and partner in crime. Francesca had also been out the night before in the local pub and judging by her expression, she also had the hangover from hell.

"Oh my god I feel so rough. My mouth feels like Gandhi's flip-flop," she laughed as she sat next to Misty. Francesca now opened her mouth and shoved it into Misty's face revealing her discoloured tongue. They both laughed as she shouted, "Look it's got fur on it". Francesca made herself comfortable before she began to ask about the night before.

"Did you get back in alright last night?" Misty nudged her right into the side of her waist, telling her to shut up, as she didn't want her brother to overhear their conversation, because if he found out about their antics, he would make her life a misery. The girls laughed as they sat on the back of the bus. Misty now felt worse than ever and knew it was going to be a long day.

The bus arrived at the school and all the kids ran down the stairs, pushing and shoving each other out of the way. Some of the older lads were pulling the girl's ponytails as they went down the stairs, this was a usual prank the lads played each morning. Remembering her knicker elastic in her hair, she grabbed her pony tail and held onto it for dear life fearing the lads would notice it and she would be the victim of endless jokes, which the entire school would have joined in on before the end of first break. Luckily she escaped their grasp and left the bus with her ponytail intact.

The noise of the pupils filtering through the gates of St Thomas More High School was similar to a crowd of football fans entering the grounds for a cup final, they were all singing and shouting and pushing each other around calling each other muppets and dickheads. The teachers who were on gate duty that morning looked like they had the worries of the world on their shoulders. You could tell by the expressions on their faces that they just wanted to be in the staffroom chilling with all the other teachers. The children now made their way to the main assembly hall, this was the highlight of each morning. The hall was large with around two hundred and fifty chairs set out in rows of twenties all facing the stage.

The morning assembly took place and the teachers spoke of worldwide news and the suffering of others. Misty wanted to shout out that she was also suffering from a hangover and to hurry up with the speech but she thought twice before she put her mouth into gear, as it had landed her in so much trouble lately. She also couldn't take the chance of having her parents summoned to school once again. The assembly finished and the two girls headed to their first lesson. The corridors were overflowing with children trying to make it to class before the bell rang. Francesca grabbed Misty's arm and led her into the toilets away from prying eyes.

"Misty, you won't believe what I done last night." Knowing she had the full attention of her friend, she continued, "go on try and guess".

Misty's face was a blank, she didn't have a clue what she was going on about. She shrugged.

"I got shagged" she shouted but then remembered where she was and lowered her voice. Misty's eyes danced with excitement as Francesca continued. "Well I was sick of being a fucking virgin and it had to happen sooner or later, so I thought fuck it, it's now or never". Both girls held each other and danced round the toilet, celebrating Francesca's night of passion. Not having any time left to talk, they both hurried to their lesson and agreed to meet at break time, so they could speak in more detail. Misty couldn't believe what her friend had done.

"You're fuckin' mental Francesca!" she laughed as they both went separate ways to their lessons.

Misty took her seat in class. She knew she wouldn't be

taking part in this lesson and headed for the back of the classroom. Sitting at the wooden desk, she took out all the books needed from her bag and placed them on her desk. This would be a decoy for the teacher she thought, as she made herself comfortable ready for a sleep. The lesson began and Misty placed her head onto her folded arms. It was time for sleep, she thought as she rested her head onto her arms hiding her face from the teacher.

Drifting off the night before came flowing back into her mind. Misty and Francesca had been dancing away in the local pub when two lads had come to join them. They introduced themselves as Kevin and Gordon. Both were kind of hunky but as usual Francesca grabbed the better looking one, who introduced himself as Kevin. His mate was called Gordon and so as not to let the team down Misty danced with him so he wasn't left alone. Throughout the night they enjoyed their company and had a really good time. Both girls hid their ages because if the lads found out they were only fifteen, they would have classed them as jailbait and kept well away. Misty already had a boyfriend whose name was Dominic and also went to the same school. They had been going steady for around eight months and she knew he thought the world of her. She had felt guilty dancing with another boy but 'what's a dance' she thought. You couldn't class that as cheating and she had continued to dance with them with her conscience clear.

As the night in the pub ended the two lads had plans for Misty and Francesca. Kevin grabbed hold of Francesca's arm shouting "Hey you're coming with me!"

Francesca laughed, "Why would I want to come with you?" He now reached for her and swung her around whilst whispering sweet nothings into her ear.

"I have got a surprise for you if you want to see it"

"Where is it then?" She replied eager to see.

"Feel inside my trouser pocket and you will feel it". As she slid her hand into his pocket both boys laughed, as they knew exactly what was going to happen. She felt around and round searching for her present but still couldn't find anything. "More to the left", he laughed and then she finally found it.

"You dirty bastard!" she shouted as she squeezed his willy tight, making him beg for forgiveness.

They all laughed and both couples went their separate ways. As they waved goodbye, Francesca walked off arm-in-arm with Kevin without a care in the world, ready for a good time with her new found friend. Misty looked at Gordon and smiled, "Do you want to walk me home then?" she asked in a cocky voice, as she didn't fancy walking home on her own at this late hour.

"Erm, go on then but first I need to look at something". Misty could tell he was rather agitated before he spoke again. "Do you want to come with me, we won't be long?" Misty wanted to head home but she was interested as to where he was going, so she agreed wanting to know more.

"What have you got to look at?" she asked. He smiled and took her by the arm pulling her closer to him.

"I hope you're not a little shit bag Misty." Misty now felt a little scared of what he had planned for her but followed him just the same.

"No way, I'm not scared of anything" she replied but you could tell by the concern in her voice she was shitting herself.

Gordon was fairly handsome and his overall appearance seemed smart enough but his eyes had something special about them. They seemed to sparkle with excitement and twinkled when he looked at her. He was eighteen but he looked older. She found his stubble very appealing. Misty knew she should be heading home but she felt excited by Gordon, something about him made her tingle inside and she wanted to please him, so off they went to his secret destination.

Gordon walked at a fast pace and Misty struggled to keep up. "Slow down will you, what's the fuckin' rush?" she shouted, as he turned to wait for her. Gordon looked uneasy and told Misty to wait at the corner of the street. "Where are you going?" she shouted but he never replied, he just disappeared into a nearby alley. The night air felt cold now and the streets were dimly lit, as she stood waiting.

Misty stood on the corner, swaying as the signs of alcohol started to take effect. 'Where the fuck is he?' she thought as she squeezed her legs together, bursting for a piss. She could see a car approaching and watched as it picked up speed, heading towards her. It looked like it wasn't going to stop, Misty's heart went into her mouth as she moved from the roadside to protect herself. Then the passenger side door flew open and she could hear a voice shouting.

"Get in, ya knobhead," Misty had to look twice, before she recognised the face of Gordon, "fucking hell, hurry up" he shouted, as she took her place in the passenger side, slamming the door behind her. Gordon drove off at speed and headed onto the main road.

Still nervous Misty began to speak "I didn't know you had a car?" He smiled at her as he turned the radio up to drown out the sound of her voice. Misty looked round the interior of the car and noticed all the wires hanging down under the steering wheel positioned between Gordon's legs, and that's when the penny dropped.

"Is this your car?" she asked anxiously. He turned to face her and sniggered but never replied.

"Have a look in the glove compartment; there is usually some music in there". Following his instructions she looked inside and pulled out several cds, as she did, Gordon looked pleased at her find and told her to change the disc.

Their journey lasted for at least an hour and his driving became quite dangerous as he weaved in and out of traffic. Misty felt her heart in her mouth on a few occasions and wanted him to stop. She knew she had to think quickly and an idea came to her.

"I need a piss. You will have to pull over before I wet meself" she shouted but the sound of the music drowned her out. Gordon carried on driving before he slowed down as he entered a dark side street.

"Come on then pissy arse" he laughed as he drove the car to a sudden halt. Misty opened the car door and hurried to a nearby fire escape that was set in darkness and out of sight from Gordon. Pulling her knickers down just over her arse cheeks, she squatted. She could just about see the car and watched as Gordon rummaged around in the front of the car. She finished, shook her bum to remove any drips, yanked up her knickers and made her way back to the car.

Sitting herself back in the passenger seat, her eyes were drawn to the empty place where the radio used to sit. "Where's the radio?" She asked and Gordon pointed to the back seat. "I can sell it tomorrow, my mate will give me twenty quid for it. It's a good one you know." He could tell by Misty's face she wasn't impressed and leaned towards her putting his arm round her chair. "You going to give me a kiss or what?" She turned her face away from him and pretended to look through the steamy window but he now pulled her head to meet his and his lips met hers.

He kissed her passionately and she could feel a strange excitement deep in her fanny. She watched as he moved the seats back enabling them to have more room. He slid over and joined her on the passenger seat. As he lay on top of her, his kiss became more intense and she could feel his hip bone pressing deep into her groin. As his tongue teased her lips, she felt completely aroused. Misty felt she was losing control and knew she would have to stop before it got any further but at this moment she couldn't control herself and continued kissing him. She felt a warm sensation emerging between her legs and they were slowly opening with a mind of their own. She wanted him so much, she could feel herself gripping his masculine body, as uncontrollable passion seeped through her veins.

Gordon loosened his trouser button and pulled his jeans half way down his legs revealing his love pole. He then moved closer to her, pulling her knickers to one side. Slowly his fingers entered deep inside her and he commented on how wet she felt, he knew it was only minutes before he could enter her. Her body tensed as he pressed himself into her and she held his shoulders as she kissed his neck. Misty dug her nails into his back as he groaned with pleasure. She knew she had to stop now because if it went on any longer it would be too late and her virginity would be gone forever. She had promised her virginity to Dominic and to lose it to a one night stand would be devastating. All of a sudden reality hit home and she had to think quickly to stop it from going any further. She quickly pulled her legs up to her chest and began to struggle, trying in desperation to remove Gordon.

"What's fuckin' up with you."

Misty lied and told him she had to be home as her parents would be worried and might phone the police. Gordon looked disappointed and began to question her.

"Why, how old are you?" Misty knew she should of told the truth from the moment they met but she didn't think it would get this far.

"Fifteen" she whispered and waited for his reaction. Gordon jumped off her and returned to the driving seat.

"Fuckin' fifteen you're jail bait you are. Why didn't you fucking tell me?" He could tell by Misty's face she felt embarrassed by the whole situation. Gordon thought for a minute and began to laugh, "Well I'm not bothered if you're not, age means nothing to me and you know what they say 'if there's grass on the wicket, let's play cricket'". Misty smiled at his attempt at humour and thought she had got off quite lightly. "Right then little school girl let's get you home" he said.

Gordon started the engine and slowly crept out of the alleyway with his lights turned off. As he did he began to talk to Misty. "Do ya wanna see me again?" Misty smiled and nodded, even though she already had a boyfriend. The only thing on her mind at that moment was to be back home in the comfort of her bed. "Right little prick teaser where do you live?" Misty gave him directions to her house and told him to park up round the corner once they had reached their destination, as she didn't want them to be spotted by any nosey neighbours.

As they approached Misty's house he reached over and started to stroke her leg. "We can finish where we left off next time we meet if you want?" he said in a sexy voice. Misty felt herself blushing as his hand ventured deeper up her skirt. She felt strange and couldn't understand what she was feeling. He had stirred something inside her. Even though she knew it was wrong she couldn't get enough of him. Gordon was like a drug and she was well and truly hooked.

As he drove into the night Misty watched him leave. Filled with excitement she made her way to her back door. She climbed onto the concrete shed, which was situated beneath her bedroom window. Hitching her skirt up she clambered on top of it and with a great tug she pulled her bedroom window open. With effort she swung her legs onto the window ledge and began to pull herself through the window. Misty rested for a minute before she made her final move; she knew she had to be quiet as a mouse as her family was sleeping and she couldn't afford to wake them. Finally she pulled herself through the window and rested her legs on the other side. 'Another successful mission,' she thought as she took her clothes off and fell onto her bed. Tiredness filled her body and the room began to spin, the brandy she had drunk earlier was taking effect. She held onto the bed for dear life and before she knew it she was sound asleep.

Misty could hear the sound of the teacher's voice shouting her name and as she opened her eyes she remembered exactly where she was.

"Are you asleep Misty Sullivan?" Misty gazed round watching all the faces of her classmates on her.

"No Miss, I just feel a bit ill and needed to rest my eyes". The teacher looked at her in disbelief and told her if she did not feel well to report to the school nurse at break time but for now she must join in the lesson and pay attention. The sound of the school bell hit the walls of the classroom just in time to save her and her classmates hurried out into the school grounds. Francesca waited for Misty as she watched her make her way down the corridor towards the exit. Seeing her face Misty chuckled, "Right yo-yo knickers, tell me all about last night". Both girls laughed as they tried to find a quiet spot, away from nosey bastards. Reaching a grass verge they sat down and each lit a cigarette they had bought from another pupil earlier.

"Come on then, tell me all the gory details, I can't believe you're not a virgin anymore. What was it like?" Misty's questions continued until Francesca finally spoke.

"My fanny is killing underneath. It feels like it is on fire when I go to the toilet". Both girls laughed as Francesca told of her night of adult fun with Kevin. Francesca continued laughing as she spoke. "After leaving you, I was well pissed. Kevin suggested we went for a walk in the park. We got on really well and before long my knickers were round my ankles and all I could see was Kevin's arse moving up and down like a sewing machine." Misty held her side as she laughed, as Francesca continued with a serious face. "It felt pretty alright though, after he finally got his knob in, it seemed to take forever. He said my fanny was as tight as a fish's arse, whatever that means". Both girls rolled around the floor; with laughter exploding inside their bodies. Francesca looked serious as she asked the next question.

"Misty" she whispered. "Tell me the truth. Can you smell spunk on me?"

Misty smelt her friend and giggled, "What does it fucking smell like?" she asked.

"I don't know" Francesca replied, "but I don't want to take the chance of my mam or dad smelling it on me. I didn't have time to get a bath this morning and I keep thinking I can smell something strange."

"Misty," she said firmly, "if I smell fishy, I want you to tell me". Francesca looked worried as her friend continued to smell her. Misty completed the task of smelling her friend and found no evidence of spunk or any unfamiliar smells much to Francesca's relief.

"Anyway never mind me, what happened with you and Gordon?" Misty looked innocent as she told her friend that Gordon and herself had just kissed, she didn't want to go into all the details, as she was already feeling quite guilty and she wanted to forget all about the night before. Misty had now decided that Gordon was a bad mistake and wanted to stay with Dominic, so for now Gordon was out of her life and she wanted nothing more to do with him, even though she still felt drawn toward him. She knew she needed to keep well away from him as it could only result in unhappiness.

The school day went quite quickly and before long the home time bell rung. Misty knew this was the time she would have to face Dominic, as they always got the bus home together each day. Misty walked to the school gates and as predicted Dominic was waiting for her.

"Come on slow coach hurry up" he shouted as she walked slowly to meet him. "We'll miss the bus if you don't hurry up" he moaned. Misty jogged a little faster to where he stood.

"I don't feel well so don't start going on at me."

"Well you were out last night, weren't you? What do you expect?" Misty hugged his arm hoping he would forgive her, as she knew he was jealous of the time she spent with Francesca. As they reached the bus stop, the bus had just left and you could see Francesca waving through the back window.

"Told you we would miss it. Now we will have to wait fifteen minutes till another one comes". Misty felt the tension rising between them. Dominic hadn't liked her sneaking out to the pub on Sunday nights. He would have preferred it had she spent more time with him studying. Dominic was a good lad and he had already designed a life plan, which was basically 'study, study, study'. Misty was part of this plan and he didn't want her getting into trouble with Francesca. She was nothing but trouble in his eyes, she had quite a bad reputation amongst the lads in school and he didn't want Misty tarnished with the same brush. The bus arrived and they sat together upstairs. Misty didn't speak and Dominic felt the strange silence between them.

"What's the matter with you?" He asked, as she looked through the window. Misty didn't reply but he knew something was bothering her. Reaching Dominic's house, Misty knew she would have to pull herself out of this daft mood she was in. All she could think of was her night with Gordon. Misty made the effort to speak thinking how much she loved Dominic and it wasn't him who had cheated, it was her. She would make it up to him, she thought as they entered his house.

They were greeted by Dominic's mother, who hugged

them both before they headed upstairs. Dominic had the perfect home, his home was beautiful and both his parents had good jobs, it was the complete opposite to Misty's domestic life. Money had never been short in Dominic's household and he wanted for nothing. Dominic was good looking and was considered quite a catch amongst the girls in school. His fair hair complimented his lightly tanned skin and his teeth were whiter than white. She knew he was a good catch and from now on she would be faithful to him. "Goodbye Gordon" she whispered under her breath, as they went up to his bedroom. From now on she thought all her love would be focussed on Dominic and Gordon would be left in the past where he belonged.

Misty dived on Dominic's bed "Let's leave the homework tonight, we can have some dirty fun if you want". Dominic smiled and dragged Misty down on the bed. Looking into her eyes he knew she was the love of his life and one day had planned to marry her.

"Kiss me tiger" she laughed as his lips connected with hers. Misty immediately started to compare his kiss to that of Gordon's and had to stop herself thinking about the other boy. She and Dominic had never had sex but they had spoken about it lots of times. They both agreed it would be a special occasion when they finally did it. She had wanted the full works. Four poster bed, soft music and soft lighting and nothing else would do – the day she lost her virginity she wanted it to be so special and a day she would remember for the rest of her life.

Misty felt so guilty about her behaviour the night before and wanted to make it up to Dominic. So she planned a special present for him, a present that he would love.

"Dominic" she whispered into his ear as he kissed her neck. "Let's take it to the next step" he lifted his head and looked at Misty's face.

"You mean have sex?"

"Yes" she replied in her sexy voice.

"What right now!" he asked with excitement in his voice.

"No you idiot. We'll plan it for tomorrow night when ya mam and dad are out". Dominic nearly exploded there and then and squeezed Misty tightly telling her how excited he was. "Don't forget protection and I don't mean putting a bolt on your room, so no one comes in". She giggled as Dominic laughed too. "Get some condoms, don't forget" she prompted. Dominic laughed and spoke confidently.

"As if I would. I don't want any little brats running around the place and neither do you."

Everything was planned for the next evening. They both decided they would lose their virginity. The time passed and it was time for Misty to leave Dominic's and head home. Dominic walked her to the door and kissed her gently "I love you Misty Sullivan you're my girl".

Misty smiled and told him she loved him too and then opened the front door. "See you tomorrow and don't forget what we need".

Dominic smiled as he closed the door. He then headed straight upstairs leaping three steps at a time. Entering his bedroom he rolled his body on the floor so he could see under his bed and just as he had thought, there they were his pride and joy staring right at him. He pulled out the old cardboard box and lifted the lid revealing his porn collection. Making sure his door was securely closed he began to 'read' them. He needed all the advice he could get and Big Jugs Monthly had quite a few tips inside, to keep a young boy well informed. Most of his friends read fanny mags and this is where they got all their tips from. As he opened the first page a big hairy fanny appeared on it and Dominic felt his heart pumping. "Oh my god he thought will Misty's fanny look like this". He examined it closer and was intrigued by every nook and cranny .

Dominic started to read one of the stories, hoping there was information on what women liked in bed but before he knew it he had excited himself too much and ended up masturbating. Once he had finished he lay motionless on the bed and just hoped when he finally had sex with Misty it wouldn't be a jerk and a squirt, because at the moment his penis had a mind of its own and the slightest thing made it grow beyond his control and often left him embarrassed trying to hold it down in his pocket. He prayed that everything would run smoothly and knew he just needed to relax and stop worrying.

Misty headed home. 'What would greet her tonight?' she thought. Every day in their house was a new drama and she didn't expect today to be any different. Since their father had left life had been hard on them especially for her mother. Misty knew she was at breaking point, so she was trying to help her as much as possible but how can you help someone who won't help themselves? Life was so dull for Misty at the moment and she just hoped her home life would change pretty soon. Reaching home she opened the broken back gate and entered the back door, where she was greeted by her two younger brothers Jonathan and Lee. Max was sat watching television and looked at his sister.

"Where's my mam?" she asked, as she rubbed Lee's hair, messing it up. Max raised his eyes towards the ceiling and gave her a familiar look. The look that let her know her mother was crying yet again. Misty walked into the kitchen and looked in the fridge knowing she had to keep things together. "Right fish fingers, chips and beans for tea everyone". The boys shouted with joy and the menu was set. Misty had become a stand in mam recently, as her mam was dealing with the break-up of her marriage. Her mother was a tablet away from a breakdown and Misty helped as much as she could. Making tea was her way of helping.

Entering the kitchen, she started to prepare tea for everyone. She opened the door that led to the stairs and listened. She could hear the sobs of her mother from the bedroom. Her body froze and she didn't know what to do for the best. Should she go up and comfort her mother or should she sort the kids out. Misty stood for a moment before heading back into the kitchen to make tea. She had decided her mother needed time alone to deal with her grief and she would speak to her later to see if she was alright, but for now she would concentrate on feeding the smaller children.

CHAPTER TWO

MISTY'S MOTHER LISA had been married to Ken for 15 years. An attractive woman, she had always looked very glamorous. Her hair was similar to Misty's, it was long and dark, with a mahogany cast. Her figure was amazing and most women would have killed for it.

'So how have I ended up like this?' she thought as she lay lifeless on the bed. Her heart was shattered and even the sound of her kids playing downstairs couldn't raise her. Lisa looked round the bedroom and gazed at the walls. They had witnessed so many arguments between herself and Ken. There were even splashes of blood still visible on the wall, evidence of Ken's drunken rages. Lisa wished the pain she felt in her heart would leave but no matter how hard she tried, it wouldn't go away. After endless sleepless nights her mind was being tormented by all the memories of their time together. She would toss around in bed most nights. Laughter seemed a distant memory and the person she once was seemed lost in a cloak of dark despair.

Lisa was one of five children and had done quite well for herself by the time she reached eighteen. She had worked as a sales assistant in a large well-known clothes store and had been promoted to manager. Working in the store had its perks and all the new fashions were modelled by her as soon as they came into the store. She was envied by lots of girls as she didn't seem to want for anything. Lisa first met Ken at a fashion show. He was a big name in the handbag industry and owned a successful company that supplied handbags to most of the high street stores. When they had first met, it was love at first sight. They spent every minute together and were inseparable. Ken was extremely handsome and he had a special glow about him; whenever he walked into a room he would fill it with laughter and the atmosphere would be electric. His only downside was that he had an eye for the ladies but Lisa had chosen to ignore that. Ken was an only child and his mother adored him, he could do no wrong in her eyes. Since his father's death his mother had signed the company over to him, as she thought she was too old to run it. By the age of twenty-two Ken was quite a wealthy young man. His only other bad habit was visiting casinos. On many a late night he had lost large amounts of money but it never deterred him and he always went back for more thinking the next time his luck would change.

The day finally came when Ken asked the question that most women dream of. The scene had been set in a romantic restaurant, dimly lit by burning candles and music playing softly in the background. Taking her hand, he kissed her fingers before he spoke.

"Lisa" he whispered softly, "I have never met anyone who I love as much as you and I need to know you will be mine forever." He pulled her closer and reached into his pocket revealing a small box. "Will you be my wife?" he asked.

Lisa's heart missed a beat and her body bubbled with love for him. He was her prince and now they would be together forever, she thought. Looking into his eyes she gave him the answer he had been waiting for. "Yes Ken. I would love to be your wife". Ken placed the ring on Lisa's finger and they kissed passionately. She was so excited and wanted to shout from the rooftops how happy she was. She had been the happiest women alive at that moment.

Everybody at home took the news of the marriage well and congratulated them both. Everyone, that is, except Lisa's father. There was something about Ken he didn't like but at that moment he just couldn't put his finger on it. He had a feeling deep in his gut about this man and he knew he would have to keep a close eye on him in the future as he looked like a 'wrong 'un'.

The big day came and Lisa became Mrs. Sullivan. The church was packed with people, as Ken waited patiently at the altar waiting for his new bride to make her presence. The church was filled with happiness and warmth, as they too remembered the times when they had made the same precious vows to someone they had loved. Everybody was happy on this day, all except for Lisa's dad, he just couldn't find the goodwill everyone felt around him. As he approached Ken at the altar, he watched how smug his face was and felt an anger in the pit of his stomach. He felt completely helpless that his daughter had made the decision to marry Ken and all he could do was sit and watch her make the biggest mistake of her life. Nobody else felt the same way about Ken as he did, so for now he would have to sit and wait for the moment he would be proved right...

The organist played as Lisa walked into the church escorted by her father. He held her arm for dear life and he didn't want to give her away. She was his baby and he felt the tears fill his eyes as they neared the altar. Ken turned to watch his bride as she approached. His heart melted as he watched her glide down the aisle. She looked like she was floating on air, as he watched her every move in amazement. He was a lucky man he thought and congratulated himself as she made her way toward him.

Lisa's dress could have come out of a fairy tale. She looked so elegant. The ivory silk hugged her body and had been designed by an old friend, a big name in the fashion industry. Sequins, diamonds, fur, you name it, the dress had it. It looked like snowflakes had been dusted all over it - what an amazing dress! As she stood next to Ken, her body shook with nerves. Her throat felt dry and her legs took on a mind of their own, she could feel them quivering beneath her dress. As she looked at Ken, he smiled at her and all the nerves she felt left her and her breathing returned to normal.

Lisa had waited for this day all her life, everything was perfect. She was so happy and couldn't wait until the priest pronounced them man and wife so they could begin their journey together. The ceremony finished much to the relief of Lisa's father. He had moaned all the way through it, Lisa's mother had to shoot him daggers to shut him up after which he sat and scowled.

As Ken and Lisa left the church as man and wife, Ken held her like a prize trophy. Everybody congratulated them and they all made their way for the ceremonial photographs. The day went well. It was truly memorable for Lisa and Ken. The reception went on until the early hours of the morning and the guests were very merry. The time finally came for the newlyweds to leave and after Ken thanked the guests they left the function room waving goodbye to everybody as they made their way to the car. They held each other close and things could not have been any better. It had been amazing and to put the icing on the cake Ken had booked the honeymoon suite in the Britannia hotel in the middle of Manchester. Ken's mother had bought them quite an expensive present - a dream house and tomorrow they would start their life together in it.

The hotel was magnificent. Everything was so perfect. Ken took Lisa's hand and guided her to their room. He was rampant for her body. He led her to the bed and slowly unzipped her wedding gown sliding it off her shoulders. The sight of her underwear made his manhood stand to attention and he couldn't wait a moment more. They made love throughout the night until the early hours of the morning. It had been wonderful and just how she imagined it would be. Afterwards they lay wrapped inside each other's arms until they finally fell asleep. It had been a special day and she would remember it for the rest of her life.

Ken and Lisa moved into their new home and things couldn't have been better. As the years passed they were blessed with four lovely children. Max, Misty, Jonathan and Lee. The children were Lisa's world and she had given up such a lot for them, even the job she loved so much. The last child, however, had taken its toll on Lisa's body and she found it hard to cope after the birth. Her weight gain didn't help the way she felt either. Lisa found it hard to get out of bed each morning and the home she loved went slowly downhill. Everywhere inside the home was covered in clutter and Ken constantly moaned at Lisa about the state of the house. He had told her to pull herself together but that just made her worse.

Ken's late nights started at this point. Many a night he wouldn't get home until six in the morning and he stunk of women's perfume as he lay next to her in bed. Lisa pretended everything was fine between them but she knew something was wrong, she just didn't want to admit it to herself. After one too many late nights at the casino, Ken returned home in a drunken state. Falling onto the bed he looked at his wife and nudged her to wake her up but she was in a deep sleep and didn't stir.

"Fuckin' wake up" he slurred in his drunken voice. He now nudged her again and this time she opened her eyes. "Look at you. You disgust me, you fucking stink and you're a fat lazy cow who's no good to nobody" Lisa stared at him in bewilderment.

"Why are you speaking to me like that? You're drunk

again and I'm not listening to you". She turned over and tried to go back to sleep but as she closed her eyes she felt her head bang against the headboard.

Ken then got up and swayed round the bedroom till he reached her side of the bed and stood in front of her. His eyes were filled with hatred, as he pulled the blankets off the bed and dragged Lisa out. "How dare you turn your back on me. Who the fuck do you think you are?" he now leaned toward her and she knew she was in deep trouble. She shook like a scared animal.

"Please!" she pleaded, "Stop it! The children are asleep in the next bedroom. You're drunk and you don't know what you are doing. Please stop for the sake of the children if not mine." He never listened to a single word she said as he kicked her hard in the stomach with brutal force causing her to scream. As she screamed he placed his hand over her mouth and threw her back onto the bed.

He looked down at her and growled, "I've wasted my life with you. I could have had so much more but look what I've ended up with a fuckin' walking wreck." He spat in her face and took great pleasure in watching her shake with fear.

Lisa sobbed throughout the night. She held her head deep into the pillow, so her tears didn't wake anyone. 'Why had he treated her so badly?', she thought, 'what had she done to deserve this and why did she still love him more than ever?' Lisa's life was now set in stone. She had gone from a loving marriage, to one filled with fear and violence. Ken had become her master and if she did not obey his demands there would be hell to pay and she would receive yet another beating.

The final straw came when Ken returned home late one night and couldn't bear his life with Lisa anymore. He packed all his belongings and told Lisa it was over. Ken had met someone new and wanted to set up home with his new lady friend as soon as possible. He didn't hide the fact that he had met another woman from her and talked quite openly about it. Lisa felt mixed emotions when he told her about his new woman; whilst feeling hate towards him she still seemed to love him even more. The very thought of life without her husband made her feel suffocated and breathless. Lisa cried rivers and begged him to stay but nothing could stop him, his mind was made up and he was leaving for good.

Lisa lay in bed and looked at the place where Ken would usually lie. He was gone forever and he had taken her heart with him. She felt an emptiness inside and her world had crumbled around her, she felt like she was falling deeper and deeper into a pit of despair and couldn't see any way back. Taking the tablets out of the bathroom, Lisa knew she didn't want to live anymore. She waited until the children had gone to school and began to take steps to end her life. She collected photographs of the children and one of herself and Ken on their wedding day and started to unscrew the lid off the tablets. Tears filled her eyes as she knew her life was about to end. One by one she threw the tablets to the back of her mouth, drinking water to help them go down. Before long she could feel her body melting into the bed and she felt so tired. She held the pictures close to her chest and waited for her life to end.

Misty had forgotten her homework that morning and headed back to the house. Never in a million years did she expect to find her mother half dead on the bed. As soon as she saw her, panic took over and she knew immediately what had to be done as she spotted the empty tablet bottle next to her mother.

"Mam, please wake up, what have you done?" she cried. Her mother was falling in and out of consciousness and she could see that she was still breathing, she knew she needed help quickly before it was too late. Misty rang for an ambulance and listened closely to the voice on the other end of the phone. The lady gave her important advice on how to keep her mother alive till the ambulance arrived. She tried to get her mother up walking round like the operator had told her but she felt like a dead weight and no amount of strength from her body could lift her to her feet.

"Oh Mam, please wake up! Please!" she pleaded. The ambulance men eventually arrived and immediately took over the care of Lisa as Misty watched sobbing.

Lisa was saved that day in more ways than one. Reaching the hospital the doctors took over from the ambulance men and placed her into a side ward. As they examined her the doctor called to the nurse to bring some solution so should would be sick and rid her body of the tablets she had taken. They just hoped it wasn't too late. Lisa was forced to drink the black liquid they gave her and almost immediately it started to work as she her vomited uncontrollably. This went on for about ten minutes and finally when the doctor was happy all the tablets had left her body, he started to relax. The doctor shook his head as he told Lisa she was a very lucky woman to be alive. He couldn't understand why a woman her age would want to end her life so soon. The doctor could see by her eyes she needed sleep and with one last goodbye he left her to rest.

After hours asleep Lisa was groggy. As she opened her eyes her vision was blurred and she found it hard to focus. As she looked round the room she noticed her sister Denise by her bedside.

"Oh Lisa what the fuck have you done to yourself" said her sister, half in sympathy, half in anger.

Lisa's lip began to quiver as she looked at her. She now pulled the pillow over her face and began to scream, "What have I got to live for? Ken's left me and I can't cope on my own. I just want to be left alone to die". She continued to cry like someone had ripped her heart out, as Denise reached over to hug her.

"We can all help you," Denise said softly, "nothing is ever that bad that you have to end your life".

Lisa held her body close and tugged at her skin. "Look at me, I'm disgusting. What have I got to live for now he's gone?" Denise felt anger inside her and couldn't hold on to the words anymore.

"What about your fuckin' kids, don't you think they need you? What would have happened to them if you were to die?" She knew her words were harsh but she was being cruel to be kind. "Your kids need you more than anything. You are selfish and need to pull yourself together. If not for yourself for the sake of your kids". Denise thought back to when they were children. Her sister was always the life and soul of the party and had never gone short of men taking an interest in her.

Denise sighed as she looked at her, she was a shadow of her former self. "I will help with the kids. We can get through this together. You have a family that cares about you and from now on we will all pull together. We all just want you to get better. Can you please try? If not for us, then for the sake of your kids."

Lisa came out of hospital after a few days. She felt embarrassed at what she had tried to do. Denise was right, her kids needed her and from now on she would pull herself out of this dark hole and tackle life without the husband she adored. As she waited at the hospital doors for her sister to pick her up she read the notices on the walls. One caught her eye and she began to read it.

"If you do what you have always done, you will get what you have always got". Lisa thought about what she had just read and it hit a nerve. The more she read it, the more it made sense. 'It was so right' she thought, 'that's what I need to do. I need to change'. And true to her word Lisa did change. She got herself a part time job in a supermarket and the weight fell off. The pain of Ken leaving was still inside her and some days she would sit and cry for hours but with everyday that passed, Lisa was getting stronger and soon she would be ready to face the world again.

CHAPTER THREE

MISTY MADE HER brothers something to eat and they all sat round the family table. She felt a deep pain inside her as she looked at the two empty places where her father and mother once sat. She remembered when things had been so much better and laughter had filled the room. That table had witnessed so much happiness but now all it could see was the empty shell of a broken family.

Misty made a cup of tea and headed upstairs to check on her mother. She worried so much about her these days. As she reached the bedroom she slowly pushed open the door, finding her mother lying face down on the bed.

"Mam" she spoke in a soft voice. "I have made tea if you're hungry." Her mother turned to lie on her back trying to disguise her tears.

"Come and sit here a minute with me love" and she patted the bed. Her voice was low as she started to speak. "Misty thanks for all you are doing, I feel like I am stealing your youth. You should be out with your friends not sat here looking after me and your brothers". She now paused. "Don't ever let a man get you like this love. Never end up like me. Promise me Misty" Misty made the promise to her mother and they held each other as Lisa continued to cry. Misty felt anger toward her father for causing her mother all this pain. He had never been to see them since he had left. Not even a lousy phone call. They could all be dead for all he cared.

Once all the jobs were done, Misty knew it was time to get ready. Tonight was the night she was going to lose her virginity and she wanted everything to be perfect. She had wanted to discuss this issue with her mother but couldn't find the courage to bring it up. Lisa had so many problems of her own to deal with at the moment and Misty didn't want to add to them. So it had to be a live and learn experience. She just hoped she wouldn't have to learn the hard way. Entering the bathroom Misty ran her bath. She took off of her uniform and slung it into the corner. Peeling her underwear off she stepped into the warm bath and submerged herself into the water. The hot water gave Misty calm as she lay there, trying to soak away all the misery she felt inside. Looking down between her legs, she knew she had to shave her fanny. It looked like an overgrown hedge and she didn't want Dominic telling everyone she had a big hairy fanny. So taking the scissors she trimmed the big mound of hair between her legs and threw all the evidence down the toilet. Her next step was to shave her other body parts, armpits and legs they were all in a desperate need of a tidy up. Looking at her body in the mirror, she started to laugh. She had really gone to town on her fanny and it looked like a skinhead haircut. Oh well she thought perhaps, he wouldn't notice it once they had a few drinks down their neck.

Misty dried herself and went into her bedroom. She started searching through her underwear draw looking at each piece. There was nothing that was remotely sexy – all her underwear was worn and torn. Surely her mother must have something sexy she could borrow. So creeping into her mother's bedroom she pulled open the drawer. A sea of coloured underwear filled her eyes. Quickly she found a matching set of red knickers and red bra. The bra wasn't her size but if she pulled the straps tight nobody would be able to tell. Completing her task she returned to her bedroom and closed the door tightly behind her. Looking in the mirror she tried on the red underwear and felt quite sexy. The bra looked quite a good fit. Now she put on her red dress and she truly looked a picture. Her shoes were black and once she had polished them they looked like new. Now she was ready, all but a squirt of perfume kept her from her destiny.

"Bye mam" she hurried out of the door. She hadn't wanted any of the family to ask why she was all dressed up, as she couldn't be bothered making up a load of lies, so a quick exit was her only option.

As predicted Dominic's parents had gone out for the evening and she could tell by his face that he was nervous. As she walked through the door she could smell alcohol on his breath. 'Orr! Bless' she thought as she looked at him, 'he must need some Dutch courage' and she giggled to herself. She too needed something to relax and grabbed a glass of brandy off the table that Dominic had left. Conversation was hard as they both knew what was about to happen. They both drank a lot more brandy and both of them were pissed. Misty knew it was now or never so she made the first move.

"Right come on then, if we are going to do this". She spoke in a nervous voice. Dominic looked at her in shock and eagerly followed her up to the bedroom.

There, Dominic put on some soft music, he had clearly planned the evening very carefully, and Phil Collins played in the background to set the scene. Misty lay on the bed and waited for him to join her. He moved his hand towards her face and kissed her. They kissed for several minutes and Misty felt excited at the thought of the next step. As he pulled her dress over her shoulders he kissed her curvaceous body revealing her sexy underwear and nearly exploded. He had never seen a woman like this before except on television or in his magazines. His moves were clumsy as the brandy took effect. He continued to kiss her and slid his hands into her knickers, fumbling around looking for her entrance. Then with a sharp pain she felt his fingers inside her. Her body quivered with excitement wanting and needing more of what he had to give her. He slid his fingers in and out of her and she could feel a wave of pleasure building inside her. Reaching down she touched his manhood and got quite shock. It felt huge and it was throbbing with pleasure. She could tell he was aroused. Dominic's breathing was intense as he suckled her ripe breast teasing her nipple with his tongue. Misty was in heaven and didn't want him to stop. Surely it must be time now for him to enter her, she thought as her body rocked with pleasure. Between her legs felt so wet that at one stage she thought she had pissed herself. Suddenly Dominic lifted his head.

"Oh I am going to be sick" he shouted as he staggered towards the bathroom. The sound of his uncontrollable wretching filled the bedroom and Misty knew that her first taste of sex was over. She had wanted more but as her eyes looked at his penis she realised it had shrunk in size and any hopes of continuing sex was over. Misty straightened her clothing and went to tend to him. Lifting his head out of the toilet, he looked up at her.

"Sorry, just give me a minute and I will be alright" but Misty knew he was fit for nothing except bed. As she guided him back to the bedroom, he apologised repeatedly. Misty laughed as she put him in bed. She placed the bin next to his bed in case he was going to be sick again.

"Don't worry" she whispered into his ear, "we can always try again, there's no rush is there". His eyes closed and Misty watched as he slept. Dominic had been sleeping at least twenty minutes before she decided to leave. She kissed his cheek and made her way to the front door. Walking back home she felt quite disappointed, she had wanted so much to lose her virginity but for now she knew she would have to wait. She also blamed herself for letting him drink so much – 'it's my fault' she thought.

The night was still young and Misty didn't feel much like going home early. As she walked up Carisbrook Street she could see a gang of people at the other end of the road. It wasn't till she got closer she recognised her friend Francesca as one of them. She could tell she was pissed as she was swaying around and her voice was louder than ever.

"Hiya Misty!" She shouted as she approached, "where have you fuckin' bin hiding?" Misty stuttered as she saw the familiar face of Gordon staring straight back at her.

"No where really, just been chillin" she replied. Francesca threw her arms round her and passed her a bottle of brandy.

"Get some of that down ya," Misty held it to her mouth and knocked it back, feeling the warm sensation it sent through her body. Francesca was all over Kevin like a rash and it was obvious they were now a couple. Gordon approached Misty and began to talk; she could feel her heart beating twice as fast as normal as he began to speak.

"Hiya sexy, where have you been hiding?" Misty knew she should have told the truth but he excited her and she wanted to keep Dominic a secret for now, so she ignored his question.

The gang finished their drinks and Francesca waved goodbye to Misty as she left with Kevin. Everyone scattered leaving Gordon and Misty alone together. Misty was pissed and her confidence poured out of her. Gordon pulled her towards him and began to kiss her and she made no fight to pull away. Then suddenly some of the earlier passion returned and Misty needed him like fire needed oxygen and began to kiss him, feeding the fire she felt inside. As they both walked off they playfully pushed each other.

"Right, you little dirty, where do you want to go?" he laughed. Misty looked at him with a blank expression and

BROKEN YOUTH

made no attempt to reply as she followed him. "Misty is quite an unusual name isn't it? Who the fuck picked your name?"

Misty laughed. "I was an unplanned child so they tell me and that's why I was called Misty. It stands for mistake". They both laughed as he repeated her name out loud. "Misty, Mistake".

Gordon took her to a local Collyhurst estate and headed towards a large block of flats. As they entered the flats the stench of urine and disinfectant hit their nostrils. It was that bad that you could actually taste it on the back of your throat. Misty held her nose until they reached the lift.

"Oh it fuckin' stinks in here as well, doesn't it?" she shouted. They proceeded into the lift and pressed their floor number. They watched as the doors shut and could feel the vibration of the lift struggling to carry them to their required floor. Feeling scared Misty asked the question she should have asked before she agreed to go with him. "Where we going then?"

Gordon smiled, "To my brother's house. He will be in bed but I'll knock him up". The lift finally reached the twelfth floor and they reached his brother's flat. There were about five other flats on that floor and each looked as scruffy as the next. Reaching the front door, Gordon knocked softly but his knock became harder as nobody answered. Finally a scruffy looking man opened the door and you could tell by his face he wasn't happy.

"Fuckin' hell! What time do you call this ya muppet? I have told you before, not to come here when it's late, don't you fuckin' listen to me?" Gordon ignored his rant and pushed passed him and beckoned Misty to follow. The hallway was so dark and the smell of sweaty socks filled the air. He led her into the front room and the man who turned out to be his brother followed closely behind. Gordon's brother introduced himself as Tom and by the looks of him, he could have done with a bath and a pan of potato ash down him. His hair was quite long and he was incredibly thin. He looked like a strong gust of wind would snap him in half. Gordon turned on the radio as his brother rolled a cig. Misty watched his every move as he sprinkled the tobacco into the cigarette paper. As she watched him further she could see him opening as small plastic bag containing a different kind of tobacco. He sprinkled the contents into his over-sized roll up and finally twisted the end of it. Tom lit the funny looking cig and sat back into the chair. After he had quite a few drags, he passed it to Gordon, "it's good shit that, so take it easy" he warned his brother.

Misty looked round the flat and she could tell that Tom had nowt. The settee had big holes in the arms and the carpet didn't reach the skirting boards. Also in the middle of the room was a small pine table which had seen better days and was ready for the skip.

"Here, Misty, try a bit of this" Gordon shouted and passed her the funny looking cig. She held it between her fingers, not really knowing what to do with it. Her heart pounded as they both watched. "Go on then take a drag, dickhead". they prompted. Misty didn't want to be seen as a shit bag, so she lifted it up to her mouth and took a long deep drag. At first she felt nothing but once she had a few more drags, her body felt strange, she felt as if everything was going in slow motion around her. Gordon and Tom carried on their conversation and noticed Misty sinking into her chair. Tom laughed as they watched.

"She's well and truly wrecked, isn't she?" he said and Gordon laughed because he knew his brother was telling the truth. Tom left the two of them together and returned to his bedroom, still laughing as he left.

"Aye our kid, I need to talk to you. I've got a job for us to look at tomorrow, so you better wake me up early". Gordon confirmed he had heard him and Tom disappeared into his bedroom scratching his nuts.

Gordon looked at Misty as her eyes rolled together. "Hey sleepy, don't be nodding off". He pulled Misty onto the settee to join him. Misty felt overwhelmed with tiredness, whatever she had smoked had knocked her for six. Gordon now lay on top of her and caressed her hair as he spoke. "I'm really into you Misty; I haven't stopped thinking about you since we last met". Misty's lips felt like they were glued together as she struggled to speak. Gordon looked at her and felt an incredible warmth flow through his body. He lowered his head towards her and attempted to kiss her. Misty knew she should be heading home but Gordon's hold on her was too strong and she didn't have the energy to fight him off. They kissed and he felt his way up her skirt. She had wanted him to stop but she was enjoying it too much. He slipped his finger inside her and moved it slowly. She felt like a volcano ready to erupt. Gordon thrust himself between her legs pressing his hip bone in between hers and before she knew it, he had entered her. Misty felt liked she was being ripped apart. His thrusts were long and hard and she yelled with pain.

Gordon put his hand over her mouth and whispered, "Be quiet, you will wake Tom". He continued to thrust deep inside her and his pace quickened and his breathing got louder. "Yeah baby" he shouted. "Who's the daddy" as his movements came to a halt. Misty lay still, as he now rested motionless upon her. 'Surely that can't be it' she thought. She had seen lots of sex scenes on TV and the women had screamed with pleasure but all she had felt was pain. Perhaps this was the warm up she thought, as she prepared herself for the finale but to her disappointment Gordon rolled off her and reached for his cigs.

"What did you think of that then babe?" he asked confidently "was it the dog's bollocks then or what?" She had wanted to say, it was fuckin' shite but somehow it didn't seem right and she didn't want to hurt his feeling so she carried on with the lie.

"Yeah it was great", she replied lying through her teeth. Gordon looked proud of himself and his performance and now lay recovering from his jerk and squirt routine. He now smoked his cigarette like the love machine he believed he was. Misty felt cheated, all she had to show for the loss of her virginity were wet knickers and a sore fanny. She had been very disappointed that there wasn't more to it and if that's all sex was about she could take it or leave it.

As they lay in silence, the reality of what had just happened hit her. She panicked as she remembered Dominic. Her mind was ablaze with guilt. 'Misty you little slag, what you have done', she thought as she straightened her clothes. Suddenly aware of the sleazy surroundings, she wanted to go home and couldn't wait to leave.

"I need to go now, can you walk me home?" she asked in a distressed voice. Gordon looked quite shocked, as he had had taken it for granted she'd be staying the night but in a way he was glad, as he could now have his bed to himself and stretch his tired body. He jumped up off the settee and pulled up his trousers. Few words were spoken as he escorted her home. It was late now and she hoped her family would be in bed. Gordon left her round the corner from her house, as she didn't want him to be spotted by her family. He kissed her on the side of her cheek but as she tried to leave he pulled her closer and whispered. "I will be in touch, if that's alright". Misty just wanted to get away, so she agreed so she could make a quick exit.

As she slid her key into the door she crept slowly into the hallway. There was no noise at all in the house and that was a promising sign telling her everyone was asleep. Creeping up the stairs she made her way to the toilet and once inside she bolted the door. Her heart pounded, as she pulled down her knickers to sit on the toilet. As she started to wee her underneath felt like it was on fire. Looking down into her knickers she could see traces of blood, she knew she wasn't on a period and she began to panic.

"Oh fuck!" Should she call her mum she thought, as she wiped herself revealing more blood. How could she, because then she would have to tell her she had lost her virginity. Misty held her head between her legs and sobbed quietly. Could she be dying? Or could this could be her punishment for betraying Dominic? They would find her dead in the morning then everyone would know she had lost her virginity and would realise she was a dirty lying slut. Misty decided that if she was going to die, she would do so in her own bedroom, so opening the door she made her way there, convinced she wasn't going to last the night. She couldn't wait to get her clothes off and she ripped them off as if they were on fire. She had wanted to get in the bath and wash the smell of Gordon from her body but she knew it was too late and didn't want to wake her family. She peeled off her knickers which were now covered in blood and knew she would have to throw them away at the first opportunity as she didn't want anything to remind her of the night with Gordon.

Lying on her bed, her head pounded. She could never see Gordon again she told herself and she would now end her relationship with Dominic as he didn't deserve what she had done to him. She could never look him in the eyes again knowing she had betrayed him. Closing her eyes she prayed she wouldn't die, "please let me live" she repeated in her mind as she drifted off to sleep hoping her prayers would be answered and she would still be alive in the morning.

"Come on lazy bones get up. Me mam's told me to get you up otherwise you will be late for school". This was the voice of her younger brother trying to wake her. Misty slowly opened her eyes and realised she had made it through the night. She lifted her head and she could see her brother leaving the room. Her body felt like she had been riding a horse. She still felt sore underneath and plodded to the bathroom. She knew there wasn't time to have a bath, so she reached for the face cloth and washed her entire body, still trying to rid herself of Gordon's scent. Finally she was ready and made her way downstairs to join her family.

She immediately looked at her mother and thought she could tell by her face she had lost her virginity, so she tried to avoid any eye contact with her. She remembered what Francesca had told her about the smell of spunk, so quickly she headed back to the bathroom to spray herself with perfume. She couldn't take the chance of anyone smelling spunk on her, so she lifted up her skirt and sprayed her knickers too. Making her way back downstairs, she shouted to her mum.

"Right mam, I'm going. I'll see you later. I'm gonna catch the bus". Misty had decided that the events of the night before would be her secret. She wouldn't breathe a word to anyone, not even Francesca.

The bus arrived and as predicted Francesca was on it. As she walked to join her, you could tell she was still hung over. They both sat and little conversation was made between them till they reached the school gates when Francesca broke the silence.

"So where did you get to last night dirty knickers?" Misty laughed as she told her Gordon had just walked her home and cleverly turned the conversation back to Francesca to avoid her deception. "Never mind me, where did you go?"

Francesca smiled as she told her about another sexual episode with Kevin. "Sex has got better now. I think I might have had an orgasm," she giggled as she continued. "My body shook, whatever he done to me and the feeling lasted for about forty seconds. I swear it was heaven you need to have one". Misty smiled and grabbed her friend's arm and headed towards the classroom.

Misty passed Dominic in the corridor and they both felt stupid. Dominic had felt embarrassed at his first attempt at sex but he smiled at her telling her he would talk to her later in the day. As she made her way to the classroom she looked like she had the worries of the world on her shoulders but her mind was already made up, she was going to end her relationship with Dominic. How could she ever be with him again now she was soiled goods? Her virginity was supposed to have been his but due to her being pissed as a fart she had made a great mistake. One she would pay for for the rest her life. The day passed slowly and she felt like she was floating around inside a bubble. Her head felt so mixed up and for the first time in her life she was missing her father. The sound of the school bell rang and she knew it was time to face her demons. She now walked to meet Dominic. On meeting neither of them made eye contact. They walked a short distance in silence before Dominic spoke.

"Misty about last night. I'm sorry but the brandy really got to me". She made no reply to him as they carried on walking. She looked like she was in a world of her own. Dominic had noticed a change in her these last few weeks and had thought all the troubles at home were now taking effect on her. Misty had everything rehearsed in her mind what she needed to say and as she began to speak tears ran down her cheeks.

"Dominic I think we should end it. At the moment there is so much going on at home and my mother needs me more than ever, I just haven't got the time for us at the moment". Looking into his eyes you could see that his world had fallen apart and he was finding it hard to breathe.

"Misty you can't do this to me. I'm sorry about last night but I felt sick. We can try again and I promise it will be better next time", he pleaded. Her heart sank as she watched him beg her for another chance. But how could she tell him she was no longer a virgin and she was nothing but a dirty slut? He would be better off without her in the long run she thought, so she continued lying, blaming her mother for their break-up.

On the bus he held her all the way home, begging her to rethink what she had just said but nothing could change her mind now. It was well and truly over between them. As they parted company it felt like her heart had been kept hostage by him. She felt shattered inside but this was her only choice at the moment.

'Goodbye Dominic' she thought, 'I will always love you' and watched him walk off in the distance with his head hung low.

CHAPTER FOUR

ISTY'S FATHER HAD moved into his love nest with his new girlfriend Julie some time ago. His business had taken a turn for the worse and he was losing money fast. Ken was a big time gambler and casinos were one of his downfalls. Julie had worked behind the bar in the casino. To start with she and Ken had just been friends but as time went on they became lovers. Ken had spent many hours in the casino and Julie knew he was quite a wealthy man. She was very attractive and a prize catch for anyone. Her hair was blonde and shoulder length and she had once been a model. She had known from the start that Ken was married but it never deterred her. All she wanted was cash and plenty of it and Ken could give her everything her heart desired. He had already bought her many expensive gifts, the latest being a new car. Julie knew she could wrap him round her little finger and get whatever she wanted and that's what she intended to do right from the start of their relationship.

When they first spoke about moving in together she made no excuses for the way she felt about his children. She had told him she wasn't very maternal and wanted holidays and to go out whenever she pleased, so for this reason she didn't want to become a step mum to his kids. Ken had thought she would change her mind in time and agreed to see them in his own time. He already felt like he had abandoned his children but at the moment he needed Julie more. Once he had settled down with her, he thought, he would find time for his kids and make it up to them the later. He just hoped by then it wasn't too late.

Ken was living his dream with Julie and they had just returned from a Caribbean cruise. Their social life was fully booked all the time and they didn't have a moment to spare. He had spoken about his children only once whilst they had been in company and Julie had given him the eyes to stop talking about them and like a fool he did. Later, when he had asked if there was a problem with him talking about his children, she told him the truth and didn't hold anything back. She said she didn't want people knowing he had already been married and had a family with another woman. She wanted everyone to believe they had always been together and didn't want reminding about his past with Lisa. She told him he had made his choice to leave his children and now he had to deal with it.

He secretly missed his children and knew he hadn't been supporting them. He always promised himself he would drop money off for them but he never found the time. He had made it to Denise's house once in a quest to sort things out but as he stood at the door she spat in his face shouting loudly at him so everyone could hear, "You no good bastard, what kind of man could leave his children behind for a bit of a dolly bird? You will end up a sad and lonely old man Ken Sullivan. I wish you nothing but misery you sad cunt". Ken had tried to speak but she slammed the door in his face refusing to listen to a word he said, telling him the kids would be better off without him and to stay out of their lives. Ken was distraught at the time and thought it was best to leave things until it settled down a bit, before he went to claim his children back into his life. Somehow that day never came.

Ken hadn't told anyone about his money troubles. All his and Julie's good times came at a cost. His business was heading for bankruptcy at a fast pace and he had tried to put it to the back of his mind but he reckoned he had about six months before the shit hit the fan and his children's inheritance would be lost forever. Whisky now became his new friend and he was drinking at least a bottle a day. He was heading for disaster and knew dark days lay ahead. But he hid his secret well, especially from Julie. Nobody was to know about his business and his money troubles except him, because if Julie got wind of it, she would be off at a shot.

Lisa's life was still in turmoil, even though she was doing her best to keep her head above water. Every day was a struggle to pull herself out of the dark place in which she found herself. Ken was never far away from her thoughts and she wished one day he would come back to her and the family and be happy again. Lisa often reminisced about the good times and forgot the life her husband had previously led her. All that she seemed to remember at the moment were the good times. The entire neighbourhood knew about herself and Ken's split and couldn't wait to discuss it with her to find out all the details. One neighbour in particular, who was quite well known as a gossip, couldn't wait to dig the knife in and cornered Lisa on a visit to the shop.

"How are you love?" she asked sympathetically and before Lisa could answer back she continued, "Well all I can say is you're better off without the no good fucker. We always said he was a no good bastard". Lisa dipped her head in shame as the woman opened fire on her. "I saw him the other day ya know, walking round arm in arm with his new fancy piece, dressed to kill she was, a right looker. He must be paying her for it, that's all I can say, because she could do a lot better than him". Lisa pictured them together in her mind and her stomach turned, feeling like a washing machine on fast spin. Lisa just nodded and agreed with every word the woman said and couldn't wait to get away. Her chest felt tight and she wanted to die there and then on the spot. Lisa had never really thought about Ken with another woman up until now. She had tried to block it out of her mind but now it was like another weight around her neck and her heart sank into her chest. The woman filled her in on lots more detail about her husband. Every word was like a bullet to her heart. Having listened for what seemed a lifetime, Lisa made her way home feeling like a wounded animal.

Denise had been a rock for her sister in more ways than one during the previous months. Many a day she had gone round to the house and found her sister still in her bed clothes. The house had been a mess and she could see she needed serious help. What has happened to my little sister she thought, as she looked at the bag of bones that she had now become. Denise knew she needed to take action to make her sister change. There's no time like the present she thought and began on her quest to help her sister.

"Right let's get this house cleaned, it's a shit tip. You need to start looking after yourself now. It's been six months since Ken left and you don't seem to be moving on. I'm your sister and love you for all the world but I can't stand to see you like this anymore".

"Do you think I want to fuckin' feel like this?" Lisa screamed, "Well I fuckin' don't, every night I lie in bed crying. He sends me no money but he's out every fuckin' night with his new tart spending his children's money. How do you expect me to feel?" Lisa cried as her sister comforted her. Denise secretly said a prayer and hoped her sister would pull through but looking at her, she knew it would take more than a miracle to repair her sister's heart.

When the tears had finally dried up, they both sat talking and agreed she needed a night out with the girls. Lisa didn't like the idea at first but when her sister worked her magic on her she came round to her sister's way of thinking.

"Right, first you need to get that hair cut, it looks like a ball of fluff." Denise saw the look on her face and realised that money was short, so she told her not to worry she would pay for a new outfit and her hair cut as a treat. Denise didn't have lots of money but any amount would be worth it, to see her sister smile again. The date was set and all they needed to do now was to sort her sister out with something to wear and get her to the hairdresser as soon as possible. Lisa walked into the hairdressers and felt amazed at the whole set up. It had been years since she had her hair cut professionally. Her hair was now long and scraggy and she remembered how it once was her crowning glory and every hair knew its place. Those days were long gone and she knew it was time for change. Lisa took a seat and was greeted by the hairdresser.

"Hi my name is John and I am your stylist today, what I can do for you". Lisa looked into the mirror and started to lift her hair up and down, trying to decide a style. Seeing she was struggling John stepped in to help. "Would you like me to help you decide? I will run some styles past you and see what you think". He now started to pull her hair in all directions as he looked into the mirror, then he brought a colour chart over, placing different colours next to her hair. "Right, what about a deep red? It will cover all your grey and compliment your skin tones".

Lisa took the advice and he set about applying the colour to her hair. He made her feel so special as he told her of the hairstyle he had planned for her. Once the colour was on, she sat watching all the other people having their hair cut, listened to their conversations and realised she was not the only person with problems. The hairdressers was like a breath of fresh air. People would come to offload their problems on each other and seek advice on certain issues.

"Right sweetheart, let's wash that colour off," John said in a camp voice. He led her to a bowl where she sat with her head back and he washed off her colour. It felt so relaxing and she could have fallen asleep there and then. The warm water washed through her scalp and she felt totally relaxed. The fragrance of the shampoo was coconut and it reminded her of happier times when she had been on holiday. John now led her back to her chair and she gazed in amazement at her new hair colour. He had been absolutely right, it looked fantastic. They had decided that Lisa was going to have a new look that consisted of cutting her hair shorter. She had been scared but John had coaxed her into it, telling her it would look great.

The sound of the hairdryer drowned out all the noise of the other customers and Lisa struggled to hear John. "Oh you look gorgeous," he shouted as he applied the final touches to his masterpiece. All the other stylists came to look at his creation and agreed it was amazing. Lisa had felt quite embarrassed at all the attention she was getting as people all gathered round her to see her new look. As she looked in the mirror she looked ten years younger and didn't recognise herself. Then, as she looked closer, she saw the woman she used to be so many years ago and promised herself that no man would ever make her feel that way again. She was back for good and couldn't wait to show her sister the new Lisa.

Denise met her sister at the hairdressers and couldn't believe the changes. She looked absolutely amazing. Even her skin looked healthier and her blue eyes were enchanting. This was the first step to her sister's new life and Denise loved it. After a long search in the shops they both found something for Lisa to wear in Primark – the shop was full of cheap clothes and lots of women shopped there. Lisa had lost so much weight lately and she could fit into a size ten. They both laughed as she tried on outfit after outfit, saying Ken had done her a favour by leaving her – she would never have lost the weight without all the stress. The shopping didn't stop there – they bought shoes, make up, accessories and they both had a great day. Heading home the girls talked of old times and their childhood and it seemed Lisa's dark cloud was starting to lift but then she remembered.

"Oh I need to ask Misty to baby-sit. I can't see there being a problem as she's been staying in a lot lately. I think she has split up with Dominic. I don't want to ask her about it at the moment as she seems very touchy and bites everyone's head off at the slightest thing but I can't see there being a problem."

The night arrived for the girls' big night out. Lisa had butterflies all day thinking about it, she hadn't been out for years and this was a big step for her. Misty had agreed to watch the kids thanks to Denise and told her mum to enjoy herself. She watched through the kitchen window as the sisters walked to the taxi and giggled inside as she watched her mum struggled to walk in her new high heels. At one stage she nearly fell over but was saved by Denise's arm. She looked truly stunning and Misty hoped this would be the end of her mother's dark days and endless crying but only time would tell. They both sat inside the taxi and Lisa grabbed her sister's arm, "Thanks for all you have done for me lately. One day I hope I can repay you".

Her sister's eyes filled up with tears as she held her tight, "Just get back on your feet. That's all I want. I know it's been hard but you know what they say, 'what doesn't kill you makes you stronger,' so enjoy yourself tonight and start living again". No more words needed to be spoken, as they both understood. Pulling up outside the pub they could hear the loud music being played.

On their way in, they were greeted by hundreds of bodies singing and dancing and the atmosphere was electric. Heading straight to the bar they ordered their drinks. As they stood waiting, Lisa felt someone squeeze her bum and turning slowly and met the eyes of an attractive man.

"Did you just squeeze my bum?" Lisa asked.

The man laughed and said "No but if you want me too I will". Lisa smiled at him shyly and slowly left the bar followed by his eyes.

The night was fantastic and Lisa had been too busy talking to see her ex-husband leave the pub with his new girlfriend. He hadn't noticed her at first but as he looked he couldn't believe his eyes, she had looked like she did when they first met and sadness ran through his veins as he suddenly realised what he had lost. To avoid a scene he told Julie he wanted to leave, he didn't tell her his ex-wife had come into the pub, as she would have only wanted to rub her nose in it and he didn't think Lisa deserved that, she had been through enough lately and didn't need any more hassle. As he left the pub he took a final look at her and knew he still had feelings for her. Lisa found some seats and rested her feet as her new shoes were killing her. From the side of her eye she could still see the man from before looking directly at her but she couldn't bring herself to make eye contact with him, as she felt too nervous.

The night progressed and Lisa was having the time of her life,. She had never danced and laughed so much in years. Why had she become a housebound housewife, she thought as she sat back down and started to remember her life with Ken. He had ripped every ounce of confidence from her and made her feel worthless and for the first time in her life she started to see him for what he really was – a controlling bastard. She thanked the lord for her lucky escape and carried on enjoying herself.

As she sat down, the man from the bar made his way to join her but she didn't mind now because she was feeling quite pissed and the chance of a bit of flirting appealed to her.

He sat himself next to her and began to speak "Hi do you mind if I join you?" He didn't wait for a response and just sat down right next to her and moved up close "My name's Robert". He now reached his hand out to shake her hand. "Can I get you a drink?".

Lisa smiled and told him no thanks. She told him she already had two drinks on the table and she was struggling to drink them. She thanked him for his kind offer and smiled at him invitingly. They both spoke for quite a long time and they were getting along like a house on fire. Lisa found herself quite attracted to Robert. His teeth were whiter than white and it was quite obvious he wasn't a smoker. Robert made her laugh all night long and her stomach ached like a young school girl giggling with her friends.

Denise came to join them and she gave her sister the wink that meant well done. She could tell Robert was a good catch and he seemed to be doing her sister the world of good. Denise could tell her sister was in good hands, so she left her to go and talk to her other friends who were sitting on the other side of the pub.

The end of the night came and Lisa was pissed. She sang loudly as she left the pub, escorted by her sister and Robert. Robert knew he had to make his move soon. It was now or never, he thought as the girls' taxi pulled up. Thinking on his feet he moved towards Lisa and asked the question. He had already decided he liked this woman and he didn't want to lose her without getting to know her more.

"Am I coming back to your house for a coffee then or what?" he joked. Both girls smiled as they dragged him inside the taxi. Lisa never thought about the consequences of bringing a man home to her house, all she knew was that she was happy and she hadn't felt like this for a long time and she didn't want the night to end here. This was living life to the full she thought, as he sat next to her in the taxi and by god, she was going to enjoy every minute of it whatever the consequences.

Lisa dropped her sister off in the taxi and made sure she got into her house safely. Once they had seen her open the door, they waved her goodbye and continued on their journey to Lisa's home. The taxi pulled up outside Lisa's house, which was in complete darkness. This was a good sign and it meant that the children were in bed and she knew she could start to relax. Robert paid for the taxi and joined Lisa at the front door. As she searched her bag for her key he pulled her close and kissed her. Lisa accepted him with open arms and kissed him back. She felt the woman inside her had been brought back to life and she realised how much she missed the touch of a man. His kiss was so gentle and she loved every minute of it. She had already decided her next move and she hoped he felt the same way too. They crept through the front door and giggled like small children.

"Be quiet" she whispered, as she pointed up the stairs, indicating someone was sleeping. Lisa was now quite nervous as nobody had ever seen her body before except Ken. 'What if he saw her stretch marks and flabby belly' she thought, 'would he run a mile?' The more she thought about it the more she didn't care. 'Love me, love my stretch marks' she thought as they lay next to each other on the settee. Lisa kicked off her shoes and threw her legs across him.

"My feet are throbbing, please give them a rub". He laughed and told her he could find other places to rub rather than her feet. Robert smiled as he caressed her feet and slowly slid them into his mouth. Lisa giggled as she felt his tongue sliding between her toes and it was surprisingly nice she thought as she began to speak. "Well come on then, tell me about yourself, are you married? Have you got any kids?"

Robert began to tell her all about his life. He had been in the armed forces for many years and travelled to most countries. He had married but was now divorced and the rest was history he said. He asked about Lisa's life but she shied away from the truth, not wanting to ruin the night with her sad stories. Lisa cuddled up to him and he wrapped his masculine arms round her. She felt so loved once more. She knew she might never see him ever again and wanted to live for the moment. They lay together and kissed passionately. She felt very horny towards him but she didn't want to have sex, she wasn't ready for that yet but she was ready for some good old fashion loving she thought as she teased him stroking his legs. They kissed some more and Lisa got lost in the moment and didn't hear the sound footsteps coming down the stairs.

Misty had woken up, with the sound of voices downstairs and as she listened she knew it was a male's voice she could hear and secretly she hoped it was her father begging to come home. She now made her way downstairs and as she opened the door she got the shock of her life, as she could see her mother lying in the arms of another man. Anger built in her as she shouted at Lisa.

"How can you be with another man, I thought you still loved dad!"

Lisa looked into her daughter's eyes and felt her pain but Misty had to realise that her father had left them and wasn't coming back. She shouted at Misty telling her to calm down, as she would wake up the others and she didn't need a big commotion at this late hour.

Misty shouted at the man "Get out of our house ya dickhead, she's a married woman, or hasn't she told you that?" Robert felt uncomfortable and began to leave but Lisa held him back, as she shouted back at Misty.

"What the fuck, do you want me to do, cry for the rest of my life? Well no more Misty, I've cried enough for your father and it's over, the sooner you get that into your head the better." Misty slammed the door and ran back to her room in tears. Lisa could hear her shouting "slag!" as she ran up the stairs. Robert told Lisa he had to go but she insisted on him staying. She told him of her problems and after a bit of persuading he agreed to stay.

Misty lay on her bed crying, waiting for her mother to come and comfort her and tell her everything would be alright but she never came. She had deserted her now, just like her father had. Misty lay on her bed and kicked her legs, with her temper exploding inside her.

She had now made up her mind to go and see her father the next day and decided she would ask Max to come with her. Misty needed her father more than ever and missed him so much. She would go and see him and surely when he saw her and Max he would surely want to come home and realise he had made a bad mistake leaving them all. This was her last hope to keep her family together she thought. If this didn't work god only knows what would happen to them all.

CHAPTER FIVE

THE MORNING LIGHT smiled through Misty's window to greet her tear filled eyes. She had waited all night long for her mother to come and speak to her but with no success. Obviously her night with her new man had been much more important than her teenage daughter's tears. As her body left her bed, she felt totally drained, her energy levels were low and life didn't seem worth living anymore.

"Morning shit the bed", Max shouted as his sister walked into the kitchen. It was quite unusual to see his sister up and ready so early. She was usually always late. He could see by her eyes she had been crying. "What's up with you mard arse?" he joked. His sister looked straight at Lisa and gave her an evil look. "What's up with me? Ask Mrs. wine and dine me over there". Max looked straight at his mother for the answers but her face remained stern, "Listen I haven't got time for all this right now. We will speak about it when I get home".

Max danced his eyes from Misty to his mam and tried to find out what was going on but they both looked at each other like gunslingers about to draw. Misty continued to speak to Max, watching her mother's face as she spoke.

"I am going to see dad after school if you want to come?" She waited for his response as he turned his face towards hers. Max screwed his face up and felt mixed emotions. He wanted to see his father but he felt anger toward him for leaving them and had previously wished him to rot in hell.

"Why are you going to see that prick? He's not bothered with us for months, all he is interested in is his new girlfriend and his gambling so why now?"

Misty shrugged her shoulders and continued to speak. "Well he is not the only one who has moved on and forgotten about this family's needs".

Lisa looked at her and knew what she was about to say. She knew nothing could stop her so she just watched and waited for her to say her piece. "Ask mi mam about moving on. Go on ask her, she had her new man in here last night. Lay together on the settee all nice and comfy. Go on ask her!" she shouted.

Lisa went red in the face and felt her blood boil. Her children knew their dad had a girlfriend, so why was she expected to live a solitary life. Max stared at his mother waiting for an answer but Lisa couldn't bring herself to speak. Why did she have to explain to them, their father didn't, she thought and remained silent.

Misty grabbed her stuff and left the house, slamming the door behind her. "She's a right fuckin' slag", she thought as she headed to school. Not far behind she could hear Max shouting her name, telling her to wait for him, she could see by his face he was angry. Once he caught up with her he began to speak. "So tell me again about last night. Why didn't you fuckin' wake me up? I would have thrown him right out the cheeky fucker. Who was it, did you know him?"

Misty told him all the details and they both decided they would speak to their mother when they got home. Her behaviour was totally unacceptable and she needed to think about what she'd done.

The day was more or less the same as any other in school. It had been three weeks since her split from Dominic and he was making her life unbearable. Since they had split, he had tried every day to win her back but because she said no, he was making her life a misery. He would flirt with Francesca trying to wind her up and when that didn't work, he spread rumours around the school about her, so her life at the moment was quite shit .Francesca was going from bad to worse. Her reputation had gone downhill and all the lads said she had more knob ends than weekends. They all knew she was an easy ride and boys just used her just for sex. Francesca and Kevin had fizzled out, he also had used her for sex, the same as all the others but Francesca couldn't see it, she thought he would come back to her one day.

Misty had decided she wanted to study as much as she could as her exams were coming up and she needed good grades to get her into college. Gordon had been out of the picture since their last meeting and she liked it like that, even though he had never been far from her thoughts. School finished and she waited for her brother to escort her to her dad's. She felt jittery inside knowing they were going to see their father. How would he react, she thought. Say he told them to go home and didn't want to see them, how would they cope? She knew she would have to go and find out either way and it was now or never. Max walked up to join her and they discussed their next move.

He too felt nervous but hid it well. Max hadn't really wanted to go but he didn't want his sister to face it alone. He had secretly been worried about her lately; she seemed to have lost that happy-go-lucky bounce about her. What Max never told her was that he knew she had been seeing Gordon and that that was the reason she had finished with Dominic. He also knew Gordon was a thief and a dead leg but until he knew for definite his sister was serious about him, he would keep his mouth shut.

The door of their father's house looked straight at them, as they left the bus. "Go on then Misty" he whispered, as he playfully pushed her. Misty's heart pounded but what was she worried about she thought after all, he was their father. They both laughed with nerves as Misty knocked on the door, she could feel tears building in her eyes as she waited for him to answer. A lady opened the door and stood looking at them waiting for them to talk. She was well and truly gorgeous, Misty thought as she cleared her throat to speak.

"Is me dad there?" The lady looked shocked and you could tell by her body language she wasn't happy with their visit.

"Ken!" She shouted in a piecing voice. "There's someone at the door for you" and she left them stood at the door as she casually walked back into to the house.

The man they saw walking toward them, didn't look like their father .He looked ancient and somewhat scruffy. When he saw the faces of his children, his face lit up.

"Come in kids, why are you stood at the door?" Max wanted to say, "Because your little hooker of a girlfriend as left us here" but he zipped his mouth for now as he didn't want to cause any trouble. Ken led them into the front room and it looked like a show house. Everything looked so new and clean and it was a palace compared to their own home. Ken hugged Misty and rubbed the top of Max's hair telling them to sit down. You could tell by his face he felt embarrassed regarding Julie's behaviour. Julie made her entrance into the room like the queen of Sheba and made no attempt to look or talk to them.

"Julie, these are my children Misty and Max". Her face remained stern and she nodded her head. Then she shot Ken a look to let him know she wasn't happy about their arrival. "Well I hope you have told them we are going out soon. We don't be want to late do we?" She said in a commanding voice. Ken looked at her and confirmed to his children they couldn't stay long, as they were going out. It looked like she had secretly sprinkled magic powder over him to make him obey her every command. Ken spoke for a while but turned his attention toward the racing on the television. He shouted at his horse and sat forward in his chair. "Come on you lazy bastard whip the fucker".

Max and Misty felt completely out of place and you could tell by Ken's face he wanted them to leave but didn't have the courage to tell them. After watching his horse lose the race he turned his head to face them both.

"How's your Looney mother these days?" he asked in a cocky voice. The children looked at each other and Max wanted to jump on him and pound his fist deep into his face. My mother he thought, the mother you made fuckin' Looney. Misty spoke quickly as she saw the anger on Max s face.

"She's alright", Misty said in a sheepish manner, "and so are Jonathan and Lee. She is working now and doing well." Misty lied to protect her mother, she didn't want him to think she was still the nervous wreck he had left behind.

"Your mother working, that's a first, it's about time she got off her lazy arse and got a job, instead of living off me for all these years" he moaned. Misty could smell alcohol on him as he passed her. Ken stood fidgeting in the mirror as he began to speak.

"Right kids I better start getting ready". This was his hint to tell them to leave but they both continued to sit there and this made him feel even more uncomfortable with the situation.

Misty now felt worse than ever, their mother didn't have time for them and now her father was acting in the same way. She felt like they were toys and now her parents weren't together, neither of them wanted to play anymore. Well at least she had seen it with her own two eyes. Her mother was right, Ken was an out and out bastard who cared for no one but himself. He walked his children to the door and couldn't wait to see the back of them. They shouted goodbye to Julie but she made no reply as she pottered about in the bedroom. Ken reached into his pocket and pulled out two five pound notes. The children looked at each other as he passed them one each but he made sure Julie was out of sight before he did. No kisses were exchanged as he waved them off, he closed the door immediately after they left and it was obvious he was glad to see the back of them. Misty felt her heart breaking in two, as emptiness filled her body. Max saw his sister was going to break down in tears, so he grabbed her arm and began to speak.

"Fat fucker isn't he and his little tart of a girlfriend who does she think she is. Well we are better off without him. He will never be a dad to us now he has got himself another woman. He is only interested in keeping her happy and has forgotten all about us. Anyway at least we got a fiver". Max giggled and tickled his sister bringing laughter back to her face. They both decided their money would be spent wisely on cigs and beer. They laughed as they made their way to the bus stop. Both children kept calling their father names, all the way home, it was sort of a therapy to rid them of him. They both decided there and then they wouldn't be going again and as far as they were concerned the man they once knew as their father was dead and gone.

Reaching home, they entered the back door and there was Lisa with the family photo album spread out on the table. As they watched her they could see piles of pictures with Ken's head cut out of them.

"What are you doing mam?" Max asked.

"Something I should of done years ago – rid myself of your father. He doesn't deserve to be in our family photo album anymore. He is not a dad, all he is interested in is his fuckin' self but from now on, I am going to take a leaf out of his book and live my life", she replied.

Max looked at Misty and decided to leave her to it. Both parents were playing a game between themselves but had forgotten about the four children they had produced together. No one was giving them a second thought. Misty headed to her bedroom. The walls had witnessed many a change to this young girl. Once sweet and innocent Misty was now changing into someone even she didn't recognise anymore.

CHAPTER SIX

MISTY WENT FROM bad to worse over time and everyone could tell that her parent's separation was having an effect. Her mood in the home was snappy and she had changed towards her mother, only talking to her when she needed to. Tonight was the first night she had been out for a long time and she was looking forward to meeting with her friends, because staying in her bedroom was driving her crazy. Misty now made no secret that she was going to the pub and to tell the truth her mother was glad of the break from her and her sarcastic comments. Robert was coming round tonight, so with Misty out of the way, it was set to be a peaceful night.

Francesca knocked on the front door and was greeted by Lisa. "Hi Francesca she's upstairs, go straight up".

"Misty are ya ready yet?" she shouted as she approached her bedroom. As she opened the door, her friend was stood there looking truly stunning. "Wow, check you out" she said as she looked her friend up and down. Misty was wearing the shortest black skirt she had ever seen, with a pink vest top. Her shoes had quite a large heel but they complimented her skinny legs.

"You're definitely copping off tonight, you look great", Francesca laughed. Misty looked into the mirror and she knew Francesca was right she was dressed to kill and she was more than ready to party.

"Come on then, let's get out of this shithole" Misty shouted. Francesca laughed and asked what was going on with her, as she noticed she was in a strange mood. Misty didn't have time to explain everything to her and replied

"Family problems, just ignore me I will be alright once we are out of here". Francesca knew all about her parents splitting up and knew Misty was finding it hard to cope, so she followed her friend down the stairs asking no more questions for now.

"See you later Lisa", Francesca shouted as she waited for Misty to find her coat. Hearing Francesca's voice, Lisa headed to the front door. "Have a nice night, don't get too drunk". Misty stared into her mother's eyes and made no comment.

"What time will you be home Misty?" Lisa asked. Misty now stood tall and spoke in a sarcastic tone.

"Whenever I get home. So make sure lover boy is not here when I do". Lisa stood and felt her blood boil.

"Listen, keep your snide remarks to yourself, I was only asking a question." Francesca wanted the floor to open and swallow her up. She felt so embarrassed for Lisa, the way Misty had spoken to her. Misty found her coat and left the house slamming the door behind as she left.

"Right I am feeling wild tonight, so let's go and get rat arsed". The girls linked each other arms as they made their way to Billy Greens, the local pub where everyone went. As they walked down Rochdale Road the men pressed the horns in their cars to show their appreciation for the way the girls were dressed and both girls laughed at the attention they were getting.

Entering the pub, the music played loudly and the atmosphere was lively. The pub drunk was dancing to some song that was on the juke box and as Misty walked past him he grabbed her hand to dance with him. Misty laughed and tried to escape his grip but he was quite strong and would not let go, "Let me go ya muppet" she shouted but he continued regardless, until a hand reached over her shoulder and took over the man's grip. "Didn't you hear her nobhead, she said let go".

The look on the man's face told her he seemed scared and he slowly released his grip. As she turned to see who had rescued her, there he stood, like a man made of iron and her heart skipped a beat as he said hello.

"Hello Gordon. Thanks for saving me, he was doing me fuckin' head in", she smiled. He smiled back and escorted her to a seat.

"What are you drinking?" he asked. Francesca now saw Gordon and joined them and answered cheekily

"Two brandy and cokes please". Misty smiled, as he left to go to the bar.

"Fuckin' hell did you see Gordon with that man's hand? He was like your knight in shining armour. I need someone like him, someone who will protect me". Francesca left her side and flitted round the pub, looking for any new talent and it wasn't long before she was in the arms of some new man. Misty watched as Gordon made his way back to her holding their drinks.

"Where's dirty knickers?" he asked as he put the drinks on the table. Misty knew who he was talking about and pointed in Francesca's direction. "Look at her she doesn't care does she?" Gordon said and Misty laughed as they watched her, chatting up her knew found friend.

"So where have you been hiding then? I've not seen you for weeks. I thought you had fallen out with me or summat". She smiled as she looked into his eyes. What had happened between her parents wasn't his fault and she was the one who had chosen to have sex with him, so she didn't know why she had ever shunned him out of her life. All of sudden she realised that all the problems she had were of her own making. He hadn't caused them, it was her who had cheated on Dominic and now she was free so why couldn't she give him a go? 'What have I got to lose', she thought as she leaned over to kiss his lips. They enjoyed a long passionate kiss and only stopped when they heard the familiar voice of Francesca at the side of them.

"Oh my god, can't you leave each other alone for a minute. You're like animals". She reached for her drink and as she did she held Gordon's neck and kissed it slowly on the side. Gordon pushed her away and you could see he was quite angry by her actions. "Will you fuck off messing around, go back to your friends over there and leave us alone".

Misty looked at her friend as she picked up her drink looking slightly embarrassed. "See you later babes, make sure he looks after you". She kissed her friend on the cheek and made her way back to the other table. You could tell Gordon was now irritated and he couldn't wait to leave the pub "Shall we go for a walk? My heads banging in here.".

Misty agreed as she could tell that Francesca had upset him but why had he reacted like that? The night in the pub was nearly over any way and they walked up the road to the takeaway. Misty suddenly felt starving hungry as the smell of the take-away hit her nose. She didn't know what was to do with her these last few days, her appetite had increased and she never felt full.

"Do you want anything?" he asked as they stepped into the takeaway. Misty wanted to order loads of food but felt embarrassed, so she just ordered chips and gravy to walk home with. Gordon didn't hold back at all. He ordered chips, pudding and gravy and it looked beautiful as he dug his fork into it. Misty picked at her food, as they started to walk off, she had wanted to scoff it down but she felt shy eating in front of him for the first time.

"Shall we go back to my brothers?" He asked as he wiped

the gravy from round his mouth. Misty didn't have to think twice before she answered, because she knew she also wanted sex, so his brothers seemed like a great idea, at least there they would have a bed.

It's funny how Misty now felt towards Gordon. She felt protected by him and he made her feel safe. He could give her all the love she needed – the love that she had been denied by her parents. Gordon took her straight to bed when they reached the flat and he wasted no time taking her clothes off. As they cuddled together their love making began.

"Before we start, have you got protection?" Misty asked.

Gordon smiled "You didn't bother last time, what's different now? Anyway I will pull it out, so we don't need to use a condom." Misty thought he knew what he was talking about and began to relax.

Gordon had plans of his own and wanted this girl for himself. He smiled at Misty as he wet the end of his penis with his spit, saying it would help get it in, as she was so tight. The sex began and not a lot had changed from the last episode. He was like a bull in a china shop, as he whacked his body against hers. Misty held her legs up as he penetrated deep inside her, she could feel his testicles banging against her bum as he slid in and out of her. The signs it was going to end filled his mouth as he chanted the usual "Yeah baby". Misty joined in with the noises so she looked as if she was enjoying it too and this made him explode. "You dirty bitch" he muttered as he collapsed on top of her. Finally he rolled off her and lay lifeless on the bed. She now cuddled up to him, as he cradled her in his arms. They spoke all night long until they heard the birds tweeting outside the window and that was when Misty decided it was time to go home.

Gordon thought this was a good idea as he had a job with his brother the next day and needed to get some rest. He kept this from Misty as his business was his own and he wanted to keep it that way.

"I didn't know you worked", Misty said in a surprised voice.

"Well it's not so much a job" he said, " but it earns me money, so what the fuck. Misty didn't delve into his work too much as she could see he was quite secretive about whatever he was doing. As she reached home he kissed her and told her to come back to his brother's house the following evening. She agreed and waved him goodbye. Life was starting to look brighter she thought as she made her way into the house. She needed some sleep desperately and plenty of it. Her body felt exhausted at the moment and she couldn't seem to find any energy. She had decided she would buy some vitamins the following day, to try and give herself some kind of boost. She had been feeling run down these last few days and had put it down to all the stress in her life lately.

Lying in bed Lisa heard her daughter come in the front door but didn't want to start a big argument so early in the morning, so she left her for now, knowing that she would have to have a talk with her sooner or later but for now it could wait. Lisa had heard on the grapevine that she was seeing an older lad and knew she would end up in big trouble if she wasn't careful. Misty' teachers had also been on the phone to her, telling her of the changes in her daughter. Her exams were coming up soon and they wanted Lisa to have a word with Misty, to see if she could make her see sense and buckle down. Lisa lay awake in her bed as she heard her daughter stumbling into her bed. Tomorrow was D-day she thought and she would confront her with all guns blazing.

The morning came and the house was alive. Everybody was getting ready for school, all except Misty. Lisa shouted her several times until finally she lost her temper. She ran up the stairs like a mad woman and charged into her daughter's room.

"I'm not fuckin' telling you again. Get up now, you have exams today and you don't want to be late do you?" Misty eyes had barely opened, when her mother pulled the blankets off her bed and yanked the pillow from under her head. "Next it will be a glass of water on you lady so move it". She knew her mother meant business and didn't wait to find out if she would carry out her threat, so jumping out of the bed, she made her way to the bathroom. Misty could smell the toast that they were making downstairs and felt quite sick. She heaved into the bathroom sink and didn't feel at all well.

Misty tried to pull herself together and headed downstairs. "Where's my school bag?" she shouted as she grabbed her coat. Still looking for her bag she moaned, "I have got an exam today and I need to revise. So if anyone has seen my bag please tell me". Lisa looked at her and wanted to say, well it's your own fault you should have done it last night but as always she didn't want to cause an argument so early in the morning, so her lips remained shut. Misty caught the bus to school and met all her friends at the school gates. They all felt nervous as she did about the exams. The bell rang and they lined up at the main hall, where the exam would take place.

Everyone found a desk and began to put all their things onto it. Misty looked inside her own bag and realised she didn't even have a pen. Looking round the hall she searched for Francesca. Once she spotted her she shouted, "Francesca!" The teacher looked up from her desk and in a loud voice shouted Misty's name.

"There is no talking allowed in this hall so whatever you want could you please ask me before the exam starts. If you need anything I will bring it, so I suggest you sit down and remain silent till the exams are finished. Misty felt the eyes of everyone gazing upon her and could feel the blood rushing to her face.

"I need a pen Miss, so stop shouting at me", she moaned.

The teacher brought a pen to her table and knelt at the side of her desk before she began to speak.

"Misty, when this exam has finished please come to my office, because I won't stand for backchat. I think you need reminding about our school rules." Misty raised her eyes to the ceiling and shrugged her shoulders as the teacher left. She could hear some of the pupils laughing in the background and she started to mutter under her breath "She can fuck right off, if she thinks I am wasting my time sat in her office revising school rules! They can shove their rules right up their arses for all I care".

The exam began and you could hear a pin drop, not a sound could be heard, except for the exam papers being turned over. Misty was hoping to do well in this subject, English literacy was her favourite subject and she often found comfort from writing poems. Misty read the paper and studied every word, hoping to fully understand the questions asked. The time flew and Misty could feel herself getting warmer and warmer as the exam was coming to an end. She felt a strange burning at the back of her throat and she felt physically sick. She blew her breath onto her face in the hope it would cool her down but the hot flush didn't pass it just got worse. The teacher ended the exam after all the papers were collected and noise once again filled the hall.

CHAPTER SEVEN

MISTY LEFT THE main hall after the exam. Her body still felt hot and clammy but she thought she would be alright once she had eaten something. She had not eaten her breakfast that morning and this could have been the reason for her sickness. The pupils discussed the test as they lined up to wait for their turn to go in for dinner. Francesca stood next to Misty as they made their way to the front of the queue, pushing all the younger kids out of the way. Misty stood and felt her body flow with heat. As she stood, she loosened her shirt, pulling it out of her skirt to let the air rise up to her chest. She still felt on fire and waved a piece of paper across her face, trying to cool herself. Francesca noticed her friend's actions and could see she wasn't looking too good. Her face had turned a funny white colour as Francesca watched her closely.

Misty could hear voices fade around her and everything went blurred, she felt her legs melt into the floor, as they gave way to her tired body. Her body fell crashing to the floor and she was no longer conscious of her surroundings. Francesca screamed as she saw her friend keel over.

"Misty what's up?" She shouted but she made no reply.

"Someone go and get help. Fuckin' hell she needs help" she screamed, "will you hurry up and get someone ya nobhead, she could be dying. Go now, instead of gawping at her. She needs help". Everybody stood frozen as they watched.

Francesca shouted yet again in a fierce voice. "Please someone get help".

Francesca rested her head on Misty's chest and prayed she didn't die, as she watched two girls running finally to get help. The two girls who had witnessed Misty fall had now run to the teachers in the dining room.

"Miss! Come quick, its Misty Sullivan. She's collapsed on the floor, I think she's dead".

The nearest teacher came running and seeing Misty lay on the floor, panicked and shouted aloud "Give her room, please give her some room".

Francesca held her friend in her arms, trying to explain what had just happened, as the teacher listened. "Right, someone go and get a glass of cold water from the kitchen staff".

Misty was now starting to come round. She could hear voices round her. She felt light headed and her body didn't feel like her own. Misty felt cold on her face that caused her to open her eyes. As they opened, she could see everybody gazing down at her. The teacher now took control from Francesca and held Misty in her arms. As she passed her a drink of water she told her to try and drink some. The water felt so refreshing as it reached the back of her throat. Misty now felt strong enough to sit up and managed to sit on a nearby chair. The teacher dispersed the on-lookers, telling them that the show was over and to head back to the dining hall.

Misty was now fully conscious as she spoke to her friend. "Fuckin' hell what happened to me? One minute I remember being in the queue and the next I woke up on the floor".

Francesca put her arms round her and comforted her as she spoke "Misty I proper shit it, I thought you'd died. I was talking to you one minute then you were on the floor, I sent one of the year threes to get help". Colour now returned to

Misty's face but she still felt shaky inside. 'At least I'm not dead' she thought, as she drank the cold water. The teacher now came back and asked if Misty was feeling any better. Once she knew she was alright she asked Francesca to take her to the medical room to see the nurse.

Misty finished her drink and slowly stood. Her legs were still shaking and with her friend's help she made her way to the nurse. "Oh, my legs feel like Elvis's, they won't stop shaking" Misty chuckled.

Francesca laughed as she held her friend tight, "Why do you think, you fainted? Have you eaten some dickey food or summat?"

Misty tried to scan her mind, to see if she could remember anything she might have eaten but nothing sprang to mind. "I think I might have just been hungry, I didn't have any time for breakfast this morning and that could be the reason".

Francesca opened the door to the medical room and asked for the nurse. The medical room was somewhere Misty had never been before. All the walls were painted white and there was a large bed placed against the wall. Francesca pulled up two chairs and waited for the nurse to come in. The girls sat chatting until they heard the sound of the nurse. As she entered they both looked her up and down from head to toe. The school nurse was quite plump and her feet looked too small for her body, it was kind of weird how her body was shaped, she looked like an egg with legs.

"Right first things first. Who's the patient?"

Francesca began to speak "Well miss. We were stood in the hall and Misty fainted". The nurse stopped Francesca right there.

"So you're not the patient then?"

"No miss it's Misty" she replied.

"Right then sweetheart, you can head back for your dinner, I only need to see the person who is ill, so off you trot". Francesca stood and tried to make her point but the nurse was having none of it and escorted her to the door.

"Miss she is my best mate, I want to make sure she's alright". The nurse smiled as she opened the door, to let Francesca out.

"If she needs any help I will call you back in but for now kindly go back to whatever you were doing so I can deal with your friend.

Francesca shuffled out of the room like a snail, shouting to her friend. "If you need me Misty, get someone to come and get me". Misty nodded as Francesca left the room, mumbling something under her breath.

The nurse pulled up a chair and seated herself next to Misty. "Right my love what can I do for you?" Misty explained what had just happened to her and the nurse took down some notes.

"Misty I am sending you home for the rest of the day and once there I suggest you have a lie down and in future make sure you eat your breakfast in the morning. Breakfast is the most important meal of the day and you shouldn't be skipping it" the nurse lectured. Misty nodded in agreement and listened carefully to what she had had to say.

"Can anyone come and pick you up Misty? I don't want you walking home alone in case you faint again" the nurse asked.

Misty shook her head and told the nurse her mam was in work. "Well what about your dad then, surely he can come and get you". Misty felt her face go red as she told her about the family situation. "I don't see my dad anymore Miss, because he doesn't live with us anymore". Misty now felt tears flood from her eyes and found it hard to hold her emotions.

The nurse realised she had hit a raw nerve and flung her arms around Misty trying to comfort the poor little girl that sat in front of her. "Oh I'm so sorry. I didn't realise your parents were no longer together. Lots of children are without two parents these days, I'm sure everything will work out in time, please don't get upset".

Misty wanted to tell her that her father didn't give a fuck and all he cared about was his new life without them but she knew her words would have been wasted, so she remained silent. Misty knew her family was broken forever and nothing could be done to fix it, so she dried her tears and put on a brave face once again. The nurse left the room once Misty had stopped crying and went to phone Misty's mother. Once she found her mother's contact number she dialled it and waited till someone answered.

"Hello could I speak to Mrs. Sullivan please, it's the school nurse regarding her daughter Misty".

The voice told her to hold the line and the nurse could hear them shouting Lisa's name in the background. Eventually she heard footsteps approaching the phone.

"Hello Mrs. Sullivan speaking."

The nurse then went on to tell Lisa about her daughter feeling unwell and she could tell by her tone, she wasn't willing to leave work to come and pick her up. The nurse told Lisa she was willing to drop her off at home but she didn't want her left alone. Lisa took a minute before she answered and it was decided Misty would go to her sister Denise's until she finished work. The phone call ended and the nurse headed back to tell Misty the news. They both got into the car and the nurse started the engine, Misty gave directions to her auntie's house as they set off. There wasn't a word spoken all the way through the journey and the nurse could feel Misty's pain as she watched her gaze through the window in a world of her own. When they finally reached their destination, her auntie came to greet them with a concerned look on her face. Misty stepped straight out of the car and headed towards Denise.

"You look like death warmed up love. Go in the house

and put the kettle on while I speak to the nurse". Misty did as her auntie asked and walked slowly down the garden path to the house.

"Hi, I am Misty's auntie, is everything alright? Her mum has just phoned me saying she felt unwell". The nurse confirmed that her niece was feeling unwell and told her about her breaking down in tears, as she spoke about her father. Denise felt rather embarrassed and didn't know what to say, so she thanked the nurse for dropping her off and headed back inside. Once inside Denise asked how she was feeling and Misty told her she still felt shaky inside.

"Right. I will make you a piece of toast – that might help. I always feel sick when I don't eat, so you have probably got that off me." Misty smiled as she watched her toast under the grill and her appetite returned. When everything was ready, they went into the front room, so they could talk some more. Denise had been right – once Misty ate the toast, she felt a lot better, at least the shakiness subsided. Misty loved spending time with Denise. She was always so understanding and they got on like a house on fire.

Denise knew Misty had a new boyfriend, as Lisa had told her previously. She also knew he was a lot older than she was. Denise was always on the ball with her sister's children and once she knew Misty had fainted, one thing sprang to mind but she knew she couldn't come out straight out and say it. She would have to go undercover and secretly interrogate her niece for the information she required.

"So I hear you have a new boyfriend, Misty. Are you going to tell me about him then". Misty smiled and felt kind of shy. She had not been able to talk about him to anyone, so this was an ideal opportunity to tell someone exactly how she felt.

"Well" she said in a proud voice, "His name is Gordon and I really like him. I didn't at first but he has grown on me". Denise showed an interest and she prompted her to continue speaking, as she knew she had to get her to talk more if she was ever going to get to the bottom of her sickness. Denise had a gut feeling she was right and continued with her investigation.

"Is that it?" said Denise, "I thought you were madly in love with him. Your mam said she thought it was quite serious". Bingo! That was it, thought Denise, as Misty began to reveal all the details about her relationship. That was for all but one detail, the one Denise wanted to know most. Denise listened as her niece continued to speak but couldn't hold her tongue any longer as the frustration was killing her.

"Do you love him?" Denise asked. Misty smiled shyly and nodded. It came as quite a shock that she had answered yes to that question but the more she thought about it, the more she realised she really loved him. Denise couldn't hold the question in any longer and needed to know now.

"Are you having sex with him Misty?"

Misty nearly collapsed as she stuttered her words, she could feel Denise watching her every move as she repeated the question.

"Are you having sex with him? Tell me Misty because there are things we need to sort out, like the contraceptive pill and other things if you are". Misty knew she needed to talk about contraception with someone and this could be the ideal opportunity to get help, so she confessed her sins to her auntie.

Denise felt sick inside when she told her she had been having sex with Gordon and without even doing a pregnancy test Denise knew the outcome. As she cast her eyes over Misty, her stomach churned 'Oh please god no, please no, she's only a baby herself', she thought as she lit a cigarette. Denise paced the front room as Misty watched.

"Are you alright Denise, you look like you've seen a ghost?" Denise turned to face her and couldn't hold back any longer.

"Do you think you could be pregnant love?"

Misty screwed her face together as she shouted "No, how could I be pregnant?" But the more she thought about it, the more everything fell into place: the tiredness and the increased appetite. Misty's head was spinning now as she tried to remember the date of her last period and everything suggested she was pregnant. Misty screamed as the reality hit home and Denise moved towards her.

"Listen don't worry, we don't even know if you are pregnant yet, so let's cross that bridge when we come to it". Denise sat with Misty and they tried to work out the date of her last period. When they had finished their calculations they decided that Misty could only be two or three weeks late for her period.

Denise ran things over in her mind. No matter how much she tried to deny it she knew deep in her gut Misty was pregnant. Denise knew she couldn't keep this secret from her sister, it was too serious, so creeping upstairs she made her way to the bedroom and used the phone to tell Lisa what she suspected.

Lisa went hysterical when her sister mentioned that Misty could be pregnant. "Don't be silly, she is still a virgin and she's only a baby herself" cried Lisa. Denise continued as Lisa sobbed at the possibility. "Oh God, please don't let her be pregnant please" she yelled. Denise tried to calm her sister down.

"Right Denise will you please phone the doctors and try and get her appointment for around five o clock" Lisa asked. "I can't stand the thought of not knowing. The sooner we find out what's up with her the sooner we can sort thing out. Will you please phone for me?"

Denise agreed but on one condition "I don't want you going spare at Misty, till we know for sure if she's pregnant or not, alright?" The phone line was quiet for a moment then she heard the timid voice of her sister replying.

"I will try Denise but it's so fuckin' hard, its one thing after the other with my kids at the moment. I am at my wits end, I don't know what I will do if she's pregnant. I don't know anything anymore" Lisa ended the phone call and in a dazed trance headed back into work. Throughout the rest of the day Lisa couldn't stop thinking of anything else but as she thought back she realised that no sanitary towels had been used, because she had checked them to see if they needed replacing and the full pack had still been there but Lisa had never given it a second thought at the time.

'Silly, silly bitch' she thought as her temper exploded inside her. Well if she is pregnant she can go and live with her fuckin' father. Let's see if him and his tart of a girlfriend can sort this mess out. Lisa watched the clock till the end of her shift, knowing she had to meet Misty to accompany her to the doctors. How would she control her anger when she saw her she thought. All she wanted to do was to dive on her and beat the living daylights out of her but she knew she had to restrain herself for the moment till she knew the truth.

Lisa's shift finally came to an end. She grabbed her coat and waved to her work friends "Can't stop got to get home early" she shouted, "See ya tomorrow". Once out of the door she walked at speed to meet her daughter. "Be calm" she muttered to herself, "don't explode, just be calm" she repeated to herself as she walked the distance to meet her daughter.

Lisa was like a woman possessed, as she marched up the hill to greet her. She felt sadness as she looked at her and in her mind she spoke desperate words. She's only a baby, please lord, please don't let her be pregnant. Misty stood waiting for her mother, unaware she knew all about her sex romps with Gordon.

"Come on, we best hurry up if we want to get there on

time", Lisa spoke in a calm manner. She knew there was no point in arguing till they had seen the doctor and he had diagnosed her. As they walked, Lisa asked what had happened at school. Misty began to tell her that she had collapsed in school but didn't know the reason why. Her tone was as stroppy as ever and Lisa had to bite her tongue as not to cause an argument before they got to the surgery. Lisa held the door open and Misty plodded in towards the reception.

"Can I help you love?" the receptionist asked. Misty waited for her mother to join her before she answered. "Erm I've got an appointment. Mam what time is my appointment?" Lisa took over the conversation and told the receptionist all the details as Misty found two seats in the waiting area.

She looked at all the other patients and wondered what ailments they each had. The doctors surgery was quite pleasant, all the walls were painted in a light yellow colour and all the furniture complimented it in a navy blue. The doctors had a system for appointments. All the doctors' names were displayed on the wall, with a flashing bulb next to them and they would call out the patients name over the speaker when it was their turn. Misty sat and gazed around, reading the notices on the wall. Her stomach churned as she knew there could be a possibility she could be pregnant but for now she tried not to worry and hid her concern well.

"Misty Sullivan, to surgery three please" the doctor shouted over the speaker. Lisa stood first and Misty slowly followed. As they walked to the room it felt like the walk of death, as fear filled her body.

"Hello Lisa how are you?" the doctor asked. He had remembered Lisa, as she had been there several times in the last couple of months. He knew of her suicide attempts and knew she had been dealt quite a bad hand lately.

"Hi doctor, it's not me for a change, it's my daughter Misty". Misty looked the doctor up and down and he looked quite ancient, she thought. His skin could be compared to that of a rhino and he seemed very solemn.

"Right young lady what seems to be the problem?" he asked. As she tried to explain, her words got mixed up and she began to panic. Lisa could see she was struggling and took over to avoid any embarrassment.

"Well doctor, she collapsed in school. I think she's got some kind of stomach bug or something like that, or perhaps even food poisoning". The doctor asked several more questions and then pulled out a little plastic tub from his desk. "Right I need a urine specimen, can you take this to the toilet and fill it for me". She felt like she wanted to laugh and felt a smile fill her face as she spoke.

"What, you want me to wee in that?"

"Yes" the doctor replied as he peered over his glasses to look at her. "Off you go young lady I haven't got all day".

Misty left the room with the plastic bottle in her hand and located the toilets. Once inside the cubicle, she pulled down her knickers and concentrated hard to wee. Nothing came out at first but after several minutes she could feel a trickle of urine leaving her body. Quickly she placed the container between her legs and adjusted her body to fill the bottle. Once she had finished she examined its contents by holding it up to the light to see if anything was floating round in it but nothing could be seen. The bottle was just a quarter of the way full and there was no way she could have filled it anymore even if she had tried all day. Her bladder was well and truly empty. Oh well it's better than nothing, she thought as she headed back to see the doctor. As she entered the room, she had no idea her mother had already told him about her fears regarding her being pregnant.

Misty sat herself next to Lisa, handing the sample back to the doctor. The doctor made no comment, as he walked over to the corner of the room and unscrewed the lid off the container. They both watched him eagerly as he searched in the drawer for a smaller jar that contained swab like sticks one of which he now placed into the urine. The doctor then headed back and sat at the table.

"Right young lady, I am just carrying out a few tests to see if I can get to the bottom of your fainting today. It should take only take a few minutes, so please be patient".

As they waited the doctor started to write in Misty's notes, asking her lots of details about how she felt just before she fainted. Several questions later, the doctor headed back to the corner of the room and examined the swab. As they watched Lisa knew it was bad news, as the doctor shook his head and rejoined them.

"Right Misty I have found out why you haven't been feeling well and I am afraid it isn't very good news." Lisa edged forward, hanging on his every word.

"Right young lady, it appears you are pregnant".

Lisa screamed and put her head in her hands. "Please no. Please Doctor. Are you sure? Please check it again". The doctor sat back in his chair and pulled Lisa's hands from her face.

"Mrs. Sullivan, the test is one hundred percent accurate and your daughter is most definitely pregnant."

Lisa sobbed as Misty gazed round the room in astonishment. The words he had spoken hadn't even sunk in. She sat there feeling numb as she fidgeted with her sleeve.

The doctor now turned to Misty "Well you have been quite a silly girl haven't you? I hope you know what this means". Misty froze and was unable to speak. He continued speaking as he watched Lisa rocking her body to and fro, unable to cope with the devastating news.

"You're not having it Misty" Lisa shouted. "You are a child yourself, how could you have been so stupid". Lisa wanted to throttle her daughter and her temper was about to explode but she knew she would have to wait till they had left the surgery so she now turned to the doctor for support. "Doctor will you tell her she's too young to have a baby?" Lisa pleaded. The doctor felt Lisa's pain as he knew the terrible time she had been through herself with the break-up of her marriage in the past. His heart melted as he watched the distraught woman swaying to and fro. He now turned his eyes to face Misty in the hope she would listen to his advice.

"Misty, you need to have a serious think about your circumstances. The choices you make now will determine the rest of your life. I suggest you go home and have a serious think about your situation."

Misty knew that he meant for her to have an abortion without him actually saying the words, she had learnt all about it in school weeks before and knew what it entailed, but for the moment she was more embarrassed that her mother knew that she had been sexually active, rather than knowing she was pregnant. Lisa thanked the doctor, and he gave them a follow-up appointment, to discuss the pregnancy further. As they stood to leave, the doctor looked at Misty with disapproving eyes and she knew then, she was in deep shit. No amount of lies could save her this time. Lisa left the surgery like a fired bullet and Misty knew it wouldn't be long before she opened fire on her. They walked away from the surgery before Lisa spoke. Then, like a preying animal she pounced on Misty, grabbing her sleeve and dragging her closer towards her face.

"You dirty little bitch. Trust you to get pregnant, all your mates are still playing with dolls and you decide you want to play with willies. You disgust me. I just hope you know that as soon as we get home I am phoning your father. Let him fuckin' deal with you, because I am sick to death of you and your troubles". Lisa released her grip and carried on her journey home, whilst Misty followed behind her, walking at a slow pace.

Misty's mind exploded with questions. How could she be pregnant? She had only had sex a few times and Gordon told her he knew what he was doing. Her heart sank with despair as she made the journey home. She knew things would definitely get worse before the night was over. Lisa looked over her shoulder and shouted her name to hurry up. She could tell her nightmare was now about to start.

Lisa threw her coat down on the chair as she entered the front room. Max and his two brothers watched her as she lit a cigarette. They could tell something was wrong as Misty made her way into the front room with a face like thunder.

"What's up with you?" Max asked in a stroppy voice.

"What's up with me? Ask Little Miss Dirty Knickers there, go on ask her" Lisa shouted.

Misty dipped her head in shame as Max continued his interrogation. "Well what's up then? Are you going to tell me or what?" Misty remained silent as Lisa took over the conversation yet again.

"Well your sister's been to the doctors today because she fainted in school. We all thought it was a stomach bug, or food poisoning but we all got a nice surprise didn't we Misty?" Lisa now screamed at the top of her voice and tears trickled down her face. "Go on tell them, or are you too fuckin' ashamed? Everyone will know sooner or later, so tell them". The silence filled the room and you could hear a pin drop, everybody's eyes were on Misty waiting for answers but she still remained quiet.

"Is anyone going to tell me what's going on, or what?" Max shouted. Lisa positioned herself back on the chair as the words left her mouth like flames leaving a fire. "She's fuckin' pregnant, that's what's happened". Max now stood over his sister in disbelief, as he stuttered his words, trying to take in what had just been said.

"What? Pregnant! Don't be stupid, how can she be

pregnant?"Then his brain clicked like a bolt of lightning who she had been seeing. "Are you pregnant Misty?" He now stood over her frothing at the mouth, awaiting her answer. As she looked at him he could see by her reaction it was true and no words needed to be spoken. He knew the truth and looked at her with disgust.

"Well what's happening now then? Surely she's not keeping it?" Lisa stared into space as she lit yet another cigarette. Her face was white with anger and she looked like she couldn't take much more.

The two younger children giggled between one another and looked at Misty with mischievous eyes. They knew they had to be quiet, as they saw Max pacing up and down the front room looking for answers to solve this nightmare. Lisa now stood and moved towards the phone.

"Well I am going to ring your father, let's see what he has to say about this mess. That's if he can pull himself away from his tart for an hour or so".

Misty's temper now broke, as she screamed at her mother. "Go on phone him, see if I care. What can he do? He deserted us months ago, so he has no right to involve himself in our lives anymore". Misty pushed passed Lisa and headed for her bedroom in tears, shouting abuse as she went. "You want to sort your own fuckin' life out and leave me alone. I'm sick of people in this house trying to rule me. Well you can all fuck off, because I'm leaving and then you can get back to your perfect life with Rob can't you".

Lisa went to run after her but Max stood in front of her blocking her path. "Just leave it will you, you both need to calm down and chill out. If you go up there now, you will both end up fighting and the problem won't be solved. Just leave her for now, you know what she's like".

Lisa grabbed the phone and dialled Ken's number. It seemed like forever before anyone answered. Eventually a woman's voice could be heard on the end of the line. Lisa hesitated before she spoke, as she knew it must be Julie, Ken's girlfriend who she was speaking to.

"Erm, is Ken there?" she asked. The woman never asked who was calling, she just shouted his name in the background and left the phone. Lisa listened carefully as she heard his footsteps approaching and her heart raced. She knew he was about to talk to her.

"Hello, Ken Sullivan speaking" he spoke in a confident manner. Lisa took a deep breath before she continued, as his voice sent shivers down her spine.

"Hello, it's Lisa," the phone went silent and she thought he had left the phone, "Hello is anyone there?" Ken coughed as to clear his throat and began to speak in a quiet tone. "Lisa why are you phoning me and where did you get my number?" he asked. Lisa could hear the panic in his voice as her anger unleashed.

"Listen Ken, I'm not phoning for me, I am phoning because I need your help. I need you to come over to my house to help sort this mess out". Ken scratched his head as he thought Lisa was still on a mission to win his love back.

"Lisa, me and you are well and truly over. There is nothing I have to say to you". His voice became quite cocky and she could hear the arrogance in his voice as he continued. "So stop phoning me, will you". Lisa screamed down the phone, to stop him speaking any more nonsense.

"Listen, will you. It's not me, it's Misty, she's in trouble and I mean big trouble."

His tone changed as Misty's name was mentioned and you could now hear the concern in his voice. "Why what's happened? Is she alright?" Lisa sobbed as she tried to tell him the news.

"She's pregnant Ken and I am at my wits end. I don't know what to do with her?" The phone line went dead, as

Lisa shouted his name. "Ken are you there? Ken please answer me" but still no voice replied. Lisa hung up the receiver and looked at Max for support.

"He's hung up on me. The bastard hung up". Lisa sat as Max comforted her.

"Mum we can sort it out between us, we don't need his help he's just a wanker and the sooner you realise that the better." Max held his mother to comfort her, feeling every ounce of her pain.

Misty lay on her bed with the covers over her head, hoping they would make her invisible to the world outside. The words pregnant rambled through her mind and it was now she realised the seriousness of her actions. Misty touched her stomach, hoping to feel the new life growing inside her body but the only movement she felt was her nerves. As she lay on the bed, she heard a car pull up and jumped to her window to see who had arrived in such a hurry. Misty's heart stopped as she looked closer at the driver.

"Oh fuck! It's me dad" she whispered as she hid behind the net curtain, watching his every move. She could tell by his face he already knew she was pregnant as he hurried up the path finally entering the house. Misty ran to the top of the stairs and sat perched on the top step, hoping to hear what was being said but the sound of the two younger boys shouting covered any information she was likely to hear.

Lisa sat at the table as she watched Ken approaching the door. Her heart nearly exploded with mixed emotions. Half of her wanted to run and meet him with her fist, but the other half wanted her to remain calm to try and sort out this terrible mess that Misty had got herself into. Ken opened the door and stepped into the front room. His face looked wild with anger.

"Well where is she then? Are you sure she's pregnant?" His voice was loud and could be heard throughout the house and Misty listened to every word as she sat shaking on the stairs. "Did you know she was having sex?" he asked.

Lisa looked at him in disbelief and shook her head. "Do you really think she would tell me that she was having sex? Fuckin' think about it, I am just as much in the dark as you". The two younger children huddled together, as they hadn't seen their dad since he left. They whispered to each other and watched his every move. Ken stood like a statue and shook his head you could tell he was debating his next move.

"Where is she now?" he asked. Lisa pointed with her eyes to the stairs but made no comment. Ken took off like a raging bull. Misty had heard the conversation between them and ran like a cheetah to seek cover in her bedroom.

As she lay quivering she faced the wall pretending to be asleep, hoping this would deter him from speaking to her but by the sound of his breathing she knew there wasn't a chance.

"Misty are you awake?" She held her breath and tried to remain as still as possible, hoping he would leave but suddenly she felt his arm on her shoulder, shaking her body like a rag doll. "Wake up and turn round. I need to speak to you". His voice was fierce and she knew she had to face him, so slowly, like a waking child, she began to turn still pretending she had been asleep. His face told her she was in deep trouble and she knew there was no escape as he placed himself on the side of the bed next to her. Ken didn't speak straight away, he looked at his child with sorrow in his heart, hoping and praying she would make the right decisions. His first thought was to throttle her but that had now gone out of the window. She was still his baby and he couldn't bring himself to lash out at her. He needed to make her see sense and by shouting he knew his words would have been wasted.

"Misty, your mother has told me what has happened. I am here to help sort this mess out. What you have done is wrong but we need to sort it out before it ruins the rest of your life". He reached to hug Misty but she moved away from him feeling quite uncomfortable. He didn't feel like her dad anymore he felt more like a stranger. Her eyes gazed over him and she could see his disappointment. He looked so old and the smell of alcohol filled the room. Ken also felt the barriers between them and his heart broke as he continued to speak.

"Misty you know you have to have an abortion don't you? There is no way in this world you could ever look after a baby, you're a baby yourself. Think about it. You know it makes sense". Misty felt the anger build inside her and it was only a matter of time before she erupted. 'How dare he come round here preaching to me' she thought.

"Dad I know what I have done is wrong but I am not getting rid of it. It's my baby and my mistake I will have to deal with it not you".

Ken's eyes widened as he listened in disbelief. "What do you mean you're not getting rid of it? You fuckin' well are, so stop right there missus. I know what's best for you and I am telling you now, over my dead body. There is no way you're having any bastard child".

Misty screamed as the words left Ken's mouth and from somewhere deep inside her she found courage to speak her mind. "It's my choice not yours. I'm not having an abortion". She now shouted hysterically. Ken watched in shock and he couldn't understand where her backbone had come from. She had always been such a good child and the girl he saw in front of him now was someone he didn't recognise. Misty continued shouting at Ken with full pelt, until he stepped up towards her face, looking like he was ready to explode. The real Ken now appeared and she was about to see him for what he really was.

"Listen you little slag, if you had kept your knickers on, none of this would have happened would it?" Ken felt his rage seeping out of his body and he had no control of his actions, reaching out he grabbed her hair and threw her onto the bed. He looked at her as she tried to break free by kicking her legs. This was the final straw Ken thought, as he pulled his hand back and swung it. His hand connected with her face. Blood spurted out of her mouth as she cried with pain. He knew he had to restrain her more to stop her wriggling, so he placed his two hands round her neck and began to strangle her. "I've brought you into this world and I will take you out, you little slag". Misty wriggled to break free from his grip but there was no use. He was much too strong for her.

Lisa heard the commotion and ran up the stairs two at a time, to see what was happening. Max followed. As they entered the bedroom, they saw Ken with his hands around Misty's neck. Lisa panicked as she could see Misty was struggling for breath.

"What's going on? Get your fuckin' hands off her" she shouted as she grabbed Ken's hands and pulled at them with all her might. Ken turned and looked directly into Lisa's eyes and the memory of her own beatings came flooding back to her. Lisa knew this time she couldn't roll up and accept it. This was her daughter he was attacking and she didn't want him beating on her like he had done with herself years before.

"Max help me please "Lisa shouted. Max now leapt to help his mother and quickly joined her and together they finally managed to free Ken's grip from round Misty's neck.

Ken stood up now and realised what he was doing. His breath struggled as he tried to speak. "Well she's a little slag, the way she spoke to me. Who does she think she is and where has the cocky attitude come from?" Lisa held her daughter in her arms as Max stood beside them awaiting Ken's next move. Lisa screamed at the beast of a man in front of her. She couldn't believe he had tried to strangle his own daughter.

"You will never change will you, you always think your

fists are the answer. Well fuck off out of my house. We don't need you. You're just a sorry old man, who will end up with nothing". Ken reached to grab Lisa but Max caught his hand before it reached her and he knew it was time to make his stand.

"You heard what she said, she told you to get out". Ken bit his bottom lip as he pulled his arm free.

"Oh do you fancy your chances now big boy?" Ken asked. Max stood like a soldier on parade and his chest expanded, as he leaned towards to Ken's face.

"Ay old man. I'm big enough and you're fucked, so if you think you have got it in ya, bring it on!"

Ken could see his son meant business and for the first time he knew he had to back down. The anger in his son's eyes told him he wouldn't stand a chance. Ken straightened his clothes and backed off towards the bedroom door, shouting as he did.

"Well you all deserve one another you lot. You're fuckin' mad the lot of you, it was the best thing I ever done, leaving you lot behind". Ken stopped as if he had forgotten something and turned to Misty speaking his final words before he left. "And you lady, get yourself to the doctors and rid yourself of that little bastard growing inside you, or do you want to end up like your mother a worthless piece of shit". Max pushed him towards the door as Lisa ran at him like a wild women.

"Worthless piece of shit. You have got a cheek. All you care about is your daft fuckin' tart and your drink." Lisa spat in his face as he left the bedroom.

"Good riddance to bad rubbish that's what I say. Once a bastard always a bastard, you will never change. I wish you nothing but sorrow, you wanker".

Ken headed down the stairs towards the door followed closely by Max. The two smaller children shouted as they saw Ken returning.

"Dad where are you going?" He made no response. He just opened the door and banged it closed as he left nearly taking it off the hinges. Max shook inside as his adrenaline level lowered. He looked at the two boys and he could see they were upset by everything that had taken place.

"Why doesn't dad love us any more Max, what did we do?" Max cuddled them both together trying to explain the best way he could, why their dad had left them. After several questions more Max finally settled them both and returned back to his mother upstairs.

The silence was eerie as Max entered the bedroom. Looking at his sister his heart melted. He had never seen her cry like this before and he knew he would have to support her whatever decision she made. Lisa held Misty in her arms and she realised how much her daughter was going to need her. She decided that today was the new start for them both. She loved her daughter so much and wanted to help her. I'll never let her down again,' she thought as she kissed the top of her head. Max watched the special moment between them before he joined them on the bed. He knew this was far from over and they still needed to sort out the matter of the baby. He waited anxiously before he spoke, giving Misty time to sit up and wipe her eyes.

"Are you alright?" he asked in a sympathetic voice. Misty wiped her eyes and gave a small smile to her brother.

"I think so but my throat feels really sore". Max rubbed the top of her head and that was enough to let Misty know he cared but he still needed to persuade her to do the right thing and slowly started to speak trying to make her see sense.

"Misty, you need to think about this baby. You're young and you don't want to be tied down do you?" Misty gazed at him as Lisa watched her with eager eyes, waiting for her response but as she spoke her tone told them her mind was already made up.

"I'm keeping the baby. I've already thought about it. I couldn't get rid of it, I know I have probably ruined my life and made the biggest mistake ever but that's my choice isn't it?" Lisa and Max both sat with concerned faces as Lisa continued.

"Does the father know about the baby? He's called Gordon isn't he?"

Misty hung her head as she replied, knowing full well her mother had known about her seeing Gordon all along.

"I haven't told him yet" she whispered. Lisa sat on the edge of the bed with hope in her heart. "Well don't you think he should have a say in it? It's his baby as well. How old is he?" Misty never got a chance to reply as Lisa carried on not letting her get a word in edgeways. "I bet he doesn't want any responsibilities at his age, does he?" Max interrupted as he had a plan that might end this mess once and for all. He just hoped it worked.

"Well why don't you go and meet him and tell him what's happened, surely he would want to know wouldn't he?" The sound of someone knocking at the door broke the conversation. They looked at each other hoping Ken hadn't returned for more trouble. Max ran to the top of the stairs to look through the window. He pulled back the curtain and peered out. His eyes focused on the figure of Francesca.

"Don't worry its only Francesca" he shouted. "Should I let her in or what?" Lisa looked at Misty. She knew she could do with someone her own age to talk to and hopefully Francesca might be the one to make her see sense she thought as she shouted to Max.

"Tell her to come up," Lisa shouted. She kissed Misty and told her she would speak to her later. As she stood to leave the room she turned to Misty and spoke in a low tone. "Misty I know we haven't been the best of friends lately but I do love you. Things have been hard for both of us you know. I just hope we can move on from this and be how we used to be. What do you think?"

Misty agreed and threw her arms round her mother, she knew she had been a nightmare lately and agreed with her mother, things needed to change between them. Lisa wiped the tears from her eyes and kissed her cheek before leaving the bedroom. This was a weight lifted off her mind and Misty knew, at a time like this she needed her mother more than ever, because if Gordon no longer wanted her, her mum was the only person she could truly rely on.

The sound of Francesca could be heard throughout the house. "Hello Mrs. Sullivan, where's the patient?" she shouted in her usual loud voice. She told Francesca to go straight upstairs as Misty was in her room. She knew it would be only a matter of time before Francesca knew the truth. She was the biggest gossip in the neighbourhood and they knew from tomorrow, the world and his wife would know of Misty's pregnancy. 'God help us' she thought, as Francesca bounced up the stairs. But as soon as Francesca saw the state of her friend, her bubbly attitude changed and she looked quite concerned.

"What's up with you? you look terrible". She looked closer at her friend and realised her lip was slightly enlarged. "What's up with your lip?" She enquired as she examined it closer.

Misty was in two minds whether to tell her friend the truth but she had no choice as she needed her to get in touch with Gordon as soon as possible. The girls sat on the bed and began to talk. Francesca knew it was something big that had happened and was eager to know every detail and she wasted no time in getting straight to the point.

"Well are you going to tell me what's happened? I can tell it's something bad by the state of your face. Have you been caught smoking?" Misty now started to tell her what had happened as Francesca looked with an astounded expression.

"It's been a nightmare Francesca. My dad has just left. He tried fucking strangling me. Look at me lip!"

Francesca looked horrified as Misty pulled down her lip to show her in detail the true state of what he had done.

"What the fuck has he done that for? Phone the police on him. He isn't allowed to do that to you. Phone child line. I know loads of people who have grassed on their parents for hitting them. Get him nicked, the fuckin' bully". Misty shook her head and began to tell her the reason why her father had lost his head.

"Well he was quite angry. I suppose I deserved it in a way". Francesca was about to go into another speech but Misty stopped her before she could go any further. "I'm pregnant and that's why he hit me. Once he found out, he came flying round here like shit off a shovel." Francesca didn't comment straight away and I don't think she didn't really took in what her friend had just told her. Then it hit her.

"Pregnant! How can you be pregnant? You haven't even had sex!" She paced the room and fired more questions at Misty and you could tell she was mortified as she continued. "Well if you're pregnant who's the dad?" Francesca now sat for a moment and racked her brains tying to think who the father could be. She looked her friend straight into the eyes and thought she had uncovered the mystery.

"Oh my God! Its Dominic isn't it?" Francesca smiled as she continued. "Dominic is the father of your child isn't he!" Misty lowered her head and slowly began to tell her she had got it all wrong. "It's not Dominic baby it's someone else's. So stop saying its Dominic's". Francesca looked puzzled and thought her friend was trying to cover up the truth but Misty soon wiped the smile off her face.

"It's Gordon's baby", she muttered under her breath. Francesca stood to her feet and the colour drained from her face. Misty could tell she wasn't happy and she looked just as angry as everyone one did when they found out her news.

"How can it be Gordon's baby? You told me you only kissed him, so stop fucking lying". Misty looked at her friend and wondered why was the big concern about Gordon being the father. What did it matter who was the baby's father, the point was that she was pregnant and needed help. Misty felt annoyed with her reaction and challenged her.

"What's the matter with your fuckin' face? What does it matter to you, who the father is? I am still fucking pregnant and need your help". Francesca realised that Misty was right and hugged her. She hid her own disappointment well as she held her in her arms. Francesca knew she had to hide her true feelings otherwise her own little secret would be out of the bag and all hell would break loose so for now she knew she would have to be supportive. After a few tears Misty broke free from her grip.

"I haven't even told him yet. I am going now to try and find him. Any ideas on where he might be?" Francesca thought for a while and told her to get ready. "I think he might be at home. I will come with you if you want, you don't want to face this on your own do you?" Misty declined the offer but asked her to walk with her till she reached her destination. Francesca agreed but secretly had wanted to watch Gordon's face when she told him the news, to see how he reacted. After a short while Misty was ready and headed downstairs to tell her mother her plans, followed closely by Francesca. Misty noticed the quietness in her friend but just put it down to shock of the news she had told her and hopefully she would come round to the idea of it, just like everyone else would. 'Time is a good healer' she thought looking towards her mother sat in the front room.

"Mum I'm going out for a bit. I won't be long just need to sort a few things out". Lisa didn't ask too many questions, as she knew she was going to see Gordon and hopefully once she came back, all this mess would be sorted out.

"Right love, don't be gone too long and phone me if you need me". Lisa smiled at Francesca and knew by her face Misty had told her everything and she wasn't too happy with the news either. Once outside both girls linked arms and huddled together to keep warm as the night had a slight chill about it.

"I'm fuckin' freezing Misty. I don't know about you but I should have put a warmer coat on". Misty smiled and told her, that she was shaking from head to toe. Nerves had taken over now and she felt quite sick.

"Oh I am so scared. I can't believe what a big mess this all is. What do you think he will say when I tell him? Do you think he will go mad?" Francesca shrugged her shoulders and gasped. She didn't really know the answer but she hoped Gordon would tell her to get rid of the baby. She also thought to herself that Misty should get rid of 'it' but she didn't want to hurt her feelings by telling her the truth, so she tested the water to try and guide her friend to make the right decision. "Well the best thing is to get rid of it isn't it. You don't want a baby at your age do you?"

Misty defended herself straight away, much to her friends surprise and she nearly snapped Francesca face off as she replied. "Well I've already decided I'm having the baby, with or without Gordon, so he hasn't really got a choice. I just think it's best if I tell him first and let him know what I've decided".

Once again Francesca remained strangely quiet and made no comment but inside she felt like a volcano ready to erupt. She knew at that moment things would never be the same between herself and her long time best friend. Once they had reached their destination, Francesca hugged her friend and tried one last time to stay with her.

"Do you want me to stay with you? Because I will if you want". Misty smiled as she left her, telling her it was something she had to do on her own but thanked her for her support anyway. Francesca stood and watched as she turned into the block of flats and once she had disappeared she headed home feeling, amongst other things, like she had lost her friend forever.

Misty's heart pounded as she waited for the lift to arrive. Once inside she pressed the floor number. She felt the lift struggle to the selected floor. Misty hated lifts and had quite a fear of being enclosed in a such a small space but the stress of telling Gordon the news took her mind completely off it.

The doors opened and revealed the landing of Gordon's scruffy flat. Stepping out of the lift, she straightened her clothes and took once last deep breath before she headed to the front door. She knocked at the door softly at first but as she stood there she realised she would have to knock harder if she wanted anybody to hear her. She knocked quite loudly this time and she could see the shadow of someone approaching through the glass panel in the door. As she listened carefully she could hear a voice shouting as they approached the door.

"Fuckin' hell! stop banging I'm here aren't I", they shouted in an angry voice.

As they opened the door, she recognised the man in front of her as Gordon's brother Tom and you could tell by his face he was none too pleased at being woken. At first he had to stop and stare at her, before he realised who she was but once he did he began to speak.

"You after our kid love?" Misty nodded and told him it was quite important and that she needed to speak to him urgently. "Well he's just nipped to the shop, he should be back in about ten minutes. You can come in and wait if you want?" Misty thought about it for a moment but didn't feel safe being alone with him. He looked like he was a couple of butties short of a picnic and had a weird look about him that unnerved her, so she told him she would meet Gordon on his way back from the shop. Tom smiled and made no effort to continue the conversation and closed the door and headed back to his pit.

Misty reached the ground floor and looked briefly outside but at the moment there wasn't any sign of him. Her body felt quite uneasy as she sat at the corner of the entrance to the flats. She knew this was the best place to wait, as this was the only entrance back inside the flats. Misty sat on the cold concrete floor, playing with her shoe laces to pass the time. It seemed like she had been sat there for hours before she stood to look outside. Looking out of the door she searched the area but still there was no sign of him. Her heart sank as she knew she couldn't wait any longer. Gordon would have to wait, she thought as she stepped out into the night to head home.

Misty had started to walk away from the flats when she heard her name being shouted. She turned to see who it was and recognised Gordon heading towards her.

She panicked and knew she would have to now tell him the reason for her visit. As he approached, she placed her hands into her pocket to try and get them warm, and stop them from shaking. She studied Gordon's face as he neared her and could tell he looked like quite pleased to see her. A smile filled the whole of his face before he began to talk.

"What are you doing here so late?" She smiled as she checked her watch before she replied.

"It's only half past nine, that's not late."

"It is for you little school girl. You should be in bed, ready for school tomorrow" he laughed. Misty knew this was the ideal time to tell him the reason for her visit and wasted no time getting the words out.

"I don't think I will be going back to school again

after today", she spoke in a trembling voice. Gordon smiled remembering his years in school and the mischief he had got up to and thought maybe she had been in trouble with the teachers once again.

"Why, what's happened? Have you been a naughty little girl again?" He asked in a sarcastic tone. Misty looked at him and the words that had been burning her lips for the last few hours flew out like hot coals from a fire.

"I'm Pregnant. I fainted in school and my mam took me to the doctors." The words left her mouth and she didn't stop for breath until the last word had been spoken. She felt like a weight had been lifted off her mind, as she waited for what seemed a life time for his reply.

Gordon stood speechless. The smile fell from his face like a lump of lead. 'Come again?' he thought as he challenged her to repeat herself.

"Did you just say you were pregnant?"

Misty fidgeted. "Yes I am pregnant and I have decided to keep it". She now watched him like a hawk and waited for his reply. His hands touched the top of his head and his fingers pulled at every strand of his hair. He was walking round in circles, puffing and sighing but still he made no response. After a few minutes he began to speak in a distressed tone.

"Who knows about this? Does your mother know it's me who made you pregnant? Oh my God Misty! You're fuckin' fifteen. I could go to jail for this. It's underage sex!" Misty bit onto her bottom lip to stop the tears from flowing. He was in a state and he had looked none too pleased with the news. Gordon now moved toward Misty and took her arm leading her back inside the flats, away from prying eyes.

"Orr fuckin' hell Misty, what am I going to do?"

Misty lowered her head. "Listen, you don't have to worry. I won't tell anyone it's your baby. My mum knows but we had a talk and she said we both needed to speak to sort out what we were going to do about the baby". Gordon sat lifeless on the floor. He knew now he would have to face the consequences of his actions, even if it meant prison.

"My dad knows as well. Look at my lip where he slapped me". Gordon moved over to her and examined her lip. As he looked into her eyes, he felt his body melt and he knew he couldn't leave her in her time of need. After all it was his baby as well and maybe this had been what he had secretly wished for. He looked concerned as he spoke. "What did your Dad say?"

Misty told of the events of the day and how her dad had tried to strangle her. After listening to all she had to say he thought it wasn't as bad as he first thought and perhaps with a little persuasion from himself he might win her parents round to them keeping the baby. Gordon and Misty sat and talked for a while, discussing the baby and at the end of it they both decided they were going to keep it. Gordon placed his hand onto Misty's stomach and began to talk to the unborn baby inside her.

"Hello little baby, I'm your dad. You're going to be so loved and want for nothing, I promise you I'm going to look after you and your mother forever." Misty looked at him. As he spoke to her unborn baby, nothing else seemed to matter. Together they could face anything and the world seemed a brighter place now she had told him about the baby. He lifted his head and kissed her. She responded and the love she felt for him seeped from her body. Misty told Gordon she needed to go home and he offered to walk her. He also asked if he could come in and meet her mother. He didn't want her to think he was running from his mistakes and he had to meet her sooner or later, so now was as good as time as any...

CHAPTER EIGHT

L ISA SAT WATCHING the clock and lit another cigarette. Denise had come round about an hour before and sat eagerly awaiting Misty's return. Rob, Lisa's boyfriend, was like a rock to her at the moment, she had told him the news and he had came straight round. He realised the stress Lisa was under and took it on himself to get the two younger children ready for bed. The two smaller children had really taken to him and looked at him as a father figure, they would spent hours talking to him and playing games. In his own right he had become a step father to them and it wasn't long before he had earned everyone's respect.

Denise opened a bottle of red wine and poured two large glasses, hoping to calm her sister's nerves. "Here get this down your neck, it will calm your nerves". Lisa took a large mouthful.

"Where the fuck is she Denise? She should be well back home by now. Say he's hit her and she's lying in a ditch somewhere. I'm going to give it half an hour more, then I am going out to look for her". Denise agreed and told her if she hadn't returned shortly, she would accompany her, as Denise was secretly starting to worry too.

Max had not long returned to the house and sat at the table with his mam and auntie. He too was starting to worry about his sister's whereabouts. He had become quite a changed person lately and Lisa put it down to his new job in the travel agents. If the truth was known she had thought he had become more feminine, even in the way he had been dressing and speaking but for now she put it to the back of her mind as she was too stressed about Misty to think of anything else. They all turned towards the back door, as they heard the gate scrape open, eager to see who it was. As they looked closer they saw Misty approaching, with a large man following closely behind her. Max stood almost immediately and pulled the back door open to watch his sister walk down the path. Lisa and Denise peered round the side of his body hoping to see who was with her.

"Gordon's with her" he shouted. "He's got a fuckin' cheek, who does he think he is coming here? Doesn't he know how much trouble he's caused without making things worse coming here rubbing our noses in it, the wanker".

Lisa sat back and awaited her daughter's arrival. Denise knew there could be trouble as she watched Max stride into the kitchen. Misty entered first but closed the door behind her, telling Gordon to wait there for a minute. Once inside she started to tell Lisa what had happened. "Mam I know you think I am daft but me and Gordon have had a talk and we have decided we want to keep the baby .He's waiting outside till you say he can come in. He wants to tell you that's he's sorry about what happened and he doesn't want to run away from his mistakes"

Lisa wanted to jump from her chair and face the man who had taken advantage of her daughter but she knew she would upset Misty so she sat with her fists clenched and agreed to meet him. 'Better the devil you know,' she thought, as Misty beckoned Gordon to come in. Lisa stood in amazement. He looked more like a man than a young boy. As she studied him, she concentrated on his stubbly face and manly features. It took a while before Lisa spoke as she was still gob smacked by his appearance.

"Hello Lisa, I'm Gordon". The roomed filled with silence and you could hear a pin drop as he continued.

"I know what I have done is wrong but I do love her and I will take care of them both. I promise you". Lisa listened, as Denise held her waist to comfort her. Secretly she held her like this as she was also unsure whether her sister would pounce on him at the first opportunity. Lisa felt surprisingly calm and sat at the table telling Gordon to sit down as well. He headed over to sit beside Misty. Once he was sat, Rob offered him a drink and Gordon accepted straight away because at the moment his mouth felt like sandpaper and he needed moisture in it so he could talk.

Max didn't return to the room. He didn't want to sit with Gordon as he knew the stories about him and he knew he was nothing but trouble. But if his sister had fallen in love with him, what could he do except sit and wait for him to show his true colours? 'Only time will tell', he thought as he headed to his bedroom, still pumping with rage at the thought of Gordon being the baby's father.

Surprisingly before the night was over, they were all getting along fine. Lisa knew she would have been wasting her breath as you could tell by both their faces that their minds were well and truly made up. She just hoped Misty wasn't making the biggest mistake of her life.

The next day, things started to move pretty quickly. It was decided that Rob would move in with Lisa and Misty and Gordon would move into his house till they found somewhere of their own to live. Lisa didn't like the idea at first but the more she thought of it, the more it made sense. Rob was over the moon at the idea. This meant he could spend more time with Lisa and the children, he was virtually living with her anyway, so it seemed the right thing to do for everyone.

Gordon was buzzing with happiness. Secretly he couldn't wait to move out of his brother's house, as things between them had got quite heated recently and they had nearly came to blows on more than one occasion.

CHAPTER NINE

A S PREDICTED FRANCESCA told everyone in school that Misty was pregnant. There was one person in particular she had taken great pleasure in telling. She had chosen her moment carefully and threw it into the conversation snidely as Dominic listened in horror.

"Have you heard the news yet Dominic?" she teased. Dominic looked towards her with a blank expression as he continued to speak.

"What news?" Francesca couldn't wait to tell him the news and went straight in for the kill loving every minute of his pain.

"It's Misty, don't tell me you don't already know..." Dominic screwed up his face and became quite angry with her as he continued to speak.

"Are you going to tell me or what? I haven't got all day" he snarled. Francesca told the news, looking like the cat that had got the cream. She seemed to enjoy watching his face as she knew he still felt something for Misty despite what he had told everyone.

"Misty is pregnant. I spoke to her last night and she told me the news. She was in a right state, because her dad had been round and opened a can of whoop-ass on her. You should see her lip where he slapped her". Dominic felt his face go bright red and Francesca could tell that he was shocked.

"Why you telling me that?" he said in a cocky voice.

"She's nothing to do with me anymore and if she wants to ruin her life that's fuckin' up to her". Dominic walked away from her, followed closely by his friends. He couldn't let anyone know how he was feeling as he wanted to pretend he wasn't bothered but deep inside, he felt like someone had stabbed a hot poker deep into his heart and the pain was excruciating. He knew there was nothing he could do. Misty had to make up her own mind up regarding the pregnancy. He just hoped she made the right choice and didn't ruin her life. Dominic had hoped that one day he and Misty would be back together again but that day seemed very distant after this news. Francesca watched him leave and felt quite pleased with herself. She hadn't really liked Dominic anyway and any chance to get one over him was welcome, she thought as she joined her classmates.

Meanwhile, Lisa was the talk of the neighbourhood. As she walked towards the school gates. She could see all the women huddled together in little groups. She could tell they were talking about her as she got nearer. Lisa smiled as she walked past them all, as they stared directly at her with smirks across their faces. 'Fuck 'em!' she thought, if they're talking about me, they are leaving some other poor fucker alone. Lisa carried on walking towards the playground wall to escape the fierce gusts of winds that had just started to circle the playground.

One lady came to stand with her. She had spoken to her on several occasions and they had become quite friendly. The lady huddled against the wall and stood at the side of Lisa, sweeping her hair away from her face before she spoke.

"See you're the topic of the playground this week." She smiled, letting Lisa know she had already heard the news, about Misty being pregnant. "My old Nan use to say worse things happen at sea. If you think about it, it's quite true. It will all work out for the best love, don't worry. Misty isn't the first to be pregnant at an early age and I suppose she won't be the last. She's just been unlucky that's all. How many of their daughters are having sex and they don't know about it?" she laughed. "People who live in glass houses shouldn't throw stones and trust me, it won't be long before the gossip is on someone else. You know what it's like in this playground for gossip; swings and bloody roundabouts. What goes around comes around just wait and see".

They shared a few minutes laughing and Lisa told her friend all about how she felt regarding Misty. Surprisingly after the conversation Lisa spirits felt quite uplifted and she knew her friend was right in what she had said. Lisa set off towards the classroom door, to meet her children with her head held high and a smile fixed firmly on her face. She looked liked she didn't have a care in the world as she cuddled her boys. If only the world knew the heartbreak she was feeling inside. The smile she was wearing was just part of her make-up and her world had collapsed with the recent news she had received.

The months passed. Misty and Gordon were now living together. Misty loved the wife's role she had been given and tried her best to keep Gordon happy. It was funny because she never really saw him. He was up at the crack of dawn and didn't return till late at night. Misty treated him like a king and as soon as he walked in through the front door, his tea was always placed onto his lap. He wanted for nothing. Sometimes Misty had got quite disheartened, as he never thanked her or commented on how nice his food was but she carried on regardless as she didn't want to upset him. She had never approached Gordon on his whereabouts during the day, or the late hours, as she didn't want to seem jealous, so she left him to his own devices to come and go whenever he pleased.

Misty was showing now and her bump was quite large. When she looked into the mirror from the side, she could tell she was pregnant. She loved being pregnant and would often hold her hand round her stomach to feel the life growing inside her. She was eager for the baby to be born and got jitters all through her body whenever she thought about it. The one thing she didn't like were the stretch marks that had started to appear on her lower stomach. Nobody had ever told her that this was a part of pregnancy. There were little silver lines, branching out all across her stomach and she hid them from everyone as she felt quite embarrassed that they had appeared on her body. Even Gordon hadn't cast his eyes on them. The other changes to her body were her breasts. They were enormous. 'Where have they come from?' she wondered as she squeezed them together in front of the mirror. She compared them to two melons, they were so big and in a way she secretly loved them as, before she was pregnant, all she had were a pair of fried eggs.

She had also been to meet Gordon's parents and she had got on with them like a house on fire. Gordon's mum wasted no time when she heard the news she was going to be a nana. This was her first grandchild and she wanted to play her part well. So at the first opportunity, off she went shopping searching for all the latest baby clothes. Even Misty's age didn't stop her celebrating. She had been surprised to say the least but the baby was on its way now and she loved the idea of becoming a grandparent. Gordon's relationship with his parents had been quite odd. He always spoke to them with an attitude and you could tell by their faces they didn't approve of how he spoke to them but in front of Misty they just grinned and bared it. There were never any hugs or kisses exchanged between Gordon and his parents and he would never want to stay at his parents' house for long. He always seemed in such a rush to get away.

Once, when Misty and Gordon's mother were alone, she had confessed to her how much of a handful Gordon really was. Apparently when he was a child his dad use to beat him up quite regularly and now as a result of this, somewhere in Gordon's mind he blamed his mother for letting it happen. You could see the sadness in his mother's eyes as she continued to tell Misty the story. She told her Gordon hadn't spoken to his father for many years. Misty always felt that's there was something wrong between them but just couldn't put her finger on it. 'Now it all makes sense' she thought as she listened eagerly.

Gordon had been about sixteen years old when things came to a head. His dad had tried to beat him for something or other and Gordon had decided to fight back. His mother rubbed her arms as she spoke and you could tell the memory of it still gave her goose bumps. The tears welled up in her eyes as she continued to speak. Gordon's mother told her how she had watched as Gordon head-butted his father to near death. She also told her when she had tried to pull him off her husband, he head-butted her as well. The injuries were horrendous she told her. Gordon's father was in hospital for over a week and they weren't sure whether there would be any permanent damage. Luckily not a lot of questions were asked in the hospital regarding his injuries and Gordon had got away with it. His mum begged her not to repeat a words she had spoken, as she didn't want Gordon going mad at her for gossiping about family business. Misty agreed, but she felt shaky inside, realising what Gordon was capable of – she just hoped she would never see that side of him.

Misty jumped as Gordon returned and the conversation between them stopped dead. You could see the fear in his mother's face, as she enlarged her eyes at Misty and shook her head slowly, as to warn Misty to end the conversation. Misty changed the conversation quite quickly, as Gordon sat to join them. She felt her heart beating with fear in case he had overheard them but luckily he was none the wiser that their talk had ever taken place. They talked about the baby and even Gordon took part in it, which surprised Misty, as he never really spoke about it. After about ten minutes Gordon stood and told her it was time to leave and as usual she obeyed his command and said her goodbyes to his parents, kissing them both on the cheek before she left. Misty could feel Gordon's eyes burning into the back of her head as she kissed his father goodbye. She felt quite uncomfortable, as he urged her to hurry up. Once the goodbyes had been said, both Misty and Gordon headed home.

Misty felt quite affectionate towards Gordon now, knowing the troubled life he had led and she felt like she needed to show him some love. So slowly, she reached to hold his arm but he moved away almost immediately and you could tell by his face he wasn't impressed. "What the fuck are you doing" he moaned. "I hope you weren't trying to hold my hand" Misty blushed as she tried to speak, to avoid her embarrassment. "Why what's wrong with that? You are my boyfriend aren't you" Gordon chuckled as he continued to speak.

"Fuckin' holding hands in the street, who do you think I am? If my mates saw me they would think I had gone soft." Misty felt well and truly rejected and knew this was the ideal time to bring up the other matters that had been playing on her mind. "Well, your mates aren't in bed with us, so what's your excuse there? We haven't had sex for ages, Oh! I forgot, you said you were scared of hurting the baby. What fucking kind of excuse is that?" she said with a sarcastic voice. "I am getting quite sick of this loveless relationship, so you better start showing me love, I have needs you know". Gordon stared at her in disbelief. He responded straight away.

"You silly little bitch, since when have you become all grown up, talking about relationships. You will get what love I have to give you, when and if I am ready. If that's not enough, you know what you can do." Misty knew he meant business by his angry tone. She now felt embarrassed for even bringing it up and knew he wouldn't talk to her for the rest of the night. She had seen this look on his face before and knew he could make her life a misery. 'He's well and truly spat his dummy out,' she thought as they walked the rest of the way home in silence.

As they reached the front door, Misty pulled out her key but from nowhere, Gordon pushed passed her and inserted his key into the front door. "Excuse me wouldn't go amiss", she said in a soft voice but Gordon made no reply. As they both entered the house, Misty turned to close the door and as she turned there he was, stood right in front of her with an evil look in his eyes. He didn't speak at first but as soon as Misty tried to move past him he pounced on her grabbing her by the hair.

"So where has all this back chat come from you cheeky little fucker. It stops now, do you hear me." His voice was fierce as he dragged her hair towards the floor. "Let this be a lesson to you, anymore backchat and I will deal with you proper. Do you understand." Misty squealed with pain as he released her, throwing her towards the floor.

He walked away from her slowly, watching her cry as she tried to pull herself off the floor. He didn't feel an ounce of guilt as he left her crying. He headed straight upstairs and Misty could hear the bath water being run. After a few minutes, she headed to the front room. Once there she switched on the television and sat patiently waiting for him to return. She had already taken full blame for what had just happened and hoped Gordon would forgive her once he had finished in the bath.

Misty sat watching television. Every noise from upstairs sent shivers down her spine, as she knew he would be returning soon. A few minutes passed and she could hear the sound of his footsteps coming down the stairs. Taking a deep breath, she got ready to eat humble pie and try and make things better between them. He walked in the room like he was proud of his behaviour and knew he was the king of his domain once more. His eyes never met hers as he pottered round. The smell of his aftershave lingering in the air and this told her that he must be going out somewhere, so before he did, she tried to make her peace with him.

"Gordon, about before. Can I just say I'm sorry? I know I went on a bit but I just get frustrated sometimes". Gordon looked at her and slowly came to join her on the chair. "I'm sorry for what just happened too but you deserved it winding me up like that. You know you deserved it don't you?" Misty smiled and lowered her head, like a small child being scolded by their parents and agreed with his every word. Gordon knew he had to keep Misty happy at the moment, as his plans for tonight didn't include her and he didn't really want to leave her whilst she was upset, so he forgave her.

He hugged her, kissing her head telling her how sorry he was. Her heart melted and she believed his every word. The moment didn't last long, before he pulled away and casually dropped his bomb shell.

"Well I better get going. I am off to the Whitegate for a few pints with my mates. You don't mind do you." Misty smiled but couldn't hide her disappointment she felt inside. She knew it would have been pointless in asking him to stay in with her as his face told her that his mind was already made up. Gordon didn't wait for a reply, he just picked up his keys and pecked her on the cheek, telling her not to wait up as he knew he wouldn't be in till late.

As soon as he shut the front door he sighed with relief. He had been worried that Misty was going to kick up a fuss about him going out and he would have ended up staying in with her to keep the peace. So their argument had come at a good time and his escape had been quite easy. Gordon walked towards the pub with a spring in his step. He really loved the way he was looking at the moment and felt so confident in himself. As he approached the pubs entrance a voice started shouting at him.

"Come on hurry up. I didn't think you were coming. I have been waiting ages for you". Gordon smiled as he picked her up and squeezed her.

"All good things come to those who wait", he laughed, "I know I'm late but a few things cropped up at home and I had to deal with 'em first. Anyway I am here now, so stop moaning and give us a kiss".

Francesca smiled as her lips connected with his, she knew it was wrong to be with him but something inside her just couldn't let him go. He had told her Misty had been a mistake and once she had given birth he was going to tell her the truth about them. Then finally they could be together without hiding their love any longer. Francesca was madly in love with Gordon and didn't care who she hurt to be with him. It was just a matter of time till they could be together and Francesca was willing to wait to get her reward.

CHAPTER TEN

ORDON HAD ALWAYS been secretive but recently his life had become even more complicated. Sometimes he had wondered how he had ever ended up in such a mess. On a few occasions he had wanted to sit down with Francesca and tell her all about his life and what he had been involved in but he couldn't take the chance on someone else knowing his secrets.

It all started when he was sat in the local pub with his brother Tom. It was just a normal Saturday afternoon and nothing much was happening except the usual old men watching the horse racing and a few lads playing cards. Everyone was chatting casually when the pub door flew open as if a gust of wind had blown it and in walked four well dressed men.

The silence was eerie, as they walked to the bar and all eyes watched them, wondering if they were dibble. The men ordered their drinks and you could tell they were all in the mood for a good session. Gordon watched them closely as he saw the largest man pull out a large bundle of cash from his pocket. Nudging his brother, he continued to watch in amazement.

"Fuckin' hell our kid, did you see all that cash he just pulled out?" Tom panicked as he told his brother to lower his tone as he didn't want the men to overhear him.

"Keep the noise down then. You don't want them to hear you do you? They look like gangsters and they won't think twice about coming over here and kicking your fucking head in". Gordon agreed but still watched their every move.

"Four brandies love and get one yourself" the larger man shouted. The bar maid smiled and knew her night had just got better. Tips had been non-existent recently, the way these men were spending it looked like a good night.

The men walked past them and sat in the top area of the pub. As they passed, the strong smell of expensive aftershave caught in the back of Gordon's throat and the smell made him think of how rich the men could be, to afford aftershave like that. The hours passed and the men got gradually louder and louder. They sang along with the jukebox and encouraged everyone else in the pub to sing along with them. Before long the men were buying everyone in the pub drinks and the atmosphere was buzzing. The night kicked in and Gordon had somehow ended up in the four men's company. He didn't mind though, as they were paying for all his drinks. Their sense of humour was brilliant and Gordon hadn't stopped laughing all night. Tom had left about an hour before and he'd been well and truly pissed as he rolled out of the pub doors. One of the men took a particular shine to Gordon and chatted to him frequently. As their conversation continued, the man revealed a bit about himself and confided in Gordon about one or two other things that he wanted to know more about. He also asked him what kind of work they did but the man remained secretive. The man drank brandy like nobody's business and eventually it loosened his tongue.

"I am a bad man" he whispered in to Gordon's ear, "I do it for the money that's the only reason I do it", his words slurred now and Gordon had to listen carefully so he could understand every word he spoke.

"To tell you the truth I wish could stop". Gordon had now heard the word 'money' and got quite excited and urged him to continue.

"Why mate, what have you done to think you are such a bad person?" The man stuttered and Gordon found it hard to understand him fully but the words he did hear, left him wanting to know more.

"Ten grand each was our last hit. Not a bad day's work is it mate? His eyes lit up at the sound of the large amounts of money. He had only ever dreamed of that much money and listened intensely as he spoke further.

"Our mate got caught on the last hit and he's now looking at a ten stretch in prison. That's the chances you take though innit mate? We all try our best for our families and sometimes this is the only choice we have to give them the life they deserve. Tell you what, I wish I could stop doing it but the money gets a grip of you and you can't live without it in the end". The man now sunk his head into his chest and his eyes started to roll.

Gordon knew he must strike whilst the iron was hot, so in he jumped without giving a second thought. "I know what you mean mate. My girlfriend is pregnant and we haven't got a pot to piss in, so if there is any work going I would be grateful". The man lifted his head and tried to focus on Gordon's face before he spoke.

"Tell you what mate. This could be your lucky day but I can't speak about it now, as I'm too pissed". He then reached into his jacket pocket and pulled out a pen. Looking round the table, he picked up a beer mat and scrawled down a phone number. Once he had finished, he passed it to Gordon telling him to ring him the following day. Gordon took the piece of paper and held it like a piece of gold. 'This could be my ticket to a better life' he thought, as he slipped it carefully into his pocket.

The night finished on a good note and everyone in the pub were pissed as farts. The four men stood to leave and waved goodbye to their new found friends. Gordon followed them to the door, holding up his new friend as he staggered out into the night air.

"Right mate, I'll ring you tomorrow and once again thanks I won't let you down. Just wait and see". The man swayed and nearly fell, before the other men took charge of holding him up. They were all well and truly drunk. Gordon returned back into the pub and sat back in his seat feeling pleased with the new friends he'd found. Minutes later Francesca came to join him. She had been busy chatting to her friends most of the night on the other side of the pub. As he looked at her he knew she had one thing on her mind. This wasn't the first time she had begged for his company. A few months before she had thrown herself at him and made no secret of what she wanted from him. Gordon had told her that she was Misty's best friend and it wasn't right but that never deterred her, she just seemed to want him even more.

As she sat facing him, he could feel the surge of warmth between his legs and he knew tonight would end with a sex romp with Francesca. Nobody in the pub had ever put two and two together and questioned their friendship. Everyone knew she was Misty's friend and found it quite normal that they should be in each other's company. Francesca felt no remorse for her actions and never once did she consider Misty feelings. As far as she was concerned Gordon belonged to her and it was only a matter of time before the world would know as well. Gordon and Francesca left the pub together, laughing and joking. Their usual place for sex was at Francesca's aunties and tonight was no different. She had been living with her aunt for the last couple of months since her mother had kicked her out. Her mother had thrown her out because she had also heard the stories about her behaviour with men and couldn't take the arguments between them anymore, so the only option was for her to move in with her auntie. At first her aunt had been quite strict about lads staying the night but over time she had come round to it and didn't mind it as long as they kept the noise down.

As they walked towards her aunt's house, Gordon felt the passion boiling between them. He hadn't been having sex with Misty due to the fact she was pregnant and he didn't really find her remotely attractive anymore. Francesca suited his needs at the moment and he was making the most of it while he could. He knew Francesca changed like the weather and could move on to some other man the following week. The night in front of him would be filled with hot, steamy sex. Francesca was one hot chick between the sheets and had no hang-ups about trying new positions.

Reaching her aunt's house, Francesca went in first to check the coast was clear. Once she had checked her aunt was in bed she beckoned Gordon to follow her. They both headed straight for the conservatory. This was the place they often used for sex, as the noise seemed to go undetected once the doors were shut. Once inside, Francesca threw Gordon on to the round wicker chair and straddled him. She looked like a woman possessed as she pushed herself roughly onto his crotch. Gordon's face exploded with excitement. She could feel his love pole beneath his pants and knew how excited he was and rubbed herself over his erection and, like a snake, hissed with pleasure.

Gordon loved the control Francesca had over him during sex. Considering her age, she knew every trick in the book. All the blood from his brain had now run to his penis and his body was now in Francesca's control. Finally she pulled his penis from his pants and caressed it slowly with her mouth. The power she felt over him excited her and she felt so in control of his every move. Gordon was now panting like a dog begging for more as she hitched her skirt up. He watched her pull her knickers to one side and slowly guided his love shaft towards her entrance. Once he was inside her she began to work her magic. She took his hands and placed them above his head and thrust to and fro on his penis. She could feel warmth travelling up from her toes and tickling the back of her neck – she was ready to explode. It was quite funny she thought, how Gordon made her feel, he knew exactly where to touch her, unlike all her other partners. All her other partners had thought clitoris was an island in Greece and had never located it during sex. Gordon was different, he knew exactly which buttons to press and it drove her wild when he did.

They breathed like racehorses finishing the final furlong in the Grand National. She rode him like a jockey and her body quivered with delight as she gazed upon him. She noticed his face started to change and she knew heaven was just around the corner for him. He groaned as his hands lowered and gripped Francesca's buttocks. He jerked her faster and faster till he felt her reach climax. Once she had come, he knew it was his turn and he penetrated her deeper and deeper. Moments later it all ended as Gordon gasped "Oh baby". Francesca rested herself on his lap for a minute, to recover. Once her breath had returned she sat herself on the chair facing him. He now pulled up his jeans and searched inside his coat pocket for his cigarettes. He lit two cigarettes and offered one to Francesca and pulled her towards him on the chair.

"That was quite good wasn't it? You're a dirty vixen aren't you?" Francesca smiled as she took a deep drag of her cigarette, feeling the nicotine travel through her body. She went on to tell him how she had read many books on what men liked in bed and he nodded, letting her know he had enjoyed every minute of her research.

As they sat, they spoke about the secret they were keeping from Misty. Francesca told him she would only wait till Misty had given birth and not a minute more. Gordon had agreed, although deep down he knew things would never be that simple but for now he pretended everything was going to plan. She lay in his arms thinking of the promises he'd made and gradually they both drifted off to sleep. The morning call of the birds made Gordon open his eyes and look straight at his watch. He didn't know he had fallen asleep. His head was banging and he felt like a bear with a sore head. Next to him he saw Francesca still asleep and then it dawned on him what the night before had led to. Lifting her body off his, he stood up and saw Francesca open her eyes.

"Why didn't you wake me? Fuckin' hell what am I going to say to Misty about where I've been." Francesca looked at him and you could tell by her face, she wasn't impressed.

"Well you weren't bothered over her last night was you? Just tell her you were with your mates having a drink. Or better still, tell her the fuckin' truth". Gordon looked at her and growled a shitty remark.

"Alright smart arse. No need to be sarky"

Francesca stretched her body and yawned as Gordon looked out of the window onto the garden. He knew he had to escape without anyone seeing him. He briefly kissed Francesca on the cheek and headed into the morning light with his head dipped to avoid detection.

"Bye" Francesca shouted. "Don't forget to phone me will you". He made no reply and made his escape.

Once outside, he walked quickly. It was early and he wanted to get back to the house before Misty was aware he wasn't home. His mouth felt dry and his head was still banging. He just hoped Misty wouldn't start going on at him when he got home, as he was nursing the hangover from hell. His hand shook as he tried to place his key into the door but once inside he listened eagerly for any sign of anyone being awake. Taking off his shoes, he crept upstairs hoping to sneak into bed without being detected. As he gently opened the bedroom door, he could see the shape of Misty's body lying in bed looking like she was fast asleep. He slowly peeled off his jeans and threw his t shirt on to floor and slid into bed trying his best not to wake her. Misty had been awake for hours, wondering where on earth he was.

She felt him sneak into the bed next to her but thought it best not to ask where he had been as she knew it would only start a big argument and she would be the one who would have ended up in tears. So for now she stayed still. The smell of alcohol overtook the bedroom and she felt quiet sick as she breathed in the fumes from his breath. Suddenly she thought she got a whiff of women's perfume but couldn't be sure exactly what kind it was. Despite this, she remained perfectly still and pretended to be asleep.

As Gordon lay at the side of her, his heart raced uncontrollably. Relieved to be back in the house, he drifted slowly off to sleep without a care in the world. Misty lay next to him wide awake. She was wondering where the hell he'd been all night and her stomach churned at the thought of him with another woman. She tried to put it to the back of her mind, because at the moment all she cared about was the life growing inside her.

Around mid morning, Gordon woke and looked at the clock. Seeing the time he rushed towards the bathroom. He was meeting his new found friends from the pub today and he didn't want to be late. He looked in the mirror and ran cold water into the sink. Once it was full he threw it across his face. The water cleansed his face but it couldn't wash away the guilt he felt inside. He had betrayed Misty big time and the guilt he felt would always be present no matter how much he tried to wash it away. Throwing on his clothes he headed downstairs to meet the sad face of Misty sitting in the kitchen, drinking a cup of coffee.

She watched his every move through the corner of her eyes, before she finally offered to make him a coffee.

"Do you wanna a drink? Or are you going straight out?" Gordon turned to face her but never made eye contact and just kept rummaging round pretending to look for something.

"No I haven't got time. I'm already late." he said in a low tone. Misty enquired what he was late for but he just told her he had some business to take care of. The conversation ended abruptly and he rushed to the cupboard to get his coat.

"Right see ya later. Don't wait up because I don't know what time I will be back". This was quite normal behaviour for Gordon and Misty had got used to it. She hardly saw Gordon anymore and she just hoped everything would change once the baby came along.

Gordon waited till he got out of sight of the house and searched in his pocket for the phone number of his new mate. Dialling the number he listened to the ringing tone and eventually he heard a familiar voice answer the call.

"Hello", the voice answered, before Gordon replied.

"Hiya mate its Gordon from last night. Do ya remember me?"

The voice laughed as he replied, "Alright mate, glad you phoned . We were just talking about you".

"All good I hope" he laughed, as the voice continued to speak.

"Right mate. We will pick you up in about ten minutes.

Meet us at the Osborne Pub on Rochdale Road. Do you know where that is?" Gordon knew exactly where it was and set off to meet them at a great pace.

Gordon's heart missed a beat as he ran to the pub. This could be his lucky break and he needed a change so he'd never have to worry about money again. He loved the lifestyle the men seemed to be living and decided he definitely wanted to be part of it. So with a quick jog, he headed toward the pub. Once there he lit a cigarette and watched the traffic go by, eagerly looking both ways to try and see them approaching. After about ten minutes a black car pulled up and a man opened the passenger door and waved Gordon to come over. Feeling a little bit nervous he headed towards them.

Once he got there, the passenger opened the back door and told him to jump in. Gordon moved his body to sit in the back seat and noticed another man sat next to him. As he looked closer he realised it was his mate from the night before. The smell of stale cigarettes lingered in the car and he felt all eyes on him before the man next to him spoke.

"Orr, I'm still pissed me from last night. I feel rough." Gordon smiled nervously as they all in turn introduced themselves, starting with the man sat next to him.

"I'm Mark and he's Wayne and the fat cunt in the driving seat is called John". They all laughed as John tried to tell them how much weight he had lost lately. He hated the fact they still called him fat but they all laughed just the same. John started to drive off and headed towards the motorway. As they set off Gordon couldn't hold his thoughts any longer. He had racked his brains all morning trying to think what work he would be doing with this new crowd but still he couldn't come up with an answer, so cautiously he began to speak hoping they would end his torment.

"What sort of work will I'll be doing then?"

Silence filled the car before Mark started to talk. Gordon could feel the eyes of John watching his every move through the rear-view mirror.

"Well ya know we're a bit dodgy don't ya?" Gordon nodded to let them know he understood what they meant.

"Well, we're bank robbers. We do what we need to do to get by, don't we lads?" They agreed as Mark continued. "Well when I say bank robbers, I mean armed robbers. We've never shot anyone though. The guns are just for show. We just use them to scare people and make our job a bit easier but we would all use one if we had to save our necks wouldn't we?" The other men agreed as Gordon listened in amazement and they started to tell him about previous grafts they had done. Gordon wondered if he had bitten off more than he could chew, as the words 'armed robber' spun round inside his mind.

The men were on the motorway for about an hour and a half and they told him they were going to look at a job. Apparently they had been watching this one for about four weeks and this was their last chance to check it out before they hit it the following week. Mark told Gordon the ins and outs of the job and the part they wanted him to play. His job would be to go into the bank with Mark and Wayne and make sure everything ran smoothly. By that he meant, any customers inside the bank were to be kept on the floor until they left .They also wanted him to raise his voice and shout a lot once inside the bank. They said it was just to scare the customers. Also he had to watch that none of them tried to phone the police. Mark explained that the shouting usually scared the people involved and the jobs were plain sailing without anyone getting hurt. All the men took part in the conversation and spoke on different subjects regarding the jobs they had done previously. At the end of it Gordon felt a bit happier and calmer and agreed to work alongside them.

John now pulled up in a parking space facing a row of shops. The parking space was off the main road and hidden from public view but still had a full view of the shops. John checked his watch and told them all it shouldn't be long before the cash would be delivered. All eyes watched the bank like hawks and nobody spoke until the van pulled up. Gordon felt sick with nerves but hid it from the others, knowing if he showed signs of weakness he wouldn't be allowed to go on the job with them. John looked at his watch and turned to face Mark.

"Right, start counting". Mark started to count as Gordon watched, wondering what an earth he was doing.

"One elephant, two elephant, three elephant". It was only when the guard stepped out of the van that Mark stopped counting.

"Right fifteen seconds. That's all we have, from him pulling up to getting out of the van". The other man started counting as well now, trying to determine how long the guard took to reach the side door where the money was coming from. Once he had walked into the bank carrying the money they all sighed with relief, as they knew the next steps were easy as they had done it loads of times before and hoped this time would be no different.

"Right Gordon. This is the point where we will take over. We will wait till he enters the bank and we will be straight in behind him. I will wave my shooter about and do my usual shit and start shouting. All I want you to do is watch our backs and make sure there are no 'have-a-go-heroes' in the bank with us. If there are, let me know, so I can remind them who the fuckin' boss is. The rest should hopefully be easy, once the money is handed over that is. All that will be left for us to do is get to the car, which John will be driving and get the fuck out of there." Gordon nodded and pretended he had taken in all the information.

All of them chatted amongst themselves and it was said there should be at least fifty grand to be earned from this hit. Gordon's eyes lit up, as he asked again the amount they expected to receive. Once they repeated the amount, he began to spend his share of the money in his mind and thought of all the luxuries he could splash out on once the job was done. They all set off back home and talked about the job they had planned. They told Gordon they had been planning this job for months and the only reason he was allowed on board was that their mate had been arrested for something else and left them a man short, so rather than lose a job they had spent so much time on, they were letting Gordon take his place. Gordon thanked them and promised he wouldn't let them down.

They ended their journey back where they began and headed into the pub for a well-earned drink. John told them all to sit down, as he was getting the drinks in. Gordon was glad of this as he only had a couple of quid in his pocket and that had to last him till his next giro, which wasn't due till the following day. Gordon sat proudly with the men and loved being seen with them. All the regulars in the pub watched him as he sat laughing with them and some felt quite jealous. Mark sat next to Gordon and took off his coat.

"Do us a favour Gordon," he asked, "just get us my cigs out of my coat pocket will you". Gordon started to rummage through the pocket and felt a large bundle, thinking it was the cigarettes he pulled it out and nearly fell to the ground when he saw what it was. It was a large bundle of twenty pound notes, held together with an elastic band. Gordon quickly replaced it back into the pocket before anyone saw him and found the cigarettes and passed them to Mark.

"Cheers mate" he replied and offered Gordon one. Gordon took the cigarette out of the packet and reached into his pocket for his lighter and held it out to Mark. "Cheers mate" he replied, as he puffed his cig to ensure it was lit properly. All of them sat speaking amongst themselves but, Gordon found himself speaking more to Mark than any of the others. They seemed to get on like a house on fire. You would have thought they had known each other years by the way they were talking.

Mark took an instant shine to Gordon and told him he would look after him. He reached into his coat pocket and pulled out a couple of twenty pound notes and passed them secretly to Gordon. "Here take this, I know you must be skint. This will get ya by till you start earning". Gordon blushed with embarrassment and refused at first, telling Mark he was alright for money but thanked him anyway. Mark pushed the money back onto his lap and told him to put it into his pocket and not to make a scene. He told him that's what mates are for and as far as he was concerned Gordon was now his mate and plus he knew he was financially embarrassed. Gordon finally agreed and stuffed the cash into his pocket, thanking Mark as he did so. He told him as soon as he got back on his feet he would pay the money straight back. Mark nodded and carried on speaking to the other men about recent events.

The day went into the night and all of them were once again pissed. The atmosphere in the pub was loud and everyone was having a good time. Mark disappeared to the toilets, shortly followed by Gordon. Once inside the toilets Gordon stood at the urinal and unzipped his pants, as he looked round there was no sign of Mark. An older man stood next to Gordon at the urinal and they chatted briefly whilst they pissed. Once the older man had finished, Gordon shouted Marks name but there was no response, so pulling up his zip he made his way to the exit. Just as Gordon was about to leave Mark popped his head from the cubicle and whispered Gordon to come over. Gordon looked puzzled but went anyway, as curiosity got the better of him.

"Hurry up and get in here", Mark whispered and before Gordon knew it he was inside watching Mark bolt the cubicle door behind him. Gordon felt a little stupid and stood fidgeting, whilst he watched Mark pull the toilet seat down. Next he watched him take some toilet roll from the holder and wiped the cistern lid clean.

Gordon couldn't think for the life of him, what was happening, until he watched Mark pull a small plastic bag out of his back pocket. The packet contained white powder as far as Gordon could see and he watched as he knelt on the floor and placed the powder onto it. Next Mark pulled out a credit card and started slicing into the powder, dividing it into lines. He looked like he knew exactly what he was doing because within seconds he had chopped out two neat lines. Mark pulled out a twenty pound note from his pocket and rolled it up to make a tube. He then watched Mark, push the twenty pound note up his nose and inhale the white powder through it. Once he had finished he turned and offered the rolled up twenty pound note to Gordon.

"Come on lad. Get a line of that. It's just what you need to keep you going after a long day's graft". Gordon hesitated at first but didn't want to offend, so with the twenty pound note shoved up his nostril, he copied Mark. Gordon felt an instant rush travelling through his body and he loved the way it made him feel. Whatever it was he had just had, he liked it and knew he would have some more before the night was out. Mark looked at his face after he had finished and laughed.

"Have you ever had sniff before, or is this ya first time?" Gordon told him it was his first time and Mark laughed, telling him he bet it wouldn't be his last now he had a taste of it. He agreed with Mark, because at the moment he felt on top of the world and full of confidence. Mark wiped the toilet lid clean and they both left the toilet cubicle together and headed back into the pub to join the others. Once seated, John looked at Gordon and knew exactly what he had been up to, as there were traces of white powder still on his nose.

"I see ya have just met your new best friend, haven't you?" Gordon looked puzzled as he listened to John continue.

"Wipe ya nose mate. There's all white shit on it". Gordon rubbed at his nose feeling quite embarrassed, whilst John started to lecture him about drugs.

"Listen mate, don't be going mad on that stuff. It's alright now and then but if you get carried away before you know it you will end up like a few of my mates who have had serious problems with it. They lost everything because of it, so be careful".

Gordon looked at John and took on board everything he had said. It was funny he had only known him a short while but he felt kind of a father figure to him. Mark came to join them and John looked at him with disapproving eyes but Mark continued to talk to him without giving John a second thought, as he was used to his snide comments regarding his drug taking. Gordon loved the way he felt inside and he kept disappearing throughout the rest of the night, back to the toilets with Mark, to get a top up of this new drug. Perhaps John was right, this drug could be his new found friend, because at that moment he loved it more than anything in his life and nothing else seemed to matter.

As predicted Francesca came into the pub looking for her usual good time. She trotted across the pub like she owned the place and came to sit with Gordon. He introduced her to his friend and all the other men greeted her. The way she was dressed impressed them all and they found it hard not to stare at the pretty little thing sitting with them. The little black skirt she wore left nothing to the imagination. Her legs were long and slender and they had quite a shimmer about them. Mark watched her with open mouth as she crossed her legs, hoping to get a glimpse of her knickers but she was too quick for him to see. Her black top showed off her breasts to their full potential. They looked firm and left Mark gob-smacked. Gordon felt quite proud of her, as she sat beside him like a devoted puppy. Misty had been a million miles away from Gordon's thoughts and he never mentioned her name throughout the night. In fact it was like she didn't exist.

The night ended and Francesca left with Gordon. They were steaming drunk. Once they got back to her aunt's house, Francesca was also introduced to the new drug in Gordon's life. Mark had kindly given him some more cocaine, knowing the night was still young and he knew he would be wanting more to see him through the rest of night. Francesca didn't hesitate to try the new drug, as she wanted to impress Gordon. When she felt the rush it gave her, she also wanted more and more of the drug. Sex between them that night was mind blowing and they both had the time of their lives. Gordon didn't want to be dominated by Francesca tonight as he was full of confidence himself. So for a change he took the lead in their lovemaking. They made love like two rabbits and never stopped till the early hours of the morning. In fact Francesca was glad when it was time for him to leave, as her fanny had dried up and she had enough sex to last her a life time. She was truly done in and ready for sleep. Gordon said goodbye and headed into the morning light. His body was still on a high and he didn't give a shit about anything.

Gordon knew Misty would still be asleep and to tell you the truth he wasn't really arsed if she was awake. His life had changed so much since he had met her and the only thing that was keeping them together was the baby she carried inside her. He now made no secret that he had come home in the early hours and woke Misty as he climbed into bed.

"Are you awake?" he muttered. She turned to face him and asked where he had been till this late hour. She could tell by his face, she had hit a nerve as he placed his face directly in front of hers.

"What have I told you about asking me where I have been? It's none of ya fuckin' business". Gordon pulled her face towards him and squeezed at it so the sides of her lips joined together. "Look at the fuckin' state of you. Do you know, I can have a much better woman than you. The women love me out there and can't understand why I choose to come home to you".

She pulled her face away from him but this only angered him more. He pulled her back and began to kiss her like an animal. She screamed for him to stop but he carried on regardless.

"Please Gordon, you're hurting me, please stop." Her words fell onto deaf ears and he started to have sex with her. He grunted like a pig as he thrust his penis deep inside her. She knew there was no point in fighting him off as he was too strong, so she just gave in and lay there excepting what he was doing to her. Once he had finished he rolled off her and collapsed beside her. His words were now mumbled and she couldn't understand a word he said. Misty lay limply next to him and tears filled her eyes. Why was he treating her like this, she thought. He was supposed to love her. Within minutes he lay sleeping and the sound of his snoring nearly took the roof off the house. Unable to sleep Misty crept down stairs and made a cup of tea. Her body was shaking from head to toe and she worried for the safety of the baby.

Switching the kettle on she stood and waited for it to boil. It seemed like forever before it was ready. Her mind was all over the place and she couldn't concentrate on anything else. Gordon had changed so much recently and happy days seemed only a distant memory. Misty leaned her body onto the kitchen worktop and cried her tears away. She prayed things would change. She just wanted him to love her, so they could have a happy life together once again.

Gordon's behaviour towards Misty deteriorated over the next few days and her mood was low. It seemed like she was in a dark hole, with no light shining in and there was no escape. Her family didn't know the pain she was feeling, as she wanted to keep it a secret, because if they found out, they would surely make things worse and she didn't need the stress at the moment.

The morning came yet again and Gordon jumped up out of bed as if he's pants were on fire and she watched him as he stumbled round the bedroom trying to find he's clothes. Misty was unaware that today was a big day for him, as it was the bank job and he was rushing so he wasn't late. Gordon's nerves had got the better of him that morning and he spent half the morning sat on the toilet shitting like a new born baby. He had felt physically sick. The job was planned for two o clock and he knew he had to pull himself together by then, otherwise his life would remain the same and his dreams would be gone forever. He shouted constantly at Misty, telling her to get the house cleaned and get herself ready, as he was sick of seeing her in pyjamas, his voice shook the house as he constantly hurled abuse at her.

"Fuckin' pyjamas, that's all ya seem to wear these days .Don't ya think it's fucking time to get ready?" Misty stood facing him ready to burst into tears but he saw the signs of her tears and headed to the front door before she started. "Fuckin' hormonal women. I can do without this shit". He left the house and slammed the front door behind him, letting Misty know she had upset him once again.

Misty was glad to see the back of him that morning and decided to phone her best mate Francesca. She could always make her laugh and cheer her up when she was down and that's what she needed at this moment. Francesca had drifted from Misty since she had been pregnant and she only saw her now and then. Misty thought it a shame as they had been such good friends. She thought she would ring her in an attempt to re-build their friendship.

"Hello long lost mate", she sniggered. The phone line went quite for a moment, her friend answered.

"Hello Misty, long time no see, I thought you was dead I've not seen you for that long" Francesca joked. Misty laughed and tried to cover up the real reason she had not been in touch. How could she tell her friend that Gordon had ruled her life these days and didn't like her having friends, so with quick thinking she lied.

"Oh you know how it is. I've just been so busy. I've meant to come and see ya loads of times but something always comes up, plus I'm feeling so knackered these days. This baby is taking it out of me. I feel like a beached whale. Wait till ya see me, I am huge". Francesca laughed and asked how far into the pregnancy she was now. She already knew the answer, as she was counting the days till Gordon would be hers forever. That's all that Francesca really cared about but for now she would play the game of not knowing anything.

"I am nearly seven months now. So only two months left. I think it's gone really fast don't you?" Francesca agreed but inside the jealousy ate away at her and she found it hard to share her friend's excitement, as she continued.

"Anyway, what ya doing today? Do you fancy coming

round to mine? We can catch up on all the gossip?" Francesca agreed instantly. In the back of her mind she had thought that Gordon might be there and she would get a chance to see him again. Francesca arranged to go to Misty's house within the next hour. The phone call ended there and they both said goodbye. Misty knew she would have to make an effort to get ready, as she didn't want her friend to see the scruffy cow she had become, so off she headed upstairs to try and make herself look half decent.

Before Misty knew it Francesca was knocking at the door. She gave herself one last look in the mirror and waddled down the stairs to open the door. As she opened it, her friend stood with a cigarette hanging out of her mouth. Misty threw her arms round her and nearly knocked the cigarette out of her mouth.

"Fucking hell! Be careful, ya nearly burnt my face". Misty apologised and showed her in to the front room. She was so pleased to see her friend and started to regret the choices she had made. Francesca was so stunning and Misty felt quite ugly stood next to her. During their time apart, Francesca had developed so much. Her breasts looked massive and she made no secret about showing them off. Her skin was golden and free from any blemishes, unlike Misty who had several spots all around her mouth and forehead. Francesca kicked her shoes off and threw her legs onto the chair. She hadn't been to her friend's house for some time and looked round noticing the changes that had been made.

"Where's Gordon today, or are you on your own?" She asked inquisitively

"No I'm on my own as fuckin' usual," she moaned. Misty began to tell her friend of the changes in Gordon and how she hated her life at the moment. She didn't go into too many details as she knew her friend was a gossip and she was scared of Gordon finding out she had been discussing their relationship.

Francesca sat forward and took in every bit of information that she gave her. She felt no remorse for what she was doing behind her friends back and kind of liked to hear that Gordon was treating her badly. Misty's eyed welled up, as she told her of the life she was leading. Francesca could do no more than hold her friend as the tears fell down her cheeks. At this moment Francesca felt sadness and guilt for the way she was being treated. Misty dried her eyes and pulled herself free.

"Oh look at me telling you all my problems, when I haven't seen you for ages, I bet you think I'm a right fucking stress head don't ya?" Francesca smiled but made no comment as Misty continued.

"That's nice perfume you're wearing, what is it?" Misty thought it strange as she smelt her friend's wrist closer, the smell was so familiar but she just couldn't put her finger on where she had smelt it before. Francesca smelt her wrist, trying to remember the name of the perfume but couldn't remember which one it was she was wearing.

"Oh it's one of my auntie's perfumes, she has loads of them and I just help myself to them whenever I want. That's one good thing about my aunt she has loads of girlie things like make up and perfumes". Francesca looked at Misty up close and could see she had really let herself go. Her hair was just shoved back into a ponytail and you could have fried an egg on it, it was that greasy. Her skin looked grey and she was right when she said she could be compared to beached whale. She was massive. Francesca focused on her belly.

"Wow you're massive aren't you? Lift your top up so I can have a proper look". Misty slowly raised her blouse, conscious of the stretch marks that lay beneath. As soon as Francesca saw them she commented on them straight away.

"Ewwww what the fuck are them?" She now proceeded to investigate them further. "They're like train tracks. Big thick train tracks. I am never having kids if this is how your body goes". Misty pulled her top back down almost immediately and explained why she had got them.

"Most women get them when they have babies. It's because your skin stretches, to hold the baby. I just hope I don't get any more, they look unsightly don't they?" Francesca made no attempt to lie to save her friends feelings, she just looked at her stomach and screwed her face up. Francesca was finding it hard to believe that a baby could do this to your body in such a short time and made the decision there and then, she was never having children.

Misty and Francesca talked of their other friends from school and what they were doing now. A lot had got jobs and were doing well for themselves, especially one person in particular. Francesca watched her friends face as she spoke of Dominic, she could tell she was still interested in him and what he was doing. It was a shame how things had turned out between them, because Misty and Dominic would have made a nice couple and had a good life together. Francesca had heard that Dominic had started an apprenticeship with some big company and it was said he was being groomed for management. When she relayed this information to Misty, she could see the sadness in her eyes as somewhere deep inside her she knew she still cared about him. The morning went well and Misty's mood was lifted. Francesca had agreed that she would visit more often, as she had also missed their chats. They both walked to the door together and hugged each other goodbye. Francesca decided that from now on she would stay well away from her best friend, because when all the truth came out, about Gordon and herself, she didn't want to make it any harder for Misty by being part of her life.

When Misty closed the door, she headed back into the front room feeling a little bit sad. Looking round the room the silence scared her. Was this how her life was going to be from now on? Surely things had to change before the baby was born, otherwise she knew she would have to move on and leave Gordon. She felt trapped inside this little world Gordon had put her in. At first it had felt nice and she loved that he was a little bit jealous about her friends but as time went on he lost interest in everything about her and he rarely spoke to her about the baby. She had always made excuses to herself about his behaviour but as time passed she knew he didn't give a fuck about her or the baby. It was funny how she now felt after seeing Francesca. It had been like a breath of fresh air and she realised what she needed to do if she was going to break out of this lifestyle she had got herself into to. Misty spoke to herself as she reached for her coat, if anyone would have heard her they would have thought she was mad.

"Well Misty Sullivan, its time you pulled yourself together and get a life", she spoke to herself. "All you seem to do is sit looking at these four fucking walls every day. Well no more girl! As from today you're going to start living your life again, with or without your nobhead of a boyfriend."

Once she had her coat on, she checked all the doors were locked and headed to her mother's house. She decided she didn't want be on her own today and Max would be in from work by the time she got to her mum's, so they could catch up with all the latest gossip, as she had not seen him for a few weeks. Once at her mother's house, she opened the back door.

"Hello" she shouted and listened for a reply but nobody answered. She walked to the bottom of the stairs and shouted yet again. "Hello, is anyone in". At that moment Max came to the top of the stairs and told her he would be down in a minute, as he was just getting changed. Misty waddled back to the front room and sat herself on the new settee. Her mother had told her all about it but this was the first time she had seen it. The settee was beautiful and she longed for the time when she could buy new things for her home, because at the moment, all the things in the house belonged to Rob and had seen better days. Misty wasn't complaining but Rob's taste in decor left a lot to be desired. Looking round the front room she noticed all the changes that had been made and was pleased that at last her mother had found her feet. It seemed like Lisa had left all the misery behind her and sorted her life out. Misty seemed to have stepped into Lisa's old life which was filled with sadness. Gazing into thin air, she thought about Gordon and his hate for her at the moment. It was only the sound of her brother's voice that brought her back into the real world and away from her depressing thoughts.

"What are you doing out of the house?" he laughed. " I thought you were a hermit these days." Misty smiled but didn't answer her brother's question. Looking at him she noticed a definite change in him. His hair now had blonde highlights in it and he had a lovely golden tan. She stood next to him and placed her pale white arm next to his.

"Look at the colour of ya. Where have you got your tan from?" Max chuckled and told her he had been going on a sun bed in Eastford Square near his office.

"I look great don't I? See if you weren't pregnant you could be doing all these things as well but did you listen to me when I told you that you were too young to have a baby?" Max watched his sister's face drop and he knew he had hurt her feelings, so he started to back pedal, trying to take back his previous comment.

"Well it's not long now before you have the baby and I'm sure you can make up for it when the baby's born. Anyway, to what do we owe the honour of this visit?" She sat back down and Max could tell something was wrong with her but didn't want to pressurise her too much, as he could see she was already close to tears.

"Fancied a change that's all", she said in a timid voice. "I'm sick of sitting in that house all day and looking at four walls". Max immediately asked where Gordon had been all day and he could tell by her face she didn't know.

"Oh he's out and about. You know what he's like, he won't be home till later. You know he's always ducking and diving all over the place. I never know where he is from one minute till the next". Max knew exactly what she meant, as he knew Gordon of old. He was a low life and as far as he was concerned he would never change. But he knew to bite his tongue for the moment as he didn't want to get into an argument with his sister.

Misty commented on the big changes she had noticed in her brother and she felt like he was trying to tell her something but she just couldn't work out what. He had told her of his new job and talked frequently about his work mate called Gary. As she listened it was 'Gary this' and 'Gary that' and she could tell Max thought a lot about him. He spoke of all the cheap holidays that were going on at the travel agency and told her that in a few months he had planned to go to Spain, with Gary and his sister. Misty was so pleased that he had got a job in a travel agency and that he was doing so well in life. Once again she regretted the path she had chosen. The rest of the Sullivan family came home within the next hour and were delighted to see Misty.

"You staying for your tea?" Lisa shouted from the kitchen.

"Err I don't know yet, why what you having?" Lisa knew that if she cooked one of her favourite meals she couldn't say no. So she shouted she was making liver and onions and mashed potato with onion gravy, knowing that Misty couldn't refuse.

"Well you should have said you were having that for tea. How can I refuse that? It's been ages since I've had it. So the answer is most definitely yes".

Both the younger children jumped for joy, at the thought of their big sister staying for tea. It had been ages since they had all sat down together for a family meal and Misty felt the warmth of her family once again. She felt quite special being at her mother's house and hadn't felt like that since she had moved in with Gordon. The two younger boys set the table and Misty helped her mam put the meal onto individual plates. One by one all the meals were brought to the table and everyone tucked in like hungry animals. Rob shouted Lisa to come and take her seat before he started eating, as he found it unfair that she was always last to sit down to eat her meal.

Lisa sat at Rob's side, like a queen sitting next to her king. Misty could see how happy they were together and regretted the hard time she had given them in the past. All the family laughed together and told stories of each other's day at work and school. She felt so happy surrounded by her family and realised how much she had missed them all. Looking round the table she made a promise to herself, that from now on she would come and see her family more often, at least three times a week. Gordon might not be happy about her choices but at that moment Misty didn't care. Her family was all she had and she needed them now more than ever. After tea Rob cleared the table and started to wash the plates. Max gathered all the other utensils and went to help him in the kitchen. Lisa lit a cigarette and sat at the table with the back door open as the two younger boys pushed passed her to play in the garden. Misty sprawled her body onto the settee and lay full length across it. Her stomach was full as she hadn't eaten like this for a long time. Her tea usually consisted of a sandwich, or sometimes just a biscuit, so the meal she had just eaten had stretched her stomach beyond belief.

"Orr mum I'm so full, I can't move."

Lisa smiled as she took a drag of her cigarette. "It will do you no harm, you're eating for two now. You don't want that little baby going hungry do you?" Misty kicked off her shoes and told her mother that what she had just eaten would last the baby till it was born. They both laughed as Lisa spoke about the birth of the baby.

"Are you getting scared yet love?" she asked.

"What should I be scared of mam, is it that bad?", Lisa smiled as she started to tell her the gruelling details of giving birth to a baby. It was quite funny to listen to them. They talked more like sisters, rather than mother and daughter – their relationship had changed with Misty's pregnancy. Misty had a few questions that had been playing on her mind and this was the ideal time to try and get them answered.

"Mum, which hole does the baby come out of? Is it ya bum hole or ya other one?" Lisa tried to keep her face straight, desperately trying not to laugh, as she explained the delivery of a baby. It was at that moment that Lisa realised exactly how much her daughter was going to need her help. Misty knew nothing about babies and how to care for one. She realised that once the baby was born, her life would change dramatically and she would have to be with Misty twenty four hours a day to start with. There was so much to learn about looking after a baby and she knew she would have to show her everything she knew to give her a chance of surviving parenthood. Lisa knew in her heart Misty would make a great mother and never doubted she would take on board any information she gave her.

The night came to an end after watching Coronation Street. Misty decided it was time to start heading home and Lisa told her she would drop her off, as she didn't want her walking home on her own, especially in her condition. She tried to persuade Lisa that she didn't need a lift but like all mothers Lisa wouldn't change her mind. Her mind was made up and she was dropping her off at home and there would be no arguing about it. Misty said her goodbyes to the rest of the family and agreed she would be back tomorrow for a further visit. Rob kissed her on her cheek and slid a five pound note into her hands telling her to get some chocolate for herself to watch television with tonight. She thanked him and walked to the car, where Lisa sat with the engine running.

It's only when she sat in the car, that she remembered she was going home to an empty house. Perhaps she should have stayed a bit longer she thought but it was too late to change her mind now as Lisa had already set off. Misty had planned a relaxing evening when she got home, she contemplated a nice hot bath with loads of bubbles. Also there was a film on she wanted to watch, a proper girlie film, so whilst Gordon was out she planned to take control of the remote control and watch whatever she wanted, without the moaning of Gordon's voice next to her. Misty wondered why on earth Gordon had to be out all day and why he didn't return home until late. She still couldn't work it out. She decided once this baby was born things were going to change and Gordon would step up to the role of being a father and if he didn't like the idea of what it entailed, he could pack his belongings and move out.

CHAPTER ELEVEN

ORDON SAT IN the pub celebrating the successful job. All the men sat together and everyone's spirits were high. Gordon had already been home and had a bath and changed his clothing. He had wondered where Misty could be, as it wasn't like her not to be at home when he got in. Theses thoughts passed very quickly however and he hurried to get ready to meet up with his friends. As he lay soaking in the bath, he tried to relax but the events of the day came flooding back to him. He had never been as scared in his whole life as he had been today. He was so glad it was all over. Gordon had brought his money home and hid his share in a black sports bag that also contained two shotguns. He had not been happy taking the guns home but the other men thought it was safer for him to take them, as he wasn't known to the police.

Gordon counted his money over and over again before he stashed it. He had never seen so much money in his entire life. In total his share worked out to be twelve thousand pounds and a few hundred quid. Searching the house he finally found somewhere safe to put it. He entered the cloakroom where all the coats were hung. The light in there was broken and nobody really ever went in there, so it seemed a good hiding place. Gordon pulled all the coats off one hook and quickly hung the sports bag on it. He replaced all the coats back to their original place and stood back to see if you could tell it was there. 'The bag is safe' he thought as he stood at the door giving it one last look, 'you can't even tell it's there' he thought as he headed back into the front room. Gordon had kept a few hundred pounds out of the bag for Misty. He knew money was tight for her and she had struggled to buy shopping these days. So writing a quick note he left a message for Misty, telling her to go shopping with the money and treat herself with what was left. He left one kiss on the bottom of the message and told her he wouldn't be home late. He knew even before he went out, he wouldn't be in till the early hours of the morning but he wrote it to keep Misty happy, knowing that she would think he was planning on coming home early to be with her.

Gordon lay in the bath for ten minutes, spending the money over and over in his mind. The first thing on his list would be clothes as his wardrobe left a lot to be desired these days. The job had all gone to plan. As planned they all got to the bank on time and waited in their positions for the van containing the money to arrive. Gordon's heart was in his mouth from the start and he kept checking his watch. Mark noticed his uneasiness and told him to relax.

"Just follow ma lead mate. You don't have to worry, just trust me. I know what I am doing". Gordon heard his heart beating in his ears, as he watched the van arrive. All the men were in position and he watched John out of the corner of his eye drive the getaway car into position. This car had been stolen the night before. It was black and a high performance. Everything was ready for action but then it all went in slow motion as far as Gordon could remember. The two men carried the money into the bank in four grey security boxes. They wore helmets with visors that covered their faces. The men looked quite old and didn't look like they would cause any problems. Gordon just hoped they handed the money over without a fight.

Pulling a scarf up over his face so you could just see his eyes and putting on a pair of dark glasses, he reached his hand into his coat where the gun was hidden and followed Mark into the bank. Once inside Mark took over as he watched nervously. He pulled out the shotgun from his coat and started waving it around like a mad man.

"Get fuckin' down on the floor now the lot of ya!" he shouted to the four customers in the shop. The guards froze at the sight in front of them. They knew exactly what was happening. Mark concentrated entirely on getting the money as Gordon dealt with the customers lying on the floor. Pulling out his shotgun, he hovered over them, shouting for them to keep their heads down and close their eyes. 'That's all I need', he thought, 'someone recognising me'. He couldn't take the chance of anyone seeing his face, so he shouted loudly for them to keep their heads flat, facing the floor. Gordon lifted his head and he could see the cashiers behind the desk holding their hands above their heads, pale with fear.

Mark continued shouting at them till all the cases containing the money were handed over. He nodded towards Gordon and beckoned to take one of the cases from him. Gordon held his gun out, still watching the customers every move as he walked over. Once he reached him Mark told him to get the fuck out of there. He wasted no time in following his instruction and made his way to the exit and all he could hear was Mark shouting, telling everybody to keep their heads down and not to move. Gordon ran as fast as he could and jumped into the car. He nervously waited for Wayne and Mark to join him. John had the engine running and revved the engine eager to get away.

"Where the fuck are they?" he shouted, "come on you pair of dozy bastards. What the fuck are they doing, opening an account?" John now fidgeted around but he never took his eyes off the bank doors. Gordon watched the bank eagerly with fear seeping out of his body. The minutes that he waited seemed like hours.

Finally Wayne left the bank with Mark following closely behind. They watched as the men dipped their heads down and ran towards the car. Gordon opened the car door and Mark jumped in while Wayne took the front seat.

"Get the fuck out of here!" Mark shouted and John sped out of the lay-by. The sound of the wheels spinning made passers-by stop in their tracks. As they pulled out, a car slammed on its brakes and just about stopped in time.

"Watch the fuckin' road", Mark shouted at John, "that's all we need a fuckin' crash." Mark looked at the car behind them and waved the gun through the back window. It was obvious the driver had seen the gun as the sound of the horn beeping behind them suddenly stopped. The car drove straight to the motorway, doing at least ninety miles per hour. Mark watched carefully through the back window to make sure they weren't being followed. Gordon sat lifeless next to him, he felt like he was on a rollercoaster. His head didn't feel like his own and his body was trembling with fear.

The men remained silent as John sped down the motorway. The drive home lasted about an hour and finally they reached their own car. All the men transferred to the other car as Mark took petrol out of the boot and sprinkled it inside the car. Everything was removed and Mark lit a piece of paper and threw it inside. Within seconds the car was in flames. The drive home took about twenty minutes and everyone was relieved to be nearly home and safe. They all headed back to John's house as planned, as they knew it would be empty and they wouldn't be disturbed whilst distributing the cash. As they pulled up outside, Gordon couldn't believe the size of it. It was like something he had only seen on television and he stared at it in amazement.

"Come on, help get these cases in the fucking house. We

haven't got all day". John whispered quietly. Mark reached for the case from the back seat and placed his coat over it to disguise it from nosey neighbours and carried it towards the house. Gordon's job was to carry the sports bag containing the guns which he did in the same way.

Once inside all four of them hugged one another and danced around the front room. The celebration went on for at least five minutes before they sat down to count their ill-gotten gains. All eyes focused on the first case as Mark attacked it with a hammer and a screw driver that John had given him. His face screwed up as he dug the screw driver deep inside the case and attacked the locks.

"Come on ya bastard. Come to daddy", he shouted as they all watched with excitement. Eventually with one last blast from the hammer, the case flew open and their reward stood looking at them. Mark emptied the case onto the table as they watched excitely.

"Right someone start counting. Put it into stacks of thousands" he shouted. Gordon had thought he had died and gone to heaven. The money would change his life forever. All the things he had ever dreamed of didn't seem that far away anymore. After time the money was all over the floor, placed into bundles. It amounted to fifty thousand pounds. Gordon immediately divided that by four in his head and realised that he had a share of twelve thousand and five hundred pounds. Overcome with excitement he jumped into the air, like his favourite football team had just scored a goal.

"I'm fuckin' rich. For once in my life I can go and buy the things I want to. Cheers lads for letting me join you. I'll be forever in your debt". Gordon's eyes filled up and the other men could see the money meant everything to him.

"Spend it wisely mate. Make sure you see something for it", said John in a fatherly voice. Mark quickly added his comments on what he thought Gordon should do with his money.

"Spend it wisely my arse. Get it spent and have the time of ya life. You could be dead tomorrow. Sex drugs and rock and roll, that's how I'll be spending mine". Mark laughed and started to kick his legs up in front of him singing at the top of his voice. John disappeared into the kitchen and came back with four glasses and a bottle of whisky. Placing the glasses on the table he poured a large amount into each glass.

"Right lads, let's have a toast. We all deserve it and a job well done to everyone. Let's hope we have plenty more jobs like this one, because I'm getting too old for all this shit and need a little nest egg for my twilight years". They all laughed as they raised their glasses.

"Job well done lads", Mark toasted as he gulped the whisky. They all followed Mark and knocked the whisky back in one and placed the empty glasses on the table. John got four sports bags belonging to his sons from a cupboard and started to split the money evenly into each bag. Each man watched and counted their share of money as it went into the bag. Once it was completed, John opened the bags containing the guns.

"Gordon I'm putting these inside your bag. My wife nearly found them the other night and I can't take the chance of having them again, so are you alright taking them home with you? Is that alright?" Gordon agreed, because at that moment he was so happy that he didn't care about storing two guns in his home. He was high on life and the guns were the last thing on his mind.

"Yeah mate shove 'em in my bag, I will sort them out later. No worries".

"Top man". John said "Saves me from the earache if the wife was to find them".

The four of them agreed they would all meet for a good piss up in the pub in a couple of hours. Wayne was the first to leave, followed shortly by Mark and Gordon. Mark and Gordon had phoned a taxi, as Mark had agreed to drop Gordon off first before he went home. The sound of the taxi beeped outside the house and Mark and Gordon left together. Once inside the taxi, they both sat in the back. Mark hugged Gordon and praised him for a job well done. Gordon felt like a young boy whose father had congratulated him on winning a football match. He leaned towards Gordon and whispered in his ear.

"Shall I get us a big bag of sniff for tonight to celebrate?" Gordon smiled and did not hesitate in his answer.

"Yeah get the biggest bag they have got, because I am well and truly celebrating tonight". Mark chuckled and grabbed him laughing, the taxi stopped outside Gordon's house ,and he arranged to meet Mark later in the pub. Gordon picked his bag up from the taxi and said goodbye to his partner in crime. Once the taxi had left he walked up the path towards his house.

Opening the front door, he dropped his bag and headed into the front room expecting to see Misty sat there but as he looked he realised she wasn't there. He ran up stairs and shouted her name throughout the house but with no reply. It was quite unusual, her not being home but for now he was kind of glad, as it gave him time to relax and get himself together before he went to meet his mates in the pub. He also knew he could always deal with Misty later when he returned home. How dare she be out of the house, he thought to himself, as he walked upstairs to lie on the bed for a few minutes to relax.

CHAPTER TWELVE

ORDON RETURNED TO the pub, as planned and joined his mates for a night of fun and games. Once inside the pub he phoned Francesca and told her to get her glad rags on and come and join him. Francesca started to ask questions about where he had got the money from, as she thought he didn't have a pot to piss in but he stopped her dead in her tracks telling her not to be so nosey. She agreed to meet him and told him she would be there in the next hour. He could tell by her voice she was excited. This was the first time he had ever phoned her to come for a drink. On the previous times he had met her, he had always been drunk and the last orders bell had always sounded.

As the men sat there Mark caught Gordon's eye and beckoned him to follow him to the toilets. Gordon knew exactly what they were going for and couldn't wait to get the fix he so desperately needed. Once inside the cubicle Mark pulled out the biggest bag of cocaine he had ever seen.

"Fuckin' hell it's like a bag of snow. How much do I owe you?" Mark told him they would sort out the money later as at the moment he too needed his fix and couldn't be bothered sorting out the money. Mark knelt onto the toilet floor and made two white lines for both of them. Gordon watched as Mark snorted the drug into his nostrils and couldn't wait for his turn, knowing the feeling that Mark was already experiencing.

"Come on move over, we haven't got all night" Gordon prompted. Mark stood up slowly and held his body closely against the wall, experiencing the full rush of the cocaine. Within seconds Gordon was down on the floor snorting his share of the drug like a Hoover. As the cocaine travelled up inside his nostrils the rush hit his brain almost immediately and the feeling inside was heaven. They both wiped the seat and entered back into the pub. Gordon was well and truly rocking. He moved over to the juke box to put on his favourite song and waited for it to play.

Then he began to sing the words loudly, encouraging the rest of the pub to sing along with him. He was so full of confidence and loved the way he felt. As he danced to the music, he made his way back to his mates, spinning and turning doing his dance moves. Once he had reached them, he took his t-shirt off and began flexing his muscles to his friends. A few ladies sat in the corner watched with lustful eyes, as they saw his muscular body.

"Get em off", one of the ladies shouted as her friends joined in the chant as well. "Get em off for the girls, get em off". They shouted as they watched him thrust his hips round and around teasing them. Mark joined in the chant and shouted with them. Before long Gordon was stripped to his boxer shorts and stood on a table facing the ladies. They all laughed and told him they wanted more. He loved the attention he was getting and straddled across one of the ladies thrusting his crutch towards her face.

The locals in the pub all came closer to watch the performance and all joined in, clapping and shouting "Off! Off! Off!". What Gordon didn't see was the shape of Francesca walking straight towards him as he was thrusting himself towards the ladies face. Francesca moved the onlookers out of the way and jumped towards Gordon.

"What the fuck are ya doing ya prick" she shouted as he

turned to face her. Once he saw her stood there the moment had gone and he stepped down off the table. The ladies tutted as Francesca passed him his clothes she had picked up from the floor. Gordon felt slightly embarrassed as he spoke to Francesca.

"Fucking hell, what's up with ya face? It's only a bit of fun for the ladies". Francesca was fuming and opened fire on him, holding nothing back.

"Oh well, if that's the case, it will be alright if I get my kit off for the lad's wont it?"

Gordon dragged her arm and pulled her to the side. She could tell he meant business and tried to calm the situation, before he exploded. He now hissed into her face with rage.

"That body belongs to me and I get jealous of other men looking at you. You are a very attractive bird, so keep ya fucking clothes on if you know what's good for you. I'm sorry for what I have just done. It was only a bit of fun". The plan had worked and Francesca calmed down. He kissed her and handed her some money.

"Here. Go to the bar, get the drinks in and stop moaning". He now shouted to his mates, to ask what drinks they wanted and he relayed it to Francesca who was already stood at the bar.

The night went with a bang as usual and everyone was in good spirits. Gordon was starving by the end of the night and wanted to go for something to eat. He asked the other men if they wanted to go for a curry or something but they declined as they all had to start heading home to their wives. Gordon stepped into the road and flagged a taxi. As it pulled over they ran to get in it. Gordon told the driver their destination. He had always wanted to eat in restaurants but never had enough money. Now, since money wasn't an issue, the world was his oyster.

"Curry Hut please mate" he told the taxi driver. "Do you

know where that is?" The driver took a few directions from him and then remembered the place he was talking about. Gordon and Francesca kissed passionately in the back of the cab as it moved off. It wasn't long before they were a step away from having sex but they knew they had to stop as they remembered where they were. Francesca could see the taxi driver peering through his rear view mirror, obviously watching where Gordon had slid his hands. This turned her on and she performed even more as the man watched agog.

Once the taxi reached its destination, Francesca straightened her clothes and stepped out of the taxi waiting for Gordon to pay the fare. She smiled at the driver as he took the money and you could tell by his face he had enjoyed the free entertainment.

"Good night love" he shouted, as he stretched his head through the taxi window. He blew her a kiss as he drove away. Gordon was none the wiser and waved goodbye to the taxi driver. They entered the restaurant like the king and the queen of Collyhurst. They were greeted by a waiter and shown to their seats. Once they were seated Francesca looked round and admired the decor. The room was decorated in a lovely red and gold wallpaper and all the fixtures and fittings matched. 'It's spectacular' she thought as the waiter came over to take their order.

He ordered lots of different things, starting with a prawn cocktail apiece followed by onion bhajis. For their main meal he ordered them a mild curry with pilau rice. Gordon gazed across the table towards Francesca and looked deep into her eyes.

"This is the life isn't it? I could get use to this couldn't you?" she smiled and agreed with him as he continued, "I'll give you some money to treat yourself tomorrow. I've had a bit of an earner today and I want to treat you. I will give you a thousand pound to rig yourself out, is that alright?"

Francesca nearly pissed herself with excitement when he told her how much he was giving her. But she played it cool as she didn't know if he was lying or not. So to thank him she leaned over the table slowly and kissed him softly for the gift he had promised. As she pulled herself back to sit back onto the chair, she froze as she saw a familiar face looking directly at her.

"Max" she whispered. Gordon asked her to repeat the words she had spoken and once again, she spoke his name.

"It's fucking Max he's just seen us kissing". Francesca hung her head low and hoped Max wouldn't cause a scene. Gordon turned and looked directly at Max and waited for his reaction but Max turned back around and left the restaurant accompanied by his friends. As Gordon watched him leave he could see his friends asking him why but Max just hurried away making no response. Gordon didn't let Max spoil their night. He knew he could conjure an excuse together before Max spoke to his sister. Anyway Misty wouldn't believe him anyway, once he had had his say the next day.

The rest of the meal went well but the mood was ruined for Francesca. That's all she needed, Misty finding out about her betrayal. Even though she wanted Gordon to leave her, the time was just not right. Somewhere, deep down, she felt guilty about the affair. Gordon saw the change in Francesca's mood and tried to make her laugh as they waited for the taxi home. Gradually her mood lifted and the party animal Francesca returned. Sitting in the taxi Gordon dug inside his pocket and pulled out his bag of sniff.

"Look what I've got for us once we get back to your auntie's," Francesca's eyes lit up like a child receiving a birthday gift, as she watched Gordon replace the drugs back inside his pocket.

Neither Gordon nor Francesca realised how much this drug was taking over their lives. They couldn't get enough of the stuff. It was fine whilst they were taking it but it was the next day that left them both feeling like zombies. Francesca had been worse, her mood the next day had left her feeling suicidal and she just couldn't seem to pull herself together. She would find herself lying in bed and feeling lifeless. Then the tears would come, she didn't know why she was crying but she was unable to stop. She had promised herself a few times that she would leave the drugs alone but when it was offered to her she always thought that this would be the last time she would have it. Unfortunately the last time never came. She was well and truly hooked and in time to come she would realise how much it had taken a grip of her.

Back at her auntie's house, they both crept in like burglars. Francesca hadn't told Gordon, that lately her auntie had been a right bitch with her. She was sick of Francesca lying in bed all day and not searching for a job. From a distance she had watched her niece go downhill and didn't like the young woman she saw in front of her now. She had once been so energetic and full of life but these days she was a waste of space and her auntie made no secret about letting her know it. She had told her that she would have to start coming in at a decent hour and boys were not allowed home with her anymore until she had sorted herself out. Francesca headed straight for the conservatory and hushed Gordon as he started to speak.

"Sssshhhh be quiet, my auntie's being a bit funny at the moment and she'll go mad if I've brought someone home". Gordon looked at her before he grabbed her by the waist and started spinning her round.

"Bet your auntie doesn't know what her sweet little niece does whilst she's in bed does she? Well get yourself over here and have a go of this. I am sure this will loosen you up".

Gordon pulled the small wooden table towards him and retrieved the bag of cocaine out of his pockets. Pouring some powder onto the table he began to split it into lines. Francesca's eyes widened as she pulled up a chair next to him, waiting for her turn. Once they had snorted the lines of cocaine they began their usual ritual of sex but Gordon knew his stay would only be short tonight, as he wanted to see where Misty had been when he called home earlier in the evening. How dare she be out he thought to himself as he began to kiss Francesca. He knew she wouldn't be doing it again once he had set her straight. 'How dare she disobey me,' he thought as he kissed Francesca.

The sex began but Gordon felt agitated and couldn't wait to get it over with. Francesca's mind was somewhere else too. Max was now holding all the cards in their lives at the moment and she didn't know whether he would go straight to Misty and tell her about the scene he had just witnessed. She just hoped he would keep it to himself. Only time would tell she thought as she began to perform a sexual act on Gordon. Once their lovemaking was over they both shared the ritual cigarette. Gordon knew Francesca would be expecting him to stay the night, so he picked his moment wisely before he broke the news to her.

"Listen I'm not staying tonight. I want to go home in case Max has decided to call round and tell Misty about us. I think it's best if I'm there, then I'll know exactly what he is saying. I'll tell her it's all lies if he turns up. What do ya think?" She didn't need time to think, she also wanted to know how Max would react, so with a quiet voice she agreed that he should go home. Francesca felt nervous as she thought Misty might knock at her door any minute and she wanted to be prepared in case she did, so she let him know she felt the same way.

"I think ya right. I can't stand not knowing whether he's told her or not". Gordon sighed with relief, he'd imagined it was going to be a lot harder than that to get away from her tonight but she took the news well and surprisingly agreed with everything he said. They both finished their cigarettes and she quietly walked him to the door, hoping not to wake her aunt. At the door he kissed her goodnight and headed home like a hurricane.

As he reached his front door, he had to bend over and catch his breath. He had run all the way home like a man on a mission. After a few moments he dug his hands into his jeans to find his key. He found it and carefully opened the door and pushed it open. The house was in complete darkness, as he sneaked slowly up to bedroom. As usual Misty was lay in a little bundle on one side of the bed. Gordon decided not to take his clothes of as yet as he wanted to deal with Misty before he got undressed. As he sat on the bed, he dug his hand into Misty back. Misty immediately jumped and turned to face the silhouette that sat next to her. Once she rubbed her eyes and focused she realised it was Gordon waking her.

"What's the matter? Why have ya woke me up?" she enquired. He made no comment but moved his legs onto the bed beside her. Before he spoke he made himself comfortable, as he knew the interrogation was about to start.

"Where have you been today?" he asked in a cocky voice. "I called home earlier to get changed but no one was in". Misty looked at him and shook her head in disbelief. "I must have been at my mum's I stayed there for my tea. Why what's the problem?"

Gordon leant towards her face and in a deep voice he spoke directly to her. "What's the problem!? You're the fuckin' problem. You're never in this house. Where's was my tea? Oh no!" He said in a sarcastic voice. "You couldn't be bothered making my tea, because you were out gallivanting weren't you!"

Misty sat up and moved away from his face. "Gordon I've been to my mum's for tea not fucking gallivanting. I haven't been to my mum's for ages and I'm sick of sitting in this house looking at four walls all day on my own". Gordon's face shown just how angry he was as he reached towards her and grabbed her hair. He gripped her hair in his hands and ragged her about like a doll, ranting into her face.

"Oh so you're sick of it all, are you? You cheeky little slut. You don't care about anyone but yourself. You're a spiteful little bitch". Gordon drew his hand back and clenched his fist. Without any warning he swung it round and connected with her eye. Her head flew to the side of the bed, as he continued to hit her like a punch bag. She pleaded with him to stop but it just fell on deaf ears.

"Get up you little lazy slut and make my fucking tea. How dare you think I don't deserve to be treated with respect? Don't I treat you well? Don't I do everything for you? All I ask is for a tea to be on the table when I come home and you can't do that one little thing for me". Gordon ragged her again before he spoke. "Get your arse downstairs and do the job you should have done hours ago". He now stood up and reached across to the shivering body of Misty. He took her by the hair and led her to the bedroom door. Once at the door he pulled her hair to the side so she was looking directly at him.

"Off you go and make my fuckin' tea. Don't get no bright ideas, about running away either because I will catch you and bring you back and it will be ten times worse then, wont it?" He released her hair slowly and watched her make her way downstairs towards the kitchen. Every part of her body was aching and she could feel her eye starting to swell. Her tears were flowing but she knew they could not help her, as Gordon saw tears as a sign of weakness and if he saw them he would punish her for being weak. So she dried her eyes and headed into the kitchen. The cold from the kitchen froze her body instantly. Her teeth chattered as she opened the fridge door and looked what she could make for him to eat. Looking in the fridge she knew there was no other option than to make him chips and something else, because if she made him a quick snack he would surely send her back downstairs to make him something proper to eat. She decided to make him sausage chips and egg. So turning on the chip pan she searched in the freezer for some sausages. Misty froze as she heard the footsteps of Gordon walking round upstairs and prayed he wasn't coming downstairs for round two but the footsteps stopped, so she carried on with relief. Finding the sausage in the freezer, she stood looking at them in her hand. Slowly she squeezed them together, pretending it was Gordon's face. Before she knew it she was spitting at each of the sausages, speaking to them like they were human.

"Fuckin' bully, hitting women. You will get what's coming to you one of these days, mark my fucking words you no good bastard" Just as she finished talking to the sausages Gordon walked to the kitchen door, looking directly at her liked a crazed animal.

"What are you making me? I don't want shite you know". Misty relayed the menu she was cooking to him and he stood there in silence.

"To tell ya the truth, I've lost my appetite. I only have hunger for you at the moment. What do you say to a bit of Gordon loving?" Misty knew she would have to say yes as she didn't want to upset him anymore. He walked towards her and she felt herself cringe with the thought of him touching her. He now touched her cheek and smiled.

"See, I only want to be cared for. I don't mean to hurt you but you know it annoys me when you're not at home when I come in. I left you some money for yourself, did you get it?" Misty nodded her head and whispered thanks as he started to kiss her trembling lips. "See I think of ya all the time. All I want is for us to be happy". He stroked her legs and started to pull her nightie straps off her shoulder. Her body froze as he started to kiss the side of her neck. Before long he had moved his lips towards hers and bit her bottom lip softly, telling her to kiss him back. Misty was crying inside but could do nothing but kiss him back. He was like an animal as he pulled her nightie up to her waist. He penetrated her deeply and she yelled as she felt him inside her but he continued without any regards to her well being. The whole episode lasted around five minutes, much to her relief. As soon as he finished she pulled her nightie back down and stood staring at him waiting for his instructions.

He pulled his jeans up and leant on the kitchen side. It was only then that he saw the true extent of Misty's eye. It was badly swollen and starting to shut, so he made his way to the freezer and opened it to find a bag of frozen carrots.

"Here put this on ya eye. It will take the swelling down". Misty turned her head away from him as he placed the bag on her eye. "I'm only trying to help. Don't be fuckin' ungrateful. It's all ya own fault. You know exactly how to wind me up don't you? And this is the result of it all. Are you going to apologize then?"

Misty stared at him in disbelief. 'Who the fuck does he think he is', she thought as she looked at him with hate in her eyes. She wished she could hurt him like he had hurt her but she knew he was too strong. Misty suddenly placed her hand to her side as she felt a burning pain shoot right across her stomach. Holding her side she dropped her head down and started to take deep breaths. The pain felt like a hot poker being pushed into her lower stomach. Gordon watched anxiously and began to move towards her. He stroked her head as he felt helpless to her pain. Looking at her face he realised she had turned a funny grey colour and he knew whatever was going on, was not good.

"What's up? Is it the baby?" He panicked as her head dipped further onto the kitchen worktop. He could tell she was in pain and he panicked unable to find the cause, as she was froze and remained completely silent.

"Misty! Fucking speak to me .What's the matter? How can I help if you won't tell me what the problem is?" It was funny but Gordon had become sober within minutes as he realised that the beating he had just given her could have had a lot to do with the pain she was feeling. He watched a few minutes more, before he told Misty she needed to lie down. He guided her to the stairs and walked slowly behind her holding her body to steady her. Once in the bedroom he straightened the bedding and placed the pillows properly onto the bed. He laid her flat onto the bed and slowly he could see the colour returning to her face.

"Do ya need a drink of water or summat?" he panicked. "You look like shite". Misty nodded and he left her to get her a cold drink of water from the bathroom. She felt the wave of pain slowly leaving her body. The pain had terrified her and she thought she was going to die. She took deep breaths and blew her breath onto her face. Hoping that her breath would cool her down as she felt like it was on fire. Gordon returned with the drink and passed it to her. He now positioned himself facing Misty and watched her with a concerned face.

"Drink it, it will cool ya down." She sipped the cold water and he slowly stroked her forehead. Inside Gordon felt guilty. Why did he behave like this, how could he hurt such a poor defenceless creature like Misty. Looking at her face, he was filled with regret and he felt sick inside. He was desperate for forgiveness for the way he had treated her. He could never look her in the face again without it. He was a coward and he knew he didn't deserve her but from now on he would change and never raise a hand to her again. That was the promise he made to himself as he lay his head on her breast, hoping she could find it in her heart to forgive the beast that lay beside her. Misty felt his tears fall onto her chest and he sobbed like a small child as he began to speak.

"Please forgive me. I'm so sorry for hurting you. I just can't control my temper. I will get help I promise ya, please forgive me". Misty stroked his head. Tears fell down her cheek as she looked at him lying on her chest. Forgiveness came within minutes because she didn't want any more arguing. Her life was terrible at the moment and she could do without all the violence. So as she held his head and told him she forgave him. Gordon hugged her waist and said he would make her the happiest woman in the world from now on and she believed him. She couldn't see through his evil lies. It would only be a matter of time before the beast would reveal his ugly head again and Misty would have to find out the hard way that the words he had spoken had been nothing but lies.

Gordon moved his body to lie next to her. He held her all through the night and she felt loved for once. He had given her extra money for herself and told her to go and get something nice to wear tomorrow whilst she was out shopping. They talked through the early hours and finally drifted off to sleep. Misty felt like all their problems had been aired out and hoped the days ahead would be filled with happiness and love.

Gordon's final thoughts before he drifted off to sleep had been so different to Misty's. His mind was ticking over thinking of Max. He knew he would have to silence him but for now he would play it by ear till Max made his move. Gordon looked at Misty's face and her eye was black and blue. He knew he would have to persuade her to cover up the truth, he didn't want everyone to know the real reason why her eye was bruised so badly. He was sure with a little t.l.c. he could persuade her to come up with a story. After all, he had promised to change and never do it again, how could she resist his charms, he thought, as he kissed her cheek and said goodnight.

CHAPTER THIRTEEN

MAX HAD TOSSED and turned all through the night. The secret he held was tearing him apart, he was in a no win situation. If he told his sister, he knew it would break her heart and he had to think of the baby. How would Misty cope on her own with a new baby? He knew she was strong but lately Gordon had sucked every inch of life out of her. Max wondered if she had enough fight left to deal with this. So for that reason he had decided to keep his secret for the moment. Max hoped he had made the right decision but one person would be getting a piece of his mind when he saw her. Francesca was Misty's best friend and the little slut had deceived his sister in the worst way possible and for that reason he would make it his business to see she got what she deserved.

He decided that once he was ready he would call and see his sister. It would be fun to see Gordon's face when he met him in the house. He would be walking on egg shells waiting to see if he told his sister the truth about him and her slutty mate. But he would play it cool he thought. Even though he had decided to not to tell Misty, he still wanted to let Gordon know exactly how he felt about his affair with Francesca. He would give him an ultimatum and tell him to end it now with Francesca otherwise he would tell his sister the truth. He expected Gordon to try and talk his way out of it but he knew he would get rid of Francesca at the first instance to save Misty finding out their secret. The baby was on its way and Max believed Gordon would not jeopardise that.

He got ready and headed downstairs around mid-morning. He was greeted by his brothers who were fighting over a toy. Lisa was trying to quiet them down as they jumped on each other, wrestling each other to the ground. As she looked at Max she noticed mascara under his eyes. Perhaps the lads had been fooling around last night she thought. They had done worse things to each other than put make-up on. She smiled as she remembered the time someone shaved Max's eyebrows off and she had to draw them back on for weeks later till they grew back.

"Are you hungry?" she shouted as he went to sit down in the front room. Max said he wasn't and told her he was going to see Misty and would grab something on the way there. Lisa thought it unusual for Max to be visiting his sister so early in the morning.

"Is everything alright?" she asked in a concerned voice. Max turned to her and made up a story that he was going round to get some music she had promised him the day before. After hearing his explanation she carried on with her business and never thought any more about it once she knew Misty was alright. Max left the house and hurried to his sisters. He had hoped to see Gordon before he left and knew if he didn't catch him now he would have to make another visit to catch him on another day. Max's first stop was at the café, he was starving. He made his order and waited patiently for it to be cooked. He had ordered two bacon and egg muffins with brown sauce on each. He had ordered his sister one, as he knew she loved bacon and eggs. The smell of bacon filtered throughout the café and Max licked his lips at the thought of eating his food. Once his order was completed he paid the lady and headed towards his sisters, with the muffins piping hot in his arms.

When he arrived at her front door he took a deep breath before knocking but once he did he pressed his head against the glass pane on the front door and watched his sister making her way towards him. As she opened the door, she reached behind it to pick up the post that had been delivered and Max couldn't see her eye. Misty panicked as her brother made his way into the hallway. He shouted for her to hurry as he told her he had brought her something to eat.

"Bacon and egg muffin, come and get it before it goes cold". Misty pottered about in the kitchen trying to think of what to say. She knew once he saw her eye he wouldn't believe any old story she told him, so she knew she would have to get her story straight before she saw him. He shouted her yet again and told her if she didn't come quickly he wouldn't be held responsible for eating her butty. Misty composed herself and slowly edged her way into the front room. He didn't notice her eye straight away as he was too busy tucking into his food but when he did, he stood straight to his feet.

"What the fuck is up with your eye?" He marched straight to her and examined it closer. Misty tried to cover it with her hand but he threw it out of the way with fury burning in his eyes. Misty tried to explain that she had banged it on the kitchen cupboard but Max knew she was trying to cover up for the bastard of a boyfriend she lived with.

"Banged it on the cupboard, my arse. Do ya think I'm fucking daft? I know it's 'im who's done this to you, why are you covering up for the nobhead?" Misty argued with him for a moment, telling him she was telling the truth but Max knew his sister was lying. She went through the story for yet a third time, trying to add lots more details to the story to make it sound more believable but he could tell she was lying through her back teeth. Max could see she was getting upset, so he backed off and tried to calm her down as he sat listening to the rest of her lies.

"Well I just hope that's the way it happened and you're not covering up for him. If he's the one who has done this to you, you deserve everything you get for lying for him". Misty tried to laugh it off and told Max she would never put up with violence in her relationship, as she had seen it with her own parents and it was something she hated. Misty was relieved when Max backed off, she knew he didn't believe her but for now she had got away with the story. Max talked over his night out and asked if Gordon had been out. Misty lied yet again and said they had a romantic night in front of the television together. She continued to lie saying that he had bought her a box of chocolates and fed them to her one by one whilst watching the television.

Max gritted his teeth as he listened to her fantasy. He had wanted to shout out the truth and tell her that he had seen her so called boyfriend out last night with her slutty mate and that his tongue was stuck down the back of her fucking throat. Looking at his sister his heart melted for her, as she was near giving birth to her child. He could tell she was doing everything in her power to make her relationship work. Even lying to him to protect the monster that had hurt her, so for now he bit his lip. Misty asked Max would he go shopping with her as Gordon had given her some money to get some new clothes and he agreed. He knew the money Gordon had given her was to ease his conscience and by the looks of his sister's face, the money had bought her silence. They both chatted for a while before they set off to go shopping. Max interrogated his sister some more about the whereabouts of Gordon but she held her cards close to her chest and refused to get into a conversation about him. He knew his sister wouldn't confide in him about the goings on with her relationship so he backed off and tried to enjoy the rest of the day with her.

Once they reached the shopping centre they searched in

all the shops for something for her to wear. Max laughed as he looked at his sister's body shape, she looked like a roley poley and was finding it hard to find something to fit. All the shops had very little maternity clothing and Misty was becoming slightly disheartened. Finally, in one of the last shops, she found a lovely black dress with red rose buds all round the edges. She immediately knew this was the dress for her and headed straight to the changing rooms to try it on. As she slipped the dress on and looked in the mirror she felt amazing. She turned all different angles in the mirror and loved the way the dress felt next to her skin. As she turned in the dress she felt a sharp pain in her side. The pain was like the one she felt last night but not as sharp. Holding her side to ease the pain she began to take deep breaths hoping the pain would pass. After five minutes she felt the pain easing in her side. She could hear her brother shouting her name into the changing rooms and popped her head out to see what he wanted.

"What on earth are ya doing? You've been ages. Are you alright?" Misty told him to stop moaning and told him she would be out in a few minutes. After she put her clothes back on she replaced the black dress back on its hanger and headed back to him. She could still feel the pain in her side but it was bearable for the moment and she made no comment to Max about it. Once she had paid for the dress, she wanted to head straight back home but Max had other plans for them. So with a smile covering her pain, she gave in to Max's plans of going for something to eat.

"I'm fucking starving," he moaned, "that bacon and egg muffin I ate earlier wouldn't fill a small child. I need something big to soak up all the beer I drank last night". Misty agreed as she thought some food would do her good. She felt quite weak and the chance to sit down for a while helped her make the decision to accompany him. Max found a small snack bar and found them both seats by the window. The waiter came over and took their order for drinks, whilst they both examined the food menu. Looking at the menu Max focussed his eyes on cheeseburger and chips.

"That will be just what the doctor ordered, cheeseburger and chips. What about you what you having?" Misty felt the pain in her side increase and covered her face with the menu. The pain felt like a wave of heat passing through her body. It started like warm air travelling up from her feet but as it reached her waist it felt like boiling water being poured on her body. She wafted the menu across her face as Max watched with concern.

"Don't tell me you're warm again. Your body clock is up the fucking wall. One minute you're hot and one minute you're cold. I'm so glad I don't have to go through pregnancy I just couldn't cope with it". The waiter came back and took their order. Misty hadn't even looked the menu due to the pain she was feeling but she pretended she had and ordered the same as her brother.

Max's mood had lifted and he felt on top of the world. He had a big night out planned that evening and thought it would be a good idea to invite his sister out with him. After all she hadn't been out for ages and the change would do her good. "So do ya want to wear your dress tonight and show it a good time?" he asked. Misty looked at him not understanding the question properly. So he repeated the question asking her if she wanted to come out with himself and a few friends from work. Max watched his sister as she touched the side of her eye.

"I don't fancy going out with my eye like this. I look horrible. I will come out in a few weeks. Just give my eye time to go down". Max smiled and shook his head, you could tell by his face he was disappointed with her decision but he knew she was right, her face was a mess and it would probably be best if she waited till the swelling went down before she went out. So after a short time, he agreed with her that she had made the right choice and carried on talking about his job and his work colleagues. Misty noticed he spoke a lot about his friend Gary. You could tell by the way he spoke he had a lot of time for Gary and they seemed to be very close and good mates.

Misty tried eating the food in front of her but had no appetite because the pain had knocked her for six. Max ate like it was feeding time at the zoo and didn't even stop for breath as he demolished the food in front of him. Once they had finished, they made their way to the bus stop and waited for their bus to take them home. The bus finally arrived and Misty felt the pain sailing through her body, as she sat down. Max was talking to her but she wasn't listening to a word he said, she was just concentrating on the pain. They reached their destination and parted company. Max told her he would see her tomorrow at their mother's house. They had a great day together and enjoyed spending quality time with one another, both agreed they should do it more often. Max waved as he walked in the opposite direction, as Misty struggled to make her way home to her front door.

Pushing the key into the door she flung it open. Her legs seemed to give way as she entered the house and she found herself on the hallway floor fighting the pain she felt inside. It seemed as if she was a bystander, watching herself from a distance, unable to take the pain away. Her breath was deep as trickles of sweat dropped from her forehead. "Please help me". She cried but no one heard her sobbing voice. Misty lay alone with the pain for at least half an hour, before she decided to try and phone her mother.

The phone seemed forever away and every step felt like ten. Dialling the number she waited for someone to answer, as she knew it would take a while as her mother was in work and the shop was always busy. At last she heard a man voice answer the phone. She struggled at first to speak, as her breath was short and the pain was intense but she forced the words out the best she could.

"Hello". The voice repeated as Misty tried to speak.

"Hello is anyone there?" Misty spurted the words out and they were fast and furious and straight to the point.

"Please can you get Lisa, it's very important. Tell her to come quick please". The male voice asked who was calling, as Misty told him it was her daughter and she needed her straight away. The sound of footsteps walking away from the phone could be heard as she waited anxiously to hear her mother voice. Misty gripped her side as the pain struck again. Holding her side she begged for her mother to hurry up to the phone. At last Lisa's voice came and as Misty heard her voice she broke down in floods of tears.

"Mam!" she screamed. "Please help me, the pain won't stop, please help me". Before Lisa could answer her daughter Misty dropped the phone onto the floor and curled into a ball, unable to take the pain any more. Lisa screamed down the phone, for her to answer but all she could hear was the sobbing of her daughter in the distance. Lisa gave up trying to get her to respond and headed back into the shop to tell her boss she had to go home straight away due to a family emergency. Her boss was quite helpful as he had also heard her daughter's voice on the phone and knew she was upset.

Lisa headed to the car like a wild woman. Her heart was in her mouth, as she opened the door to her car. She started the engine and her mind was working overtime, thinking what could be possibly wrong with her daughter. The journey seemed to last forever. 'Why is it any time you're in a rush you have to stop at every set of traffic lights', she thought as she revved her engine waiting for the traffic lights to change. At last, the light finally changed and she continued her journey with haste to her daughter's side. Pulling up near her daughter's house, she parked the car on a nearby car park and hurried towards the front door.

The door was closed firmly shut as she pounded on it. Looking through the letter box she could see Misty curled in a ball on the floor. Lisa felt completely helpless as she shouted to her to open the door. After a few minutes of watching her on the floor, there was only one option left and that was to try and kick the door open. Lisa knew the door wasn't that safe, as Misty had mentioned it on several occasions and had said anyone could open the door with a slight push. So with that in mind Lisa turned her back to the door and pressed on it with all her might. Nothing happened on her first attempt and she knew she would have to find more strength to get to her daughter, so with one last burst of energy, she pushed with all her might against the door and the door came flying open.

Lisa stumbled onto the ground as the door opened. The pain she had incurred in her shoulder took a back seat for now as she made her way to Misty.

"Misty, Misty", she shouted as she tried to look at her face but there was still no response. Lisa panicked as she tried to think of her next move. Looking at her, she prised her hands away, to reveal a pale white face. Misty slowly opened her eyes and tried to speak to her mother, her words were muffled and hard to understand, so she moved closer towards her face so she could hear.

"Mam please takes this pain away, please". Lisa cradled her child like a new born baby and rocked her slowly in her arms .Her heart melted as she tried to find out where the pain was coming from. She never thought in a million years it would be the pain of the baby inside her. Lisa noticed droplets of sweat dropping of her brow and stoked it away with long gliding movements.

"What do you think the pain is?" Lisa asked in a calm

motherly voice. Misty took a deep breath before she replied and Lisa could tell the pain was getting worse as she watched her daughter doubled up.

"I think its food poisoning . It must be something I've eaten because I have never felt pain like this before. The pain keeps coming and going but each time the pain gets worse." What Misty had described sounded like labour pains and she knew she needed to act fast to get her daughter the help she needed.

Lisa kept her thoughts to herself as she didn't want to frighten her daughter but the more she watched her the more she knew this was labour. Lisa left her propped against the stairs as she headed to the front room to phone an ambulance. Once they answered she explained her daughter's condition and told them of her fears for the baby. The lady on the other end of the phone told Lisa how to cope until the ambulance arrived. One of the things the lady told her was to put a cold cloth onto Misty's forehead and keep her cool. She also told her to make sure she had water for her to drink as she didn't want her getting dehydrated. Lisa listened carefully to all the instructions and hung up the phone and headed to the kitchen to get the cold cloth to put on her forehead. As Lisa ran the tap she could hear the wrenching scream of her daughter in the hallway. Filling a glass with cold water she ran straight back to her daughters side.

"Here, drink this cold water it might help. The ambulance is on its way so it won't be much longer, just bear with it a little bit longer". Lisa looked at Misty's face fully for the first time and noticed her black eye. "What the hell has happened to your eye?" Lisa turned her face to look at the eye in more detail but Misty pulled away and screamed with more pain. Holding her daughter's hand she could feel her fingers digging deep into her hands and she knew she couldn't ask any more questions about her eye, she just hoped Gordon had nothing to do with it, because if he had she wouldn't be held responsible for her actions. Misty screamed like a banshee, as Lisa watched her helplessly. Folding the cold cloth she placed it onto her forehead hoping it would cool her down.

The ambulance sirens could be heard in the distance and Lisa felt relieved that Misty was going to get some help. Once inside one of the ambulance men made his way straight to Misty and examined her. Then he took her blood pressure. The other ambulance man took down Misty's details from Lisa and asked her medical history. Once he had enough information he headed back to Misty and joined in the examination. Misty lay flat on the floor as they placed a funny object on her belly to listen to the baby's heartbeat. Lisa could tell by his face that things were not looking good. Almost immediately after listening to the baby's heartbeat, they went into emergency mode. It took no longer than five minutes and Misty was in the back of the ambulance and heading straight for the hospital. Lisa held the ambulance man's arm before he started the engine and pleaded with him to hurry up.

"Is it the baby?" she cried. The man looked at her and nodded and spoke with great concern.

"Listen we need to get her to the hospital as soon as possible if there is any chance of saving this baby. I just hope it's not too late". The ambulance pulled out of the car park with sirens blazing heading straight for the hospital. Lisa's body shook, before she could get in the car to follow the ambulance to the hospital. Please lord, please don't let her lose this baby. It means so much to her and she's only a child, how could she cope with such a loss, Lisa thought as she held her stomach. She opened the car door and felt physically sick. All the blood seemed to have drained from her with the shock of what she had just witnessed. Lisa sat in the car and tried to clear her head before she set off towards the hospital.

Her heart pounded as all the questions raced round her mind but she knew the first thing she had to do was to get to the hospital to be with her daughter.

Misty was met by two doctors. The ambulance men quickly informed them of her condition as they wheeled her into the examination room. Misty felt barely conscious as they wheeled her into a white room with only a bed in it. The doctor asked her a few questions before he examined her stomach area. Misty had told him she was seven months pregnant and exactly where the pain was coming from. After several tests the doctor asked if he could do an internal examination to complete his test. Misty wasn't quite sure what he meant at first but once he explained the procedure she was more than happy for it to take place. She couldn't cope with the pain much longer.

The doctor asked Misty to take off her clothes and put on a gown. The nurse who was in the room helped her as she could see she was in immense pain. The nurse knew she was only a young girl and her heart went out to her. How could a young girl like this end up in such a horrible situation? It was a crying shame she thought as she helped the young girl in front of her to get ready.

Lisa hurried straight through the hospital doors and located her daughter just before the examination took place. The doctor told Lisa exactly what he was doing and was very helpful with any questions she asked. She had tried to phone Gordon and let him know what was happening but each time she rang, there was no answer. Unknown to Lisa, Gordon was out on a secret date with Francesca. The doctor confirmed what Lisa thought and tears trickled down her face as he continued to speak to Misty.

"Well young lady, your baby has decided it won't wait another two months. It's going to be a hard next couple of hours but I will give you something to ease the pain, if that's what you want."

Misty nodded and asked how quick she could have pain relief as it was worse than anything she had ever experienced in her life. The doctor called the nurse and asked that Misty be moved to the delivery suite. He also told her as soon as she got there to administer a pain relief. He did tell the nurse the name of the drug but Misty was in too much pain to listen to what it was called.

Whilst the nurse was moving her, Lisa made her way to the pay phone in the waiting room, to try and contact Gordon for the second time. Anger filled her as she visualized her daughter lying in pain without Gordon by her side. The phone rang for what seemed like an eternity before Gordon answered with a cocky tone.

"Gordon, its Lisa. You need to come to the hospital straight away. It's Misty, she's in premature labour". The phone line was quiet for a moment before Gordon spoke.

"What do you mean labour? She's not due for another two months. Is the baby alright?" he asked in a concerned voice. Lisa didn't want to go into details over the phone and told him she would explain everything once he got there.

"Hurry up, she's in a bad way", she told him before she put the phone down. Lisa searched her pocket for loose change to let the rest of the family know what was going on and she also phoned her sister Denise to ask her to pick the children up from school as she didn't want to leave the hospital till she knew everything would be alright with Misty. Lisa made all the necessary phone calls but stood at the phone debating whether to make a call Ken. After all he was her father, she thought as she lifted the phone to dial his number.

Misty lay in the delivery suite and looked round at all the equipment placed round the room. She was afraid and didn't know what was going to happen. Would she be holding her baby later in the day, she thought or was it going to die. The questions floated around her mind as the pain relief finally kicked in. She was feeling quite light headed as Lisa walked back into the room.

"Mam what's happening to me. Am I going to lose the baby? They keep talking in medical terms and I don't understand a thing they're saying. Please tell me what's happening". Lisa felt all emotions rise to the back of her throat and found it hard not cry as she tried to explain in the best way possible what was happening.

"Listen love, there are lots of things they can do to save the baby. That's what all these machines are for. Let's not be negative for now. We will talk to the doctor and make him explain exactly what's going to happen. I've just phoned Gordon and he's on his way. Hopefully he won't be long". Lisa took hold of her daughter's hand and squeezed it gently telling her to brave but she could feel in her gut that Misty would need to be more than brave for the events that were soon to take place. She just hoped they could save the baby, as she knew if the baby didn't survive Misty would be completely devastated.

This baby had been Misty's world for the last seven months and without it, she couldn't even imagine how her daughter would begin to cope. Lisa said a prayer that everything would be fine but she knew she needed more than a miracle if the child had any chance of seeing the light of day. She just hoped the lord above would answer her prayers.

As time went by, the pain returned to Misty and no more pain relief could be administrated as the baby was just about ready to be born. She howled with pain as Gordon finally entered the room looking white in the face. He watched the team of medical staff take their positions round the room and placed himself directly next to Misty in a chair next to the bed. Misty howled like her life was about to end as the doctor examined her further.

"Please stop the pain please. I can't take it anymore. I'm just so tired". The doctor looked directly at her and told her that the time had come for her to deliver her baby. He told her she would have to listen to everything he told her to give the baby any chance of surviving .He then introduced two other doctors who were situated at the corner of the room.

"These doctors are here for the baby. Once you have given birth they will take over the care with the baby. They will give one hundred percent to try and save your baby but for now we need to concentrate on getting the baby out as quick and as safe as possible".

Misty rolled about with pain and didn't reply. Gordon looked at the doctor and introduced himself as the baby's father. The doctor shook his hand and explained in detail what was about to happen. The doctor couldn't help smelling alcohol on Gordon's breath as he spoke to him and he told him he hoped he wasn't going to cause any trouble in the room, as his main priority was the patient and he wanted to concentrate solely on her. Gordon felt completely embarrassed as he spoke to the doctor but he promised he would be no trouble as his main concern was also his girlfriend and his unborn child.

Everyone took their positions and the long struggle to give birth began. Misty's legs were placed in two iron stirrups, making it easier for the doctor to see as she tossed and turned on the bed. The doctor gave her another internal examination and announced that she was ready to start pushing. Lisa had gone to sit outside in the waiting room, as she couldn't stand to see her daughter in so much pain. The screams could be heard outside the delivery suite and Lisa covered her ears to drown out the sound of her child's screams. Rob and Max had come to join her and give their support but when they heard the screams from the room they both looked at each other and knew it wouldn't be long before Misty gave birth.

The doctor and nurse were now coaxing Misty to breathe through the pain she was feeling, but she was finding it so hard. She felt like her bum was being torn apart and couldn't cope any more.

"Fuckin' hurry up will you. I can't do this anymore" she pleaded. Misty tried to cry but her tear ducts had dried up. Within seconds of her speaking the doctor told her he could see the baby's head.

"Right young lady. I need you to push when I say and make it the biggest push you have ever done. You are nearly at the end, so I need you to give it everything on this next push". Misty listened to every word and as soon as he gave the order, she pushed with all her might. The screams could be heard through the hospital and everyone watched with their hearts in their mouths. She was such a young child and to be going through all this pain was a crying shame, the doctor thought as he dipped his head further between her legs to see how far the baby's head was out. Almost immediately he could see the crown of the baby's head and knew one more good push from her and the baby would be out. He told Misty that if the next push was a good one the baby would be definitely born.

Misty sat herself up on the bed and made herself comfortable for the last push. Her strength had returned and she felt in control for the first time during her labour. Gordon held her hand and told her it was nearly over and just to be brave a little bit longer. They all waited for the labour pain to return and within minutes the wait was over. Misty stuck her chin into her chest and pushed and pushed with all her might. Her scream had now turned into a groan that sounded like a cow. The other doctors were now at the side of the bed, waiting like preying animals to take the baby. The final pain lasted for a few minutes and then the baby was born. Misty collapsed on the bed and tried to take in everything that was happening.

Gordon watched as the doctors took the baby over to the corner of the room. They placed plastic tubes down its tiny throat, to try and help the baby to breathe. He could tell by their faces they were fighting a losing battle. The doctor placed his fingers onto the baby's chest and started knocking it quite firmly. For the first time Gordon caught a glimpse of his child as the doctors opened the blanket in which it was wrapped. His body froze as he could see the little bundle lay lifeless in their arms. As he stood he could see the sex of his child.

"My little boy," he sobbed, "please help him please!" he called to the doctors. The nurse in the room told Gordon to sit down and let the doctors do their job, as they were trying their best to revive the baby. He sat down once more and turned to Misty who was being attended to by the doctor.

"It's a little boy. I've just seen him, he looks so small .Oh Misty I hope he's gonna be alright". Misty eyes now turned to the corner of the room and focused on the infant lay on a small plastic mattress. When she saw all the pipes attached to him her heart nearly stopped beating. She watched every move they made and watched their faces for any sign of success. Minutes passed and still nothing had changed and she could tell by the doctor's face it hadn't been successful but hope still floated round in her body and she didn't give up thinking her child would survive. Half an hour had passed before the doctors finally gave up trying to save the baby. They wrapped him in a little green blanket and lay him in an incubator next to where they were stood. The doctor finally turned to see the grief stricken faces of Gordon and Misty. This wasn't an easy thing to tell them, even for an experienced doctor.

"I am so sorry. We tried our best to revive your child but he just wasn't strong enough to survive. I know this is not easy for you and there is no easy way to say this but I am truly sorry from the bottom of my heart at the loss of your child". The doctors slowly drifted from the room. Only one nurse remained but she was keeping herself busy, cleaning up all the tools that had been used and trying to keep a low profile. Everything seemed like it was going in slow motion around Misty and her eyes filled yet again with tears of sorrow. It felt like a thousand knives had been thrown at her, as she held herself tightly, rocking like a small child.

"No" she shouted at the top of her voice. "Please tell the doctors to come back. They need to try again". She climbed off the bed in search of the doctors but her energy level was low and she tumbled to the floor. The nurse ran over to where she lay and helped her to her feet.

"Come on love, you need to lie down. You have just given birth, you will end up haemorrhaging if you don't lie back down". Misty held the nurse's arm and shouted at her.

"Given birth, I know I've given birth. I want my baby. I want my baby to live, so get the doctors back to try again to help save my baby". The nurse felt her pain and comforted her the best she could as Gordon stared into space, as if he was in another world.

Once she was back on the bed, Gordon stood and walked over to where the baby lay. Looking at the nurse, he asked if it was alright for him to hold the baby.

"Of course love", she spoke in a calm voice. "If you sit down, I will bring him over to you". Gordon walked slowly back to his chair and watched every movement the nurse made with his son. Once she had wrapped the baby up in a little blanket she approached Gordon with sympathetic eyes. "Here you are. He's beautiful isn't he?" Gordon took the small bundle from the nurse and held it with tears trickling down his face. Misty turned to face him and sobbed as they both set eyes on their son for the first time.

The baby was fully formed. His skin was quite transparent

and you could see his veins. His hair was fair and even eyelashes were present on his eyes. Gordon opened the blanket and looked at the baby's body. He paid quite a lot of attention to the baby's toes. He stroked every toe individually and softly felt his little legs. Tears from his eyes fell onto the baby's skin and he wiped them with the slightest of touches. Wrapping the baby back inside the blanket, he kissed his head and whispered 'Goodnight mate', into his small delicate ears. Misty watched as he passed her the baby. As he did her body shook with fear.

"No I can't hold him, please hold him for me". Gordon withdrew the baby from her and continued to cradle him in his arms, as Lisa returned back into the room. Lisa's face was bright red and her eyes were swollen from tears she had shed. She went straight to Misty and held her tightly. No words needed to be spoken because their tears said all that needed to be said.

"Mam he's dead. My little baby boy is dead". Lisa remained speechless till Gordon told her to have a look at her grandson lay in his arms. She bent her body close to the baby and kissed him on the cheek, but felt unable to speak, as though her lips were clamped shut. They all sat in silence for a few minutes and none of them could take their eyes off the baby in Gordon's arms. Something had died inside Misty that day and nothing would ever replace the baby she had lost, his memory would stay with her till her dying breath .He would always be in her thoughts. Misty silently said her goodbyes to her son but she could never let him know how much she loved him.

The nurse pottered round the room and you could see she needed to get Misty ready to take her to the ward. It had been nearly two hours since she had left them in the room, as she thought they needed to sit and hold their baby for the last time before he was taken took away. The nurse finally told

Gordon and Lisa she needed to get Misty up to the ward and they both thanked her for her help. Gordon wanted to run outside and scream. He didn't know how to deal with what had just happened and his emotions were ready for exploding, so this was an ideal time for him to say goodbye to Misty and get out of the place where he had witnessed the death of his son. He kissed Misty briefly on her cheek and hugged Lisa as he left the room. He didn't have words for Misty except that he would be back to see her tomorrow. He was a broken man and he needed to be alone to deal with his grief.

As he left the room he walked straight into Max but no words were spoken. Max's face looked like he wanted to kill him for what he had done to his sister but he knew this wasn't the time or the place to deal with it. Rob patted him on the shoulder as he left and told him to be strong. But little did he know he was going back to meet Francesca and finish the rest of his night with her to drown his sorrows.

Misty lay on the bed lifeless with Lisa by her side. The nurse told her that she was ready to go up to the ward and started to transfer her to a wheelchair. She struggled as her legs left the bed, and her body shook with shock. Once in the wheelchair she looked at Lisa with the question she had dreaded hearing on her lips.

"Mam what's going to happen to the baby?" Lisa looked at the nurse for an answer but the nurse was too busy to hear the question. Misty asked the question again and this time the nurse answered.

"Don't you worry darling. We will take care of the baby. Most still born babies go into a communal grave. There will be no need for a funeral, so in a way it's a blessing you don't have to go through that as well after what you have just been through". Misty was quiet as they started to leave the room. Her heart told her she needed to hold her son before she left, as she hadn't held him since he had been born.

"Please can I hold my son before I leave him" she begged, "I would never forgive myself if I never held him in my arms". The nurse agreed and pushed her to her baby. Misty asked the two of them to leave as she wanted to be alone with her baby to say her goodbyes. As she picked him up she could feel a wave of emotion leave her body. She examined every part of his body and kissed each of his fingers. Words were hard to speak as she held him close to her chest but finally she managed to whisper to him as she looked into his face.

"I'm so sorry you didn't survive. I would have loved you with all my heart", her voice choked as she tried to free the final words from her mouth.

"I'll never forget you Dale. You will always be in my heart and never be far from my thoughts. Goodnight God bless son". Misty placed the baby back inside the incubator and sat back into the wheel chair. The nurse had watched her through a small glass panel in the door and knew she was ready to leave.

"Please don't leave him here on his own, will someone come and get him now?" she cried. The nurse assured her as soon as they left the baby would be attended to and Misty left with inner peace knowing her son wouldn't be alone.

The ward was dark when they arrived and the sound of an old women coughing could be heard throughout the ward. Once at her bedside the nurse helped her out of the wheelchair onto the bed. The nurse saw the pain in her eyes and felt her own heart strings being pulled.

"Time is a good healer love. You will soon feel a lot better. Just look after yourself and may God be with you". The nurse patted the top of her head and left her bedside. Slowly all the curtains were closed round her bed and Misty was left alone for the first time.

The side light at her bedside barely gave off any light. She stared round the room and listened to the sound of the nurses talking in a nearby office. She was so tired but her eyes would not give in to the sleep they so desperately needed. Her mind could not get rid of the picture she held in it of her child and every time she closed her eyes the picture was there larger than life. Emptiness was the only word that could describe the way she felt. The baby that once kept her awake at night inside her body was now gone forever and all that was left was an empty space. Misty couldn't even bear to look at her stomach as she lifted the bed sheets. The lump she had nurtured for so many months was nothing but an empty shell. All that was left was the stretch marks on her body to remind her of her child's existence. Misty could feel blood running down her legs and needed to go to the toilet. She didn't want to bother the nurses, so off she went on her quest to find the toilet. As soon as she stepped out from behind the curtain surrounding her bed, she was greeted by a middle age women in the bed facing her. Misty asked for directions to the toilets and the women told her in a soft voice

"Just down that corridor on the left, do you need some help?" She thanked the lady but told her she would be alright and headed towards the toilets. The area where the toilets were situated was dark and poorly lit, due to the time of night. Once she found the lights, she bolted the door behind her. As she looked at her legs, blood had trickled down them. Looking round the toilet area she found a box of sanitary towels next to the toilet, which the hospital had provided for patients use. Looking at them she thought they resembled surf boards. They were enormous but at the moment she had no choice as she needed them to stop her bleeding all over the place. Once she had finished cleaning herself up she crept back towards her bed, as she didn't want to wake all the other patients.

Reaching her bed, the lady facing asked if she was alright and Misty nodded. She would have liked to have chatted more to the lady. Misty could tell she was having trouble sleeping but her own body needed to rest as it was completely exhausted by the day's events.

The sound of the tea trolley woke Misty in the morning. She could hear them offering cups of tea to the patients and it wasn't long before they were at her bed side.

"Good morning young lady. Would you like a cup of tea?" Misty replied yes, as her mouth felt so dry. There was a strange taste in her mouth and she hoped the cup of tea would remove it.

The nurses opened the curtains around her and passed her a steaming hot cup of tea. Looking round the ward she noticed it was filled with a lot of older women and she felt slightly out of place. Cleaners entered the ward and started their daily chores. As she watched them they seemed so full of energy, unlike herself.

Misty felt tired as she had been restless all through the night. She knew she needed to pull herself together before any visitors came, as she looked like death warmed up. Finishing her cup of tea she took herself off to the bathroom. She didn't have any toiletries but the nurse gave her what she needed to clean herself up. Her legs were weak, as she stood to fill the bath with water. The mirror on the wall was completely covered with mist as the bath filled. Pulling the gown off her quivering body she stepped into the bath with caution. Slowly she submerged her entire body beneath the water. The warmth of the water enveloped her skin and she felt like someone had wrapped a warm blanket round her. Within seconds the water turned bright red with the blood she was losing and she sat up straight in the bath. Her baby's empty space stood staring at her as she washed her body. Slowly she glided her hands over her stomach and cried. Guilt now set into her bones and she blamed herself for the loss of her child. It must have been her fault, she thought as she went through the days before, thinking of all the things she had done. Misty finally narrowed it down to her going shopping, perhaps she had needed to rest more and she had not listened to her body when she had first got the pains. If only she had stayed at home and put her feet up, she thought, her baby would still be alive today. She got out of the bath.

Wiping the steam off the mirror she caught the first glimpse of her saddened face. She looked ten years older. Her eyes were swollen from her tears and her hair looked like she had been dragged through a hedge. She couldn't bear to look at her face any longer and moved away quickly to get ready. The knock at the door startled Misty as she was getting ready and she ignored it at first till it eventually got harder.

"Hello", she shouted and waited for a reply. "Misty are you alright?" She shouted back she was fine and hoped the nurse would leave her in peace to get ready.

"Misty, you have visitors, should I tell them you won't be long?" Her heart stopped for a moment and she knew she would have to face them. She felt like a failure and couldn't stand the thought of everyone blaming her for the death of her son. The walk back to her bed seemed like the walk of death and she could feel everyone's eyes on her as she climbed back onto the bed.

Lisa looked worse for wear as she too hadn't slept a wink. She had already been to her daughter's house to remove all the baby things before she was allowed home. Lisa had cried as she put the entire baby wardrobe into a suitcase, to take them home with her. The job was heart wrenching but she knew it had to be done. She didn't want her daughter crying unnecessarily when she got home. Gordon had already taken the cot and pram round earlier that morning and all that was left was the clothes. The silence round the bed was uncomfortable, till Gordon eventually spoke.

"Did ya sleep alright. You look knackered" Misty shrugged

her shoulders and shook her head.

"I didn't sleep at all. Every time I closed my eyes I could see his little face". Misty's emotions took over her once more as tears flooded from her eyes. "His name is Dale. I think he deserves that doesn't he" Gordon looked at Lisa for help as they both watched her sob her heart out. "I feel like a failure. It's my fault he died I know it is". Lisa stood to soothe her but was angry at her for blaming herself.

"It's nobody's fault love. Sometimes it just happens but nobody's knows why. Don't you go blaming yourself .You will make yourself ill if you carry on thinking like that". Gordon's head now dipped down with shame, as he also felt guilt. He had blamed himself for hitting her the night before and knew that was the probable cause of her labour. He kept his guilt to himself as he reached to Misty to comfort her but he knew he was the one to blame.

"Sssh. Please don't cry," he whispered into her ear, "we'll have another one, just wait and see. It will take time to get over this but we can do it together can't we?" Lisa looked upon them both and thought they needed time together, so discreetly she edged away from the bed and headed for the exit.

Just as she reached the exit she saw Misty's father heading up towards the doors. Her heart jumped into her mouth as she hadn't seen him for a few months. He looked so old she thought as he approached and his clothes looked worn. This wasn't the man she married so long ago. He looked more like a tramp. Their eyes met like gunslingers at high noon but Ken was the first to talk.

"How is she?" he slurred. Lisa could smell alcohol on his breath as he spoke and it gave her flashbacks of their time together. She took a deep breath and filled her lungs with air. She didn't want to appear nervous to him, so she spoke slowly and calmly.

"She's heartbroken. I don't know what to do with her. I just hope she gets through this". Ken saw his chance to comfort her and tried to place his arms round her but she shoved him away, letting him know she didn't need his comfort.

Nobody had seen Ken for months, so they were unaware that Julie had left him. Apparently she had moved on to a new victim, who was much wealthier than Ken. Ken's money had been gambled away a long time ago and he barely had enough to live on these days. He had found his comfort in the bottle of whisky he drank every night. Looking at Lisa he realised he still loved her with all his heart. She looked great and at that moment he realised what he had lost.

Lisa looked at Ken and was surprised that she felt sadness for him. He looked a mess. His face was unshaven and his personal hygiene left a lot to be desired. She directed him to Misty's bedside and watched as he staggered toward her. Gordon held Misty as she wiped her tears away but he didn't know whilst he was holding her she had smelt the smell of perfume again all over his body. Misty stomach turned as the smell of perfume filled her nostrils. She knew she was not imagining it this time and knew he must have been with another woman last night. She thought about raising the issue to him but the time and place was all wrong and other things were more important at the moment. He would keep, she thought as she heard a familiar voice at the end of her bed.

"Hello love, how you feeling?" Misty's eyes met her dad's and she was shocked to see him. Gordon released his arms from round her and sat back in his chair. Ken struggled for words to say but Misty was the one who made the first move.

"Dad you look a disgrace. What's happened to you?" He pulled his chair up closer to her and began to tell the story of Julie leaving him. He looked at his child with hurt in his eyes. She was his baby and he deserted her just like all the other members of his family. It was strange but bridges were built that day round Misty's bedside. Even when Lisa returned everyone spoke calmly. Ken had promised Misty he would always be there for her and her brothers from this day forward. He promised to keep off the drink and said he would try and sort himself out. Lisa was a bit sceptical but went along with it anyway, telling him he needed to, as he was a total mess. The doctor made his rounds onto the ward and surprisingly told Misty she could go home. He told her she would be much better off at home instead of being stuck on the ward all day and perhaps he was right, she did need friends and family round her more than anything, to help ease the pain she was feeling inside.

Walking back through her own front door made Misty aware of how final everything was. The baby was gone from her body and all that now was left was a memory. Lisa stayed for a few hours and made tea for everyone but Misty's appetite was far from normal. Placing her body on the sofa she took the horizontal position and tried to rest. Max called to see her but once he saw Gordon was home his stay was short. Max had been sorry for the loss of his sister's baby but somehow he thought it was for the best. Rob called to see her as well and brought her two younger brothers. As soon as they saw her they ran and threw their arms round her neck. Jonathan cried as he spoke to her.

"I'm sorry your baby died Misty. We wanted to play with him when he was older". Lisa tried to stop him talking but Jonathan being Jonathan continued. "Is he an angel now Misty?" Lisa told him again to be quiet but Misty answered his question.

"Yes he's an angel and he will be watching over you both making sure you are safe. If you are ever in trouble he will be there to help you". Lisa felt a large lump form in her throat and fought hard to try and stop the tears but as Misty continued telling the boys about him she lost the battle and had to leave the room to deal with her despair.

Night time drew closer and Lisa said goodbye, as she wanted Misty to get as much rest as possible. Hugging her once again she left Misty and Gordon to be alone. The silence was disturbing as they both sat there once Lisa had left. Neither of them knew what to say to each other and it was hard to talk. Misty could tell Gordon was agitated as he paced the front room.

"I'm going out for a bit. You will be asleep soon anyway, so I won't be missed will I". Misty agreed as her eyes were closing and needed sleep and to tell you the truth he wouldn't be missed, not by her anyway. Gordon left the house and Misty climbed the stairs to bed. Once she entered the bedroom she noticed all the baby things had been removed. Walking to the window she gazed out of it and tears fell. She felt like everything had gone. Even the way she felt for Gordon was in doubt. She fell onto the bed and closed her eyes but the vision of her son still pictured there. She found a book to try and take her mind of it. She pulled the covers back on the bed and tried to get comfortable. As she got into bed her eyes met a sparkling object. She picked it up and examined it closer. She couldn't believe what she had found. It was a gold diamond earring. Fury hit her as she knew the bastard Gordon had had someone in their bed the previous night.

Misty was too exhausted to think, she lay on the bed and slowly drifted to sleep, knowing she would deal with Gordon as soon as she was stronger. He would pay, she thought, as her eyes closed and he would pay big time.

Gordon had secretly gone to meet Francesca, who suggested he could leave Misty straight away, as there was no baby to consider any more. He gripped her neck and told her never to mention his baby again. As for leaving Misty, he told Francesca to have a bit of heart. He still promised to be with her but that she would have to wait until Misty was better. The truth was he would never leave Misty and especially not for a tart like Francesca. He had loved sex with her but that was it. In his own strange way, he loved Misty and thought he wanted to stay with her.

Gordon spent the usual night in the pub with Francesca and his friends. He was legless when he decided to return home to Misty. The drugs he had taken were still floating round in his system and he still felt horny as he lay next to her in bed. First, he kissed the back of her neck, hoping for her to wake up but Misty was in a deep sleep. He continued kissing her neck and pressed his manhood deep into her side. This time she awoke and looked straight into his eyes.

"What are ya doing?" Gordon smiled from cheek to cheek and asked if she wanted to make another baby. Misty turned away from him and told him he was drunk and to leave her alone but he persisted in keeping her awake. "Misty I want to make another baby with you. I love you so much you don't understand". Her temper now exploded and all hell broke loose. She searched for the earring she had found as Gordon watched not knowing what she was doing. Finally she found it and pushed it into Gordon's face.

"Love me do you? Well what the Fuck is this. I found it in our bed, so don't even think about lying to me, you dirty bastard. I'm lying in hospital after losing our son and you're here shagging some slut in our bed. That's not love. You disgust me" Gordon grabbed her by the throat and dragged her down to where he lay. He had forgotten to check the bed that morning, as he had been running around getting all the baby's things together for Lisa before she got home. Gordon had to think quick and responded.

"What do you take me for? Do you think I would have someone in our bed while you lie in hospital, just after you had lost our baby? You're fuckin' mental". Misty dived at him and sunk her nails deep into his eyes.

"You lying bastard. You dirty lying bastard", she shouted as he threw her off the bed onto the floor. He now stood and walked to where she had fallen. He kicked her repeatedly as he held his eyes in pain.

"You stupid slag. If it wasn't for you our baby would still be alive. You can't even carry a baby, you fuckin' freak". His words could no longer hurt Misty. She picked herself up and spat right in his face.

"I'm a freak. Take a look in the mirror nobhead". Gordon grabbed her once more but this time instead of hitting her he became quite aroused and started to kiss her.

"Getting quite brave aren't you answering me back?" She struggled to break free from his grip but he held her down by her hands and laughed into her face. "You need a good shag, to get all this aggression out of you don't you?" She continued to fight him off with all her might but he forced himself inside her.

"Please Gordon stop it" she cried but he continued to penetrate her. Blood seeped from her, as his movements got faster. The blood didn't deter him, he just kept on going till he ejaculated. Once he had finished he rolled off her and lit a cigarette. At first she lay still but she felt her body starting to shake and rushed to toilet to be sick. Her head stayed down the toilet for many minutes and she finally lifted it out to get a drink of water. As she looked down her legs, they were filled with blood. and she wet a sponge to remove the stains from her legs.

Her mind was doing over time as she returned to the bedroom, she wanted to attack him again as he lay there with a smirk on his face but she knew he was too strong for her. Her time would come she thought as she headed down stairs to sleep on the sofa. He would get exactly what he deserved for the way he had treated her and it was only a matter of time before he got his comeuppance. Gordon didn't speak a word as she passed him, grabbing the spare blanket but he knew one thing for sure - the timid girl he had once known had gone forever and a new Misty had taken her place - it shocked him and he didn't like it.

Misty took her place on the sofa and stared round the room. How had she ended up like this, she thought as she watched the clock tick away. She knew from this day on she would not be the weak Misty she had once been. From this day on she would fight and refuse to except the cards life had thrown at her and change her life forever. Misty still needed to say goodbye to her child. She found the only way she could express herself was through poetry. She had always enjoyed writing at school and found she could express her thoughts best that way. So with a pen and paper she sat through the night saying goodbye to her son, whilst Gordon slept upstairs.

Why is the cradle empty?
Why is my heart broke?
Why will you never wear, your little knitted coat?
Why is your pram empty?
Why are you not by my side?
Why can't I hide the tears, I store here deep inside?
Why will I never forget that day, you were born?
Goodbye my little angel, my heart will be always torn.
I will always love you and remember you and that I have sworn.
Goodnight, God bless, kisses from me to you
Goodnight God bless, I will always love you.

Misty read the poem over and over again. Then she folded the paper into a small square and placed it in the lining of her purse. She vowed to always carry it with her, to help her feel that her baby was still part of her. The morning light was starting to break through when Misty finally found sleep but she didn't sleep for long as the sound of Gordon getting up woke her from sleep. As he entered the room she pretended to be asleep. She felt him kiss her head and felt her body stiffen.

"Sorry" he whispered, hoping he would get a response but Misty lay lifeless, hoping he would leave her alone. Then she heard the front door close and she knew Gordon would be out all day once more. She lay for a moment before getting up. She felt a terrible burning in her chest and pulled her nightwear up to see what was going on. As she saw her breasts her eyes widened. They were like two mounds of fire. They felt rock hard and were twice the size they had previously been. Misty panicked and ran straight to the phone to call her mam, she knew she would be at home as she had taken a week's holiday from work to look after her.

"Mam it's me. You need to come round here quick, my chest has exploded and it feels like it is on fire". Lisa told her it to calm down. She would be there shortly and there was no need to panic. Misty replaced the phone and sat feeling her breasts until her mother arrived. Lisa was greeted by the worried face of her daughter. Misty wasted no time and pulled her top straight up revealing two rather enlarged breasts to her mother. Lisa smiled as she looked at them and tried to keep a straight face but they were enormous and she couldn't hide her amusement. Misty smiled too as she prodded them.

"Mam these can't be normal. Please tell me they will go away. I can't stand them, they feel like they're are on fire". Lisa searched her pockets and handed her a tub of tablets.

"Get a glass of water and take these one of these four times a day and those big balloons will be gone in no time". Misty wasted no time and headed straight for the kitchen to get a drink. Lisa explained that Misty's milk had come in because she had given birth. Lisa sat with Misty for hours and spoke about the baby. It had been quite helpful to Misty as a lot of her questions had been answered. Lisa noticed Gordon wasn't at home and asked his whereabouts but Misty just told her he was out on business and didn't say any more about him. Lisa thought Gordon would have stayed at home with her, at least until she was up and about but how wrong could she be about a person she thought as she started to make breakfast for them both.

Misty cleaned herself up and washed her hair. She still felt strange without her bump but was slowly getting use to it. As she got ready she thought about her friend Francesca. It was peculiar that she hadn't been to see her. She had thought she would have been one of the first people round to see her after losing the baby but she decided she would phone her later and find out why.

Walking back into the front room she noticed her mother had cleaned it from top to bottom and the smell of lavender could be smelt throughout the house. Lisa looked at her and thought she looked ten times better. It was amazing what a nice relaxing bath could cure. Lisa jumped at a loud bang but as she looked she saw it was Gordon returning to the house, holding a large box with a ribbon round it. Lisa immediately took back all she had thought about him leaving Misty in the house all day. This must be the reason he had left early, she thought as she watched him carry the box into the front room.

Misty's eyes watched as he carried the box to where she sat. He had seemed to have forgotten last night had ever happened and carried on as normal. Lisa noticed all the scratches round his eyes and asked how he had got them but he lied and told her his mother's cat had done it when he tried to move it off the sofa. He was a convincing liar and Lisa didn't suspect in a million years that her own daughter had done it. Everyone sat in place, as they waited for Misty to open the box. As the silence fell, noises could be heard coming from the box and everyone looked at each other as Gordon smiled.

"Are you going to open it or what" he asked. "I suggest you open it pretty soon before it breaks out". Breaks out, Misty thought, what kind of clue was that. She racked her brains as she moved towards the box. Slowly she untied the ribbon and pulled back the flaps. As soon as the box opened a little pair of brown eyes stared back at her. Once it was opened fully the little creature jumped for joy. Misty's eyes lit up as she picked the small puppy out of the box. It was a little Yorkshire terrier who was wagging its tail at incredible speed and obviously glad to see her.

"Oh it's lovely isn't it?" Lisa spoke as she went towards it to stroke its head. Misty agreed and looked towards Gordon. Why was it that he would always make her feel so sorry for him as she looked at him directly in eyes. He walked to where she was sat and now stroked the dog, as his other arm slowly cradled round her shoulder. The house filled with laughter as they watched the little puppy play round the front room. The kitchen already had a dog hatch from when Rob lived there so the dog would have full access to the garden when it was a bit older. The only problem was they would have to make the hatch a little smaller as at the moment a human could fit through it. Misty had asked Gordon to do this job several months before but as usually the job was left. She and the others played with the puppy for hours and finally she came up with a name for him. Everyone laughed when she said his name.

"Butch is his new name. I think he thinks he's a lot bigger than what he is so I will give him a big dog's name to match his personality". They all agreed about the dogs name and from the first moment of meeting Butch, Misty and the dog became inseparable. Somehow the new member of the house filled a big emptiness in Misty's heart and day by day the pain she felt in her heart would lessen.

Misty coped in a funny way over the next few weeks and the loss of her child seemed to get easier. She decided that she would enrol in college and try and make something of her life. After all she had nothing else to do with her time. It took Francesca two weeks before she visited Misty but things had changed between them. Misty couldn't put her finger on exactly what it was but something had definitely changed. When she visited, she looked as if she had the worries of the world on her shoulders. Her once attractive friend now looked shabby and scruffy. Misty tried to talk about what had happened to her but Francesca just brushed it off and refused to talk about it. Misty also noticed a love bite on her neck and laughed about it, asking who the new boyfriend was who had chewed on her neck. But once again she brushed it off and didn't give a clue to the identity of her new love.

It was only when her friend left that she thought of how off hand Francesca had been with her. Misty had to almost beg her to come round that day and she could tell she was there under protest. Something was playing on her friend's mind and she hadn't even spoken about the loss of Misty's child and that was unlike Francesca – usually she wanted to know the ins and outs of a cat's arse but this time she didn't ask a single question. Misty sat and thought for a while but came to the conclusion that Francesca would tell her when she was good and ready. So without further concern Misty started on the job she had been putting off for weeks.

The cloakroom was dimly lit as she entered it. Gordon had promised to put another light in there but as always she was still waiting. The room smelt of old shoes. The shoes were scattered all over the floor and she nearly tripped over one as she reached for the light. The coats hung on the pegs were piled six coats to each peg and she knew there was no turning back now she had started. Today was the day she had set to clean it out. As she started to sort out all the shoes that were lay on the floor, the smell of sweaty feet hit her throat. Gordon had so many pairs of old trainers lying about in there and the smell was horrid. The shoes were finally sorted out and she had almost cleared the floor area. All that was left now was to sort the coats. One by one she took the coats off the pegs, laughing as she did. Some of the coats in there were ancient. Rob had left several coats there as well so she placed them into bag to take to his mother's to give them to him. As she pulled the last few coats off the peg she noticed a black sports bag hanging underneath. At first she didn't think anything of it and placed it on the floor but as she did she realised it carried some weight inside it whatever was inside it.

Slowly she unzipped the bag and opened the door wider to let in more light to better see its contents. At first glance all she could see was plastic bags on the top of it. But as she pulled out the first bag she realised what was in it. Her heart stopped as she gazed at the object in front of her. Oh my god she thought as she realised exactly what it was she was holding cautiously she held the shotgun in her hands and examined it. Misty then ran straight to the front door. Her heart raced as she slid the middle bolt onto the door. She didn't want anyone discovering what she had found, especially Gordon. As she searched deeper into the bag she uncovered yet another shot gun and a large amount of money. She had never seen as much money in her life and her hands shook as she tried to put everything back where she had found it. As she placed the last bundle of money in the bag temptation overcame her. 'He won't miss it' she thought, as he was always pissed and didn't know what day it was sometimes and if he did realise she would sneak it back and no one would any the wiser. Before she knew it she had two bundles of money in her hands ready to stash and felt excitement flow through her veins as she thought where to hide it.

Misty ran up the stairs like a wild woman and hid the two bundles of money. That was disturbance money she thought, as she ripped off the bath panel to hide her cash. For every time he had hurt her or made her cry this was the price he was going to pay. She headed back to the cloakroom and quickly threw all the coats back on the peg. She emptied the shoes back into their previous position. and the room then looked untouched. She didn't want Gordon knowing she had even been in the room, so she left the room exactly how she had found it.

Misty took herself off to the front room and sat putting all the pieces of Gordon's life together. It all finally made sense. The phone calls he received and the way he left the room to speak, it all made sense. Misty now lit a cigarette and a cunning plan started to transform in her mind. Misty somehow felt power over Gordon now. She wouldn't let on she knew about his antics and she would keep the information to herself until she needed to use it against him. As she exhaled, it seemed that for once in her life she no longer felt like the underdog. A big smile appeared across her face, as she thought of more cunning plans against Gordon. 'Revenge would be sweet' she thought, 'in time Gordon will pay for all this' but for now she would zip her lips and carry on like nothing had happened. After all, she had all the time in the world to plan his downfall.

As time passed, Misty's life didn't change for the better. Gordon still led her a dog's life but still she put up with his violent behaviour. The violence got progressively worse and on one occasion she ended up in hospital. The only positive change was that Misty now had quite a large amount of money behind her. She kept taking a share of the money out of the sports bag every time Gordon did a job. The money she was saving was her 'payment' for living in this hell hole with him. But she knew it wouldn't last forever and planned to leave him in time.

Gordon seemed to be doing quite well. The bag was overloaded with cash these days and never empty. At one stage Misty counted over twenty five thousand pounds in it, so she knew he wouldn't miss the small amount of cash she took for herself.

Gordon was at an all time low. All he did was get pissed and stuff his face with kebabs and takeaways. His weight had gone up and he had a big beer belly. Misty would often compare him to a pot bellied pig, as she looked at him He was rarely home and that's how Misty preferred it. On the occasions he was home she couldn't bear to be in the same room as him. He made her skin crawl whenever she looked at him. Even when she watched him eat her stomach turned at the beast who sat in front of her.

Gordon depended on cocaine now. He and Francesca couldn't get through a day without it. The drug had gripped them both by the throat and wasn't about to let them go. He now had to go on every job Wayne planned, even if it was a bit risky. The lifestyle he had adopted needed money and lots of it. They both knew they were hooked on the drug but ignored their dependency, thinking somehow it would go away.

Francesca's affair with Gordon had also turned sour. Over time he treated her with little respect and he wasn't afraid to let her know who was boss and that usually meant with his fist. Her looks had gone downhill and somehow as Misty was on her way up in life, Francesca was certainly on her way down.

CHAPTER FOURTEEN

KEN LOOKED ROUND his front room and searched the floor for his bottle of whisky. His eyes could barely focus as the effect of the whisky took over his body. Time and alcohol had taken their toll on Ken. This once successful businessman was now just a shell.

Julie had long gone out of his life and moved on to her next victim without a second thought. That's when all his problems really began. He drank to drown his sorrows but his sorrow never left him and neither did the whisky. He lost their house, as he couldn't keep up the payments on it. He now sat in a bed-sit in the middle of council estate in Harpurhey, wishing his life would come to an end. He had told himself this house would only be for a short while but a year and a half later he still stared at the damp filled walls.

This was the place he spent most of his time as he rarely went out these days. He would gaze out of the window with his whisky in one hand and a cigarette in the other wishing he was dead. Night after night he would drink till he fell asleep and he couldn't remember anything that had taken place the following morning. His appetite was low and to eat a piece of toast was a task in itself. Usually after eating anything he would wretch and throw it back up. He knew his health was suffering and recently he had started to cough up blood. He promised himself he would visit the doctor but it was always too much of an effort to make an appointment.

The time Ken spent alone was filled with regret. He often reminisced about his life with Lisa and regretted ever meeting Julie. But his biggest regret was his children. He hadn't seen them for months and he didn't blame them for not coming to see him, who would want to come and see a drunken old fool like him? Lisa had been right when she told him he would end up a lonely old man, because as he looked in the mirror, that's what exactly he was. Misty had told him she would visit him soon but her own life took all her energy and she never found time. Ken saw Max the day before whilst he was with his friends and shouted at him to get his attention. You could tell by Max's face he was embarrassed as he left his friends to join him. Ken looked at the young man coming towards him and felt proud that he was his son. He had turned out to be a handsome young man and Ken felt the love pass throughout his body as he hugged him tightly.

Max hid nothing of his thoughts. His father looked one step away from being a tramp. His breath stunk of alcohol and his clothes were stained and dirty. Max wasn't afraid to let him know.

"Dad you look rough. What the hell have you been up to?" Ken hung his head in shame and playfully pushed his son to hide his shame.

"You look great son. See you get the good looks off your old man don't you?" Max smiled and asked his dad where he was going. Ken was on his way to the off licence to get yet another bottle of whisky but he lied and told Max he was just going to the shop to get a loaf of bread. They both chatted and Max arranged to come and visit his father the next day. As Max left his father, his heart sank as he watched the frail old man walking away into the distance knowing he desperately needed help.

Max returned to his friends but his father still played on his mind. He hadn't looked too well, he thought and he would make it his business to go and see him the next day to make sure everything was alright.

The next day came and Max had persuaded Misty to come with him to visit their father. At first she refused saying she had other things to do but once Max told her of his concern he soon changed her mind. They both stood outside the door and knocked quite loudly. The net curtain was all scuffed up on the front door and by the looks of it, it was ready for the bin. After a few moments Ken opened the door wearing an old white string vest and a pair of denim jeans. The pants hung off his waist and were held up with a black leather belt. As Misty looked at him her eyes filled with tears.

She blamed herself for not visiting more. His weight seemed no more than that of a small child and he looked like he hadn't eaten a good meal in a long time. He led them both to the front room and as they entered they were shocked. Ken had tried to clean the place up before they came but everywhere still looked dirty. Misty couldn't hide her feelings and let her tongue loose on her father.

"Dad what's happened to you? It's a pig sty in here." Immediately she started to pick up old newspapers off the floor and clean the place. Ken was weak as he collapsed on the chair and he was finding it hard to talk with all the excitement of their visit. After a few minutes he regained his breath and watched as Max and Misty cleaned up. Misty couldn't help but notice all the empty bottles of whisky scattered round the front room. As she placed them into the bin she looked at her father disapprovingly before she spoke.

"Dad why are you drinking all the time? You will kill yourself if you carry on." Ken knew what she was saying was true but it was too late to stop now. His life couldn't continue without the whisky. He had tried in the past to give it up but his body shook uncontrollably without it and the pain stopped when he drank again.

Misty and Max didn't stop cleaning until the house was gleaming. When they'd finished they both sat exhausted. They watched as Ken coughed in his chair. At first they didn't take much notice but as he continued they both stood up at the side of him, patting his back as they could see he was distressed. It didn't stop and he started coughing blood. Immediately they agreed it was time to phone the ambulance and they waited anxiously until it arrived. Ken had turned grey and his lips were purple and trembling. His eyes rolled as he lay back in the chair struggling to breathe. "Dad we've phoned an ambulance. Try to sit still till they get here". Ken made no movement and they tried desperately to keep him awake.

The ambulance arrived after about five minutes and took Ken straight to the hospital. Both Max and Misty accompanied him in the back of the ambulance. The ambulance men placed an oxygen mask on his face and told him to take deep breaths. Ken was starting to relax when an almighty cough was followed by even more blood. The ambulance man helped Ken sit up. Reaching the hospital he was taken straight to see the doctor. Firstly they stabilized his breathing and gave him some medication to relax. Within minutes Ken was sleeping like a baby. The doctor spent hours at his bedside. They took blood samples and did all kinds of other tests trying to determine what had caused him to collapse. Max filled in all the necessary paper work regarding Ken and he and Misty waited anxiously at his bedside, waiting for any news regarding their father's health.

Ken looked as if he had already died, as they watched over him. His body was lifeless, as the oxygen mask filled his face as he still struggled for breath. Misty had phoned Lisa and told her the news. At first she didn't seem interested but after a bit of persuasion from Misty she told them she would be there shortly. Max and Misty spoke softly at his bedside and both feared the worst. As the doctor entered the room,

Max asked if there was any news on their father's health. The doctor pulled up a chair and sat beside them. As he lifted Kens medical notes off the end of the bed he began to read the information they held.

"Your father is not a well man. We're doing our best for him but it's a long road ahead of him. All our test results haven't come back yet, so I can't tell you exactly what's wrong with him. I think we will know more in the morning. I just hope he's a fighter". They both thanked the doctor, as Misty sobbed and reached for her father's hand.

"Oh Dad, what's happened to you. Please be strong and fight through this. I know we haven't been to see you much but you left us, all four of us. What did you expect?" Max patted her shoulder as the doctor left the room leaving nothing but sadness flowing through their bones. As Lisa walked into the room, shock hit her. She knew Ken wasn't well but the man that lay in front of her barely resembled her husband. Taking a deep breath she walked to her children to comfort them, trying not to look at Ken as he lay on the bed.

"Mam I think he is going to die". Lisa held her children closely to try and take away the hurt they felt inside.

"He will be fine, don't worry .He is in the best place now. They will do their best for him. Once he's been here for a few days he will be on the mend. Mark my words". Lisa lied to her children to try and keep them calm, because as she looked at Ken she realised how ill he truly was. They all sat with Ken as darkness fell. The doctor told them to all go home as Ken was being moved to the ward and if there was any change in his health he would phone them straight away. After a short discussion they agreed to what the doctor had said and left the room.

"Goodnight Dad," Misty whispered, "we'll be back in the morning, so you get some rest and try to make yourself better." She kissed his forehead as she left and hoped he would make it through the night as she couldn't now imagine her life without him. She decided there and then that she would visit her father every week at home if he pulled through and she promised herself to try to be the good daughter she once had been. This was Misty's wakeup call regarding her father. She knew she hadn't bothered with him much lately, perhaps if she had he wouldn't be lying on the bed in front of her. Guilt overwhelmed her and she knew if her father pulled through, she would do everything she could to help him.

They all headed home in Lisa's car and Misty was the first to be dropped off at home. As she kissed her mother goodnight she noticed her lights were on in her house and that could only mean one that Gordon was home early. She watched her mother drive away and entered her home to be greeted by the solemn face of Gordon.

"Oh so you have decided to come home, have you?" Gordon hovered round her swaying from side to side and it was quite obvious he was pissed.

"Gordon, don't fucking start. My Dad's been rushed to hospital, he's really ill". Gordon looked at her with disgust before he began his usual tirade of abuse.

"Since when have you given a shit about your Dad? You haven't seen him in ages. He left you a long time ago or have you forgotten that?" She stood in front of him and looked him straight in the eyes. She knew she was dicing with death but she couldn't take the torment anymore. Her voice trembled as she started to talk.

"Listen, he's my Dad and he needs me at the moment. What do you expect me to do? Leave him on his own whilst he is ill?" Gordon reached to grab her but as he did Misty clenched her fist tightly and swung it with all her might towards his face. The fist connected with an almighty blast and Gordon lost his balance and stumbled to the floor. She knew he would try and beat her now but she was ready. No more was she going to be a victim. She knew she had to stand up for herself once and for all instead of cowering into a ball on the floor as she usually did. She looked now where the lamp was situated behind her on a table. And before she knew it, it was in her hands and she was launching it over Gordon's head . Her words fired out of her mouth like bullets as she continued to hit him. Years of torment had finally taken their toll and she couldn't take it any more.

"No more will I be a victim. You have hit me for the last time, you dirty no good fucka. Is that all you can do? Beat up women?" She shouted at the top of her voice as Gordon protected himself with his hands over his head. She continued to whack the lamp across his head and knew she was hurting him. Misty was like a wild woman and once she started she found it hard to stop. That was until she saw blood pour down the side of his head and it was only then she thought he had had enough. Gordon sat on the stairs holding his head, as she passed him to go to bed. She didn't even stop to see if he was alright .Her words were strong as she made her way upstairs.

"Oh and if ya think you can beat me at any other time be prepared, because I will stick a knife right in ya. I will go to prison for it rather than have you think I am your punch bag for the rest of my life so be warned". Misty walked up to bed as her body trembled inside. She had meant every word and she could tell by Gordon's face he knew she meant business.

Gordon spent the rest of the night downstairs on the settee. He knew he had overstepped the mark this time and wanted to give Misty time to cool down. He had never seen her like this before and realised how upset she must have been to act the way she did. He lit a cigarette and sat in the front room staring round in the darkness. He would leave her to sleep for now and tomorrow he would deal with her.

Misty slept well that night. She placed the cupboard behind the door, so if Gordon tried to come in she would be awake and ready for him but the night was quiet. Morning crept inside her bedroom and the sound of kids shouting outside woke her from her sleep. Somehow she felt a bit scared at what she was about to face beyond the bedroom door but slowly she pulled back the cupboard and made her way to the bathroom, firmly locking the door behind her. Once she had finished washing her face and brushing her teeth, she started to get ready. She listened at the door before she came out but heard no sounds. She was half expecting Gordon to be waiting for her but there was no sign of him. Misty packed a small overnight bag, as she thought she would stay the night at the hospital with her father. She had worried about him all night and couldn't stand the thought of him being left alone whilst he was so ill.

Misty walked downstairs and could smell bacon. As she walked to the kitchen, there stood Gordon frying bacon. He smiled at her as if the night before had never happened.

"Do ya want a bacon butty?" She stood and couldn't believe the picture in front of her. He had never made her breakfast. She refused his offer and told him she wouldn't be home tonight as she wanted to stay with her father in hospital. He walked to her she felt fear run through her as she waited for him to attack her. To her surprise he placed his arms round her and softly hugged her.

"I'm sorry about last night. I shouldn't have started on ya, knowing your Dad was ill. If you need to stay with him its fine by me". Misty was waiting for the catch but it never came, he just continued to hug her and watched her every move as she left. He shouted to her to tell her Dad he hoped he gets better soon, as she was closing the door. This behaviour wasn't at all in character and she knew to be on her guard as he would be hatching a plan to pay her back for last night. It would be a matter of time before he took his revenge. She just hoped she would be ready for him when he did.

Her mind raced as she set off to the hospital. She had arranged to meet her mother and Max there. Today was the day when Ken would have get the results of his tests, she just prayed everything would come back clear. As she waited for the bus, she thought of happier times when life seemed so easy. How things had changed since she had left school. She never thought she would say it but schooldays were the happiest time in her life and she wished she had concentrated more during the time she spent there. Misty felt regrets, not just for her schooldays but for ever getting involved with Gordon. Life would have been so much better with Dominic. He had loved her with all his heart and she had messed that up big time. Regrets, regrets she thought as the bus approached. Misty wanted to turn back time and be happy again but she knew life had dealt her a hand and it was now up to her how she played it.

The corridor in the hospital gleamed as she walked down it. The cleaners were out in full force, cleaning all the ledges and walls. Hospital wasn't a good place to be, it was filled with misery and tears for most people. One lady walked passed her and she could see her eyes were red through crying, she looked like she didn't have the strength to walk and looked totally exhausted. Misty smiled gently at the lady but you could see she had had the life knocked out of her and wasn't in the mood to be polite to anyone.

Reaching her father's bedside, she was greeted by Max and her mother. Lisa wasn't going to come but she felt it was unfair on her children to be left on their own to deal with Ken. Rob had been very understanding about the whole situation and told her to do what she must and that he would support her in anything she decided. That's what Lisa loved about Rob. He was so laid back and kind hearted .He was a real gem of a man. Ken still looked like death warmed up and he clearly hadn't moved an inch all night. The doctor was due on his ward rounds soon, so hopefully they would know what was wrong with their father and they all prayed it wasn't bad news.

Max spoke of the holiday he had booked. He was off to Benidorm the following week. This was to be his first holiday without his parents and he was so excited.

"Who ya going with?" Misty asked and she could see her brothers face go slightly red with embarrassment. "Well there is myself and Gary and his sister up to now". Misty looked at him and he avoided eye contact as he continued to speak.

"It was only me and Gary going at first but since his sister split up from her boyfriend , she's jumped on the holiday with us. It's kind of letting go of the past holiday," he laughed. "I've told her we're not staying at Heartbreak hotel and I don't want any tears once we're on holiday. If she wants to do any crying for her ex she can do it away from me. I'm going for a good time and I've told Gary we are not nursing her all the holiday and he's agreed." Misty smiled as she listened to him going on. She could do with a holiday herself but at the moment that was the last thing on her mind.

The sound of the doctor walking towards them made them all turn round and face him. He took Ken's notes from the end of the bed and started to read them with a concerned face. He had brought his own information along with him too. He had several pieces of paper contained in a plastic wallet. After reading them he checked Ken's temperature and checked his pulse whilst looking at his watch. Once he had finished he asked if they would like to join him in the small office at the end of the ward, so they could discuss Ken's illness. Looking at the doctor's face Lisa knew it wasn't good news and prepared herself for the worst. Once in the room they all sat in the four chairs, round a small oval table. They all looked concerned as the doctor began his speech.

Once they had introduced themselves he took a deep

breath and continued. "I'm afraid it's not good news. I have looked at your father's results and the x-ray shows us there is a large dark shadow covering his left lung. I've carried out lots of tests to determine what the shadow is and the results are not looking good". All three of them sat on the edge of their seats, praying he wasn't going to say the dreaded words. Lisa held her two children's hand tightly as he continued.

"I'm afraid your father has cancer. We are trying to get him in for treatment as soon as possible but chemotherapy is our only hope to try and shrink the cancer. I don't want to lie to you. I want to be as honest as I can and tell you how bad this really is. The chances of him surviving are very low". Misty sobbed and couldn't control the sound of her heart breaking in her chest. Lisa also felt crushed with the news but knew she had to be strong for the sake of her children. It was Max who spoke first and surprisingly he was quite calm.

"How long has he got doctor?" Max asked, hoping the doctor would say years. The doctor looked at the family and knew it must be heartbreaking for the family. He himself found it hard to speak the truth but knew he had to tell them the devastating news.

"If he has chemotherapy, he could live another three months, without chemo, he's looking at weeks". Max gulped as he felt emotion hit the back of his throat.

"Is it that bad doctor?" Max sighed, trying to come to terms with what he had said. "Can't you do anything else for him; surely there must be something else". The questions raced around Max's brain. The doctor was really understanding and tried to answer every question they asked but the outcome was always the same, no matter how much they wanted it to be different their father was definitely going to die before the year was out. The doctor finally left the room and told them they were welcome to stay for a while. He told the nurse to take them a cup of tea, as he knew they could be there for some time. The door shut behind him and the room was silent. Each of them was lost in their own thoughts, unable to take in this latest information. This room must have seen so many families' tears over the years although no amount could save someone who had lung cancer.

The time seemed to fly by as they sat together in the small room. It was a moment they would all remember for the rest of their lives and not for good reasons. Misty felt like her heart had been ripped out and squashed onto the floor while Lisa had mixed emotions. She didn't know if it was hurt she felt for her children's sadness, or hurt for the man she once had loved. Max kept his feelings to himself. Somehow it didn't seem right that he should break down and cry. He was a man and men don't cry, he thought, they are supposed to be a rock for everyone else, so for now he held his emotions and comforted his family.

They walked back to join Ken at his bedside. Somehow the way they looked at him had changed. Misty looked at his old thin face and stroked his forehead as he slept. She looked at every line on his face and every hair on his head. She needed to remember everything about him and make the most of the time they had left together. Ken slept deeply as they talked round his bedside. The medication the doctor had given him had knocked him out and he would only wake up for short periods of time. He looked like a man twice his age and the years of drink had left their mark on his face.

They talked all day round his bedside remembering the good times they had shared together and they each told memorable stories about Ken. Even Lisa found it in her heart to speak of the good times she had shared with him and laughed loudly as she told of the time he carried her all through the streets when they were younger. It was funny because as she spoke of the good times, the bad times seemed to take a back seat in her mind. It was like they never existed and Ken had been the perfect partner. Misty had planned to stay the night at the hospital, before she had found out the devastating news but right now all she wanted to do was run and never stop till she was a thousand miles from the hospital. Somehow that was her way of dealing with things. If she wasn't there with him and wasn't at the hospital she could sort of put it to the back of her mind and pretended it wasn't happening. Somehow this method always worked for her. It kept her calm and she could find something to do to take her mind of it if she was at home, so she decided she would go home tonight to deal with her sorrow and pain alone.

They all stayed till late in the evening and Ken had woken up for a short time. He had smiled at his children and thanked them for bringing him to hospital. As Ken's eyes met Lisa they shone with love. He thanked her from the bottom of his heart for coming and he knew this was the time to right the wrongs he had ever done to her. Ken had a gut feeling his days were now numbered and wanted to free himself of his torment. His children had been let down by him and he could never give them back the time he had stolen from them. He wished he could turn back time but knew that was impossible. He had nothing to leave to his children. All his money had been gambled away a long time ago and the rest spent on whisky. He felt worthless as he lay on the hospital bed and his spirits were at an all time low. The children he had neglected were all he had in the world and he looked at them with heartache in his eyes, knowing he had to make it up to them. He wondered if this was the pay back he deserved for the life he had led. He knew the time he had left would be spent rebuilding relationships, he just hoped it wasn't too late.

A coughing fit now attacked Ken and he struggled to breath. Lisa passed him the oxygen mask and he placed it fully over his face, trying to regain his breath. The nurse had heard the coughing and came to assist. She told his family that Ken needed to rest now, as he needed all his strength for the days that lay ahead. They all kissed him goodbye and walked reluctantly out of the hospital ward. As they reached the exit Misty felt like she was suffocating and needed to get into the fresh air as soon possible. Her palms were hot and sweaty and she felt like she needed to vomit. Lisa felt the same way and as they reached the main doors they both gasped for breath. As they headed for the car park, all Misty wanted to do was cry but somehow her tears wouldn't come. She needed to go home and be alone. They journey home was in complete silence and nobody had the strength to speak. Nothing could undo her father's condition and all they could do was pray he didn't suffer.

As they pulled up outside Misty's home, she kissed her mother and said goodnight. Lisa hugged her and told her to brave. Max's head was dipped low as he sat on the back seat. No matter how much he tried to conceal his pain, his eyes betrayed him.

Misty stood at the front door and watched them leave. She could hear Butch barking as she inserted her key into the door. As she opened the door Butch came running towards her, with his tail wagging rapidly. She picked him up into her arms and kissed his head. She loved him so much and he had helped her through many a night of tears and pain. His love was unconditional and she knew he would help her through the pain she was now feeling in her heart. Misty walked into the front room and saw the television was still turned on. As she went to switch it off she saw Gordon's shoes near the side of the table. She screwed up her face at the thought of him being home and hesitated going up to bed knowing he was there. Still holding Butch in her arms she crept up the stairs to bed, as not to wake Gordon. As she neared the bedroom door, she froze as she heard giggling noises coming from her room. Something in her heart told her whatever was behind the door was going to hurt her one way or the other. She searched deep in her body to try and find the strength she needed to continue. Taking a deep breath, she slowly pulled down the handle of the door. As the door opened she caught the first glimpse of a woman and her heart stopped as she looked closer. She could see her sat on Gordon riding him like a bucking bronco. Misty couldn't see the women's face fully till she lifted it up but as she did there, right in front of her, was the face of her best friend Francesca.

Gordon was the first to notice her as she stood at the door He immediately threw Francesca from his body and jumped up looking for something to cover himself. As Francesca turned to see the figure at the door her face went white. Gordon stuttered as he tried to speak as Francesca searched for her clothes frantically.

"I thought you were staying at the hospital tonight with your Dad?" He spoke in a trembling voice. Misty didn't answer him and ran toward him like a women possessed. As she reached him she shouted with all her might.

"You dirty low life bastard". Her hands clenched together as she attacked him but all he did was hold her arms to stop her from hurting him. Misty finally broke free and jumped over the bed to reach Francesca. As she reached her she punched her right in her cheek and grabbed her long locks of hair, swinging her round like a rag doll.

"You dirty fucking slut. You're supposed to be ma best friend". Gordon was now beside them trying to release Francesca from her grip but Misty was not letting go for love nor money. She wanted to hurt her, like she had never hurt anyone before. Gordon finally freed Francesca and threw Misty onto the bed, as Francesca shouted at the top of voice.

"Tell her Gordon. Tell her ya love me. Go on fucking tell her". Francesca now stood with her hand on her hip and began to tell all the details about their love affair. "He's been with me since you got pregnant and the only reason he stayed with ya was for the sake of the baby. He felt sorry for ya and that's the only reason why he fucking stayed with ya". Misty looked at Gordon as he stood over her looking like he had seen a ghost and she knew Francesca was telling the truth. Misty tried to remain calm but anger had taken a grip on her and wasn't letting go. She stood on the bed and jumped landing straight on top of Gordon. She wasted no time in sinking her nails straight into his face. They scuffled for a while before Gordon finally lost his temper and punched her in the face.

"You barmy bastard, get the fuck off me", he shouted, "who do ya fucking think you are?" He now restrained her on the bed as he shouted to Francesca to go home. Misty tried to free herself but Gordon was too strong. All she could do was watch as Francesca got the rest of her things together and headed for the door. Before she left she stood holding the door open and spoke to Gordon.

"Why don't you just fucking leave her? She knows everything now. I thought that's what you have been waiting for". Gordon looked up and gave Francesca a look that could kill and she knew to leave without speaking any further. Misty jerked about the bed trying to break free but Gordon squeezed her arms till the pain was unbearable. Misty shouted so Francesca could hear every word she spoke, as she made her way down the stairs "Don't think it's over ya little slut. I will see ya again and this dickhead won't be there to stop me, so fucking watch out". Francesca made no reply as she left the house but knew she had hurt her friend big time. She felt slightly ashamed of what she had done but she loved Gordon that much nothing else seemed to matter, not even her best friend.

Gordon listened for the front door to slam shut and knew

Francesca had left. He was aroused by the fighting and as he looked down at Misty, all he wanted to do was kiss her. Her eyes looked like a sea of blue and her lips looked so seductive.

"Misty I'm sorry. It just happened. I love you more than life its self and don't want to lose you. Francesca is just a dirty slut. I would never leave you for her". She looked at him with hate in her eyes. Everything made sense to her now. All the late nights, everything. How could she have been so stupid not see what was right in front of her own very eyes. Her skin crawled as he bent his head down and tried to kiss her.

"Get your dirty fuckin' hands off me, ya wanker. Are you right in the head, to think I would ever go near you again? You're a dirty low life bastard. I want you out of this house now". Gordon now stood and realised she meant business. He paced the floor and stared out of the window. Misty felt calmer and realised she was the one calling all the shots.

"Pack all ya fucking stuff. I want ya out of this house now. I don't want to ever set eyes on you again." He turned to face her and told her he was going nowhere. Misty had to think quickly and knew her next sentence would make him see sense.

"Well we'll see about that. I'll phone the police to get rid of you then." The word 'police' made him shiver and he knew he couldn't risk the dibble being involved, so he made one final attempt at calming her down.

"Please Misty I'm so sorry. I don't want to leave". Misty now stood and picked up the phone and looked at his face. "Do I need to phone the police, or are you going?" Gordon hurried and got ready as quickly as he could with Misty watching his every move. He told her he would be back tomorrow to collect his clothes, as he didn't think now was the time to start packing them.

"Don't ya worry about your clothes, as soon as you have

left I'll pack them and take them to your mam's. The sooner all your stuffs out of here the better". They headed to the front door and she opened it as Gordon stood struggling for words.

"I still love you Misty. I know you're angry at the moment but you can't just end it like this". Misty spat in his face as he walked passed her. Her eyes were full of hate toward him, she told him never to darken her doorstep again and pushed the rest of his body out of the door. Once the door was closed she fell to the ground and reality hit home. She felt anger more than anything. Anger for being such a fool and not realizing what was going on right in front of her eyes. Butch came to join her and she held him and sank her face into his fur.

"Just me and you now mate," she whispered, "I'll never let you down, I will always be here for you don't worry". Butch just looked into her eyes, as if he had understood everything she had said. He licked her face softly and she smiled as she softly stroked his fur.

Minutes later she went to the kitchen searching for bin bags to pack his clothes. Once she had found them she ran up stairs and pulled his clothes out of the wardrobe and threw them straight into bin liners. Once she started it only took around fifteen minutes to free her bedroom of any signs of him. All that was left now was his shoes and coats. She carried all his bags downstairs and placed them near the front door. Finally she entered the cloakroom to collect all the rest of his belonging. Entering the cloakroom, she started to pull his coats off the peg, when the familiar sight of the sport bag caught her eye. She slowly pulled it down and unzipped it hoping Gordon hadn't removed its contents. As the light shone in the bag she realised all the money was still intact. Bundles of cash stared back at her. She thought for a moment and planned her sweet revenge for Gordon. She quickly carried the sport bag out of the cloakroom and placed the two shotguns inside it. She knew he would be back sooner or later for the money and she needed to think of a plan quickly before it was too late.

The next morning she concocted a cunning plan. She would go to the hospital and get her father's house keys. If he asked why she was taking them she would tell him she was going to check everything was alright and to bring him his mail. Also this was an ideal opportunity to get her father some clean underwear and other bits he might need. Misty arrived at the hospital very early that morning. Her father was still sleeping heavily as she sat by his bedside. Slowly she opened the drawer next to his bedside and sneakily took out the set of keys for his house. Misty kissed her father's head and headed straight back to her home.

Her heart pounded as she opened the front door. She just hoped she wasn't too late and Gordon hadn't taken the money. She ran upstairs and crawled under her bed pulling out the sports bag. Without delay she phoned a taxi and waited for it at the window. Before she left she cautiously took one of the shotguns out of the bag and hid it amongst her clothes in the wardrobe. She had big plans for it, she thought as she threw her clothes over it to disguise it. This was her protection when Gordon decided to return and she knew exactly what she was going to do with it once he did. The sound of the taxi outside made her jump and her heart was in her mouth as she made her way downstairs. Everything was running according to plan and once she had the money safely hidden away her sweet revenge would begin. Misty hadn't told anyone about last night. She wanted to wait till the money was safe before she could even think about anything else and now the taxi was here, her plan was nearly complete.

She gave the taxi driver directions and sat in the back holding on to the sports bag for dear life. She looked for any signs of Gordon in the area but the coast was clear, he was probably still sleeping she thought as they reached her father's home. Misty paid the taxi and entered the house. The smell of stale cigarettes still filled the air as she entered. She quickly looked round the house and then emptied the contents of the bag onto a table. Once she had finished counting, she rubbed her hands together with excitement. All in all she counted twenty seven thousand pounds. She laughed to herself at the thought of Gordon's face when he knew his money was gone. She was powerful for the first time in her life and felt like she ruled the world. 'Revenge, sweet revenge' she thought as she placed her hands all over the cash.

Misty cleaned the house from top to bottom and it smelt fantastic once she had finished. She changed all the bedding from the bed and replaced it with fresh smelling sheets. Her last job was the most important and she now had to find a hiding place for the money. She eagerly looked round and finally found a hiding place in the bottom part of her father's bed. Pulling out the drawers at the bottom of the bed she quickly shoved the bag deep into the bed base. Once it was concealed she returned the drawer to its original position. Misty stood back and made sure you couldn't tell there was anything hidden there. Once she was happy, she returned to the front room and tried to gather her thoughts. She decided that first she would to go to her mother's home and tell her of the affair between Gordon and Francesca. Another important job was to have the locks changed on her front door as Gordon still owned a key and she knew he would try and get back in the house later that day. Misty also planned to get a key cut to her father's home as that way she could come and go whenever she pleased and no one would be none the wiser.

Misty left her father's house and walked the rest of the way to her mother's. She was surprised that she didn't feel heartbroken at the thought of Gordon and Francesca being together. She had stopped loving Gordon a long time ago and lost all respect once he had started beating her. She felt free from the chains that had shackled her for such a long time. The feeling was indescribable and she loved it. This was the first day of her new life without Gordon and if this was how it felt, she knew the days ahead were worth living once more.

CHAPTER FIFTEEN

ISTY ENTERED HER mother's house and greeted her family as they sat round the table having breakfast. The two younger children looked like they had been crying and it was quite obvious they had been told about their father's illness. Lisa was rushing round like a blue-arsed fly trying to get the family ready for the day ahead. Max looked at his sister and instantly knew something was troubling her but thought he would wait till they were alone before he asked. Rob stood near the back door and encouraged the younger children to hurry, otherwise they would be late for school. Lisa had already phoned in work and asked for the day off as her nerves were quite bad and she felt shaky inside. The boys hurried their breakfast and finally gathered all their belongings they needed for school. They kissed everyone and followed Rob to the car, whilst he moaned about how late they were. Lisa sat at the table and sipped her cup of tea.

"I just can't believe your dad is so ill. Life's too short isn't it? I haven't slept a wink all night. How did you sleep Misty?" Misty took a deep breath and relayed the night events to Max and her mother as they both listened with disbelief. Max couldn't look at his sister as he already held the secret of seeing them together a long time ago. Lisa cursed and called Francesca every name under the sun and couldn't believe how low she had sunk.

"Dirty little cow. She's nothing but a cheap tart. Wait till I fucking see her, she'll get a piece of my mind that one. Cheating on your best friend, that's the lowest of the low and him... words can't describe the fat fucker. I hope he gets his comeuppance he's too full of himself for his own good". Misty stopped her mother there and asked would she help her get his clothes to his mother's house as soon as possible and most importantly help get the locks changed.

"Of course I will. I just hope I don't see him otherwise he'll get a piece of my mind. You're not staying at home tonight. Come and stay here for a few nights and let things calm down, because you know he won't leave you alone if he knows you're at home". Lisa was looking quite concerned now as she tried to come to terms with what had happened.

"What about Butch, mum? Can I bring him with me? I can't leave him there on his own and I'm not staying here without him". Lisa hugged her as she spoke.

"Bring Butch with you, that's not a problem, as long as I know you're safe and away from that bastard, I don't care who you bring with you". Lisa passed her cigarettes round and they each lit one up. "Oh I don't know, when it rains it pours in this family. I'm sure we are cursed".

Misty and Lisa went to the house whilst she got some clothes together and picked up Butch. Lisa had arranged with Rob to get the locks changed that same night and Misty felt more at ease knowing Gordon couldn't get into the house. After loading the car with Gordon's clothes they set off to his mam's house to inform her of what had happened. Misty felt quite nervous and wanted to do this as quickly as possible.

"Mam I don't want you to start shouting when we get here. I want you to wait in the car. All I want to do is hand over his stuff and get away as quick as I can". Lisa agreed to remain in the car, even though she wanted to run in the house and give him a piece of her mind but for her daughter's sake she remained seated, as she knew it would keep for now. Misty walked up towards Gordon's mam's house and looked at the bedroom windows, making sure Gordon hadn't seen her approaching. Knocking at the door felt like waiting for a death sentence to be passed but within moments Gordon's mam opened the door with a smiling face.

"Hello love, come on in". Misty looked at her with sad eyes and started to pass the bags containing his clothes. Once Misty had explained what had happened his mother shook her head and said he deserved everything that happened to him. She had not seen her son for a few weeks and the thought of him returning home to her horrified her. She apologised to Misty for her son's behaviour and wished her good luck without him.

"He will never get anyone like you again love. He's made the biggest mistake of his life losing you and I hope he's happy with himself. It won't be long love before he's back with his tail between his legs, begging you for forgiveness trust me." Misty dipped her head and slowly left her. She felt sorry for his mam as she knew Gordon would make her life a misery whilst he stayed with her.

She waved as the car pulled off and watched as his mam started to carry all the bags inside her house. Lisa asked if she was alright as they drove to the hospital and she replied yes but Lisa realised she hadn't seen her daughter shed a tear and thought it strange that she was dealing with it all so well. She was unaware that her daughter had stolen Gordon's money and was planning her revenge even as they spoke. Max was already at Ken's bedside as they entered the ward. Misty kissed him and sneakily dropped the keys back into the drawer and nobody was any the wiser. Ken seemed a little more alert today and he was sat up in his bed speaking.

"You don't have to spend all your time here visiting me you know. I will be quite fine honestly". Lisa told him to shut up being stupid, as he was ill and needed his family round him at a time like this. Ken cleared his throat and sat up in his bed.

"While you are all here, I need to get some things off my chest. I know what happened between you and me was wrong. I can only look back now and cringe at the life I led you. You are a beautiful woman and I didn't deserve you. I knew that from the moment I met you. Can you ever forgive me?"

Lisa blushed with embarrassment as he spoke and she had to tell him to stop, before her emotions got the better of her. "I forgive you Ken but all we want is for you to get better. This isn't the time or the place for raking up the past". Ken now looked at his children and bit his bottom lip to try and stop the tears from flowing. He needed to say the words he had stored in his heart for many years.

"I know I haven't got a lot of time left but I need to tell you both how much I love you. I love your two brothers as well and hope you can find it in your hearts to forgive a selfish old man. I never thought of my family when I was living my life and it's only now that the years have passed I regret everything that I've done. "

Misty and Max smiled at him and told him he was forgiven. Misty had a few issues with him though and couldn't let them lie even as he lay dying in front of her. She needed to tell him exactly what he had done and how selfish he had been forgetting about his children.

"Dad I can't understand how you could have forgotten about your kids. You were like a different man, especially when Julie was about. We needed you more than ever and you turned your back on us. I do forgive you Dad but I will never understand why you did it". Ken shook his head and agreed with her and tried to explain why it had happened.

"I know you're right love. I just got caught up with myself

and the beer and once I started drinking I couldn't stop. Julie was a mistake and I know now she was a money grabber because once my money was gone, she didn't waste any time moving on to her next victim". Misty had now said her piece and felt like years of frustration had been lifted. It felt good to get it off her chest. It had troubled her for so many years and now finally her question had been answered. Max sat fidgeting and he seemed a bit uneasy before he spoke.

"Since we are all getting things off our chest, I need to get something off mine". Max paused for a few minutes before he regained the courage to finish what he had started. His body fidgeted around and his words took a while to leave his lips.

"Mam, Dad I'm gay. I have been for the last couple of years or so and its tearing me up inside keeping it from you". Misty smirked as she looked at her brother and thought he was joking. Lisa and Ken were speechless. It was Misty who broke the silence and started to laugh and joke with him.

"Does that mean we can now swap clothes? Wow! You can even come shopping with me and help pick my outfits". He smiled at her and told her to be quiet, as he wanted a reaction from his parents. Looking at them, he knew things weren't as bad as he first thought. This secret had kept him awake night after night for months and now finally he felt like a weight had been lifted from him. Lisa slowly kissed his cheek and pulled him toward her.

"Arthur or Marther it doesn't matter to me. You're still my son and whatever floats your boat, is up to you". Max felt emotional and tears streamed down his cheeks with relief. Max now looked at Ken for approval and wasn't disappointed with his response.

"Like your mother said, you're our son and if it makes you happy nothing else matters. But one thing, please tell me you don't want to change your name to Maxine or something".

They all laughed and somehow round Ken's bedside that day a family was pulled back together.

Ken watched his family leave as he settled down to sleep. Tiredness filled his eyes and within moments he was fast asleep. Max and Misty huddled together as they left. They were laughing over Max's confession. Misty had so many questions to ask and she wasn't wasting any time asking them.

"Are ya the giver or the taker" she laughed as Max playfully pushed her.

"It's not like that, you muppet. It's just the same as a man and a woman's relationship. Misty was intrigued and wanted more information.

"Are you in a relationship, or are you a bit of a player?" Max couldn't believe all the questions she was asking but he answered them anyway as it was good to get it all off his chest.

"My boyfriend is Gary who I work with". Her mouth dropped as she took in this revelation.

"Gary! He's gorgeous. No way is he gay. What a waste of a man". Max sniggered as he whispered into her ear. "And he's all mine. You can look but don't touch". The laughing never stopped as they sat in the car and once they were moving, Lisa took over in her turn in asking questions.

"Does that mean I have to put pink bedding on your bed now son?" They burst into laughter and somehow Misty's problems seemed a million miles away.

At home Misty and Max went straight to his bedroom to talk some more about his 'new' sexuality. Once they had sat on the bed Max jumped up with excitement as a thought entered his head.

"Come on holiday with us next week. There is nothing to stop you, we will have a ball. Gary's sister's coming and she has just split up with her boyfriend, so you will be both in the same boat." Misty refused almost immediately knowing she couldn't afford it. Then with a sparkle in her eye she remembered Gordon's money. She had her own savings as well and she could use that if she really wanted to but she still made excuses as to why she couldn't go.

"I can't afford it", she said feeling quite deflated. Max knew if he chipped away at her she would finally see sense and come on the holiday of a lifetime so he carried on in his quest for her to come.

"Mi mam will help you pay for it. Ya know she will". Misty knew she couldn't let Lisa pay for it, so she told Max about a small amount of cash she had saved.

"I've got four hundred pound in my bank. I was saving it for driving lessons but I'm sure they could wait, couldn't they? But what about Dad? We can't leave him whilst he is so ill. Who will visit him? Say he takes a turn for the worst while we are away. No I couldn't go and leave him. It's not right."

Max searched for an answer and disappeared out of the room to go and speak to his mother. He told her of their plans and told her why Misty wouldn't go. Lisa marched straight up the stairs and sat on the bed beside her.

"Misty, this holiday will do you a world of good. I will go and visit your Dad and take your brothers to see him each night with Rob, so there is no reason why you can't go. If money is a problem me and Rob can help out". Misty smiled and thanked her but knew she couldn't take any money.

"Oh mam, thanks." Her eyes welled up and the recent events hit home with an almighty bang. She had mixed emotions regarding Francesca. How could she do such a thing to me she thought, as she remembered all the times she had been round to her house whilst she was with Gordon. Misty stood up from the bed and declared she would go on the holiday. She laughed with Max and told him she was going to have the time of her life. He grabbed her arms and danced round the bedroom celebrating her decision. Max had failed to tell Misty a little secret concerning the holiday and wanted to keep it to himself. An old friend of Misty's had booked to go to the same week and secretly he hoped they might bump into each other but for now he kept this to himself and just hoped things would work out for the best.

The week ahead was filled with rushing around for Misty. She had to spend a day at the passport office to get her passport in time for the holiday and she shopped and shopped like she had never done before getting together all the clothes she needed. Misty spent hours packing and her suitcase looked like it was going to burst. She had to sit on the top of it, to close it but eventually it was done and she was ready to party with her brother in sunny Spain. On the night before they were due to fly out they both went to see their father. They explained to him that Lisa would be coming to see him and he wasn't going to be left alone. He told them to have the time of their lives and not to worry about him. They both hugged him and left to catch their flight. Misty hoped she wouldn't regret leaving him but looking at his face, he looked as well as she had seen him in a long time, so that helped her feel better about the decision to go.

No one had seen sight or sound of Gordon since she had left to stay at her mothers but little did she know he had visited her home a few times trying to unsuccessfully gain access. It was just a matter of time before he would get a grip of her and God help her when he did. His blood was boiling, knowing his money was in the house.

Max carried their suitcases into the airport as Misty kissed her mother goodbye. Lisa felt quite upset as she parted company with them both. The tears she cried were tears of happiness for a change and she loved the thought of them both going away on holiday together.

"Have a great time. Don't worry over anything. Butch is safe with us and Rob will keep a check on your house, so go and enjoy yourself". They parted company and Misty ran into the airport to find Max. She was full of excitement and she felt so happy inside. She could hear Max shouting in the distance and once she located him she started to walk towards him. As she approached she noticed a girl stood with them. She looked quite attractive and she was dressed in a bright pink dress.

"Misty, this is Sue." The girl smiled and they both began to speak. Within minutes they were like old friends, you would have thought they had known each other for years the way they carried on. Gary hugged Max and Misty felt quite shocked to see they were so in love. She could see her brothers eyes light up as Gary stroked the side of his face as they spoke. Everybody checked their luggage in and headed for the bar to get a few drinks before their flight. Misty watched through the window, all the planes landing and taking off and her stomach churned but she knew once the vodka hit her, her nerves would be calm and she would be ready for flying. In fact she would be ready for anything that life threw at her.

Sue and Misty swapped life stories and each of them had a horrific story to tell regarding relationships. Sue spoke of her split with her boyfriend and told her of their violent relationship. Pulling up her dress she showed Misty a scar on her leg and told her that was where her boyfriend had burnt her with an iron, because she wouldn't iron his clothes. Misty looked shocked as she spoke of all the things she had been through, she thought it had just been her who put up with a violent boyfriend but as she continued she knew she wasn't alone and felt slightly less embarrassed talking about her ordeal with Gordon.

The flight was called over the tannoy and everyone made their way to the plane. Misty and Sue were so caught up in conversation they didn't even realise that they had walked all the way onto the plane. Everyone sat and the air hostess went through all the emergency procedures. Misty had jumped in the seat first nearest to the window and Sue sat next to her. Max and Gary were situated behind them .Max leaned over the seat and grabbed Misty's hair playfully.

"Bet your glad ya came now aren't you sis? Beats sitting at home staring at four walls, doesn't it?" Misty agreed. How right he was. That's all her life had been lately, sitting and staring at four walls. She knew something had to change and hopefully this was day one of her new start. The pilot now came over the loud speaker and introduced himself and the other pilots. He told them all that they were about to take off and for everyone to put their seat belts on until they were airborne. Sue grabbed Misty's arm and sunk her head into it.

"Oh this is the worst part. I hate taking off. Once we are up in the air I can handle it. I just wish they would just hurry up". Sue hid her head in Misty's arm till it was all over, as Misty chuckled. As Misty looked out of the window, it was like saying goodbye to all her problems in her life and especially Gordon. Sadness filled her once more as she thought of the way her life had turned out. Surely happiness would find her someday and give her the life she deserved, all she could do was live in hope.

The flight went well and everybody was cheering as they landed in Spain. Some little children were crying as they made their way to the exit. You could tell by their faces the flight had taken it out of them and they were now very restless. The door of the plane opened and almost immediately you could feel the heat from outside. Passengers fussed around taking their hand luggage out of the overhead compartment and making sure they hadn't forgot anything. Misty looked over the seat towards Max and she could see him and Gary holding hands. The love they had found together seemed so special and you could tell they were happy.

"Come on love birds", she shouted. "Can't you keep

your hands off each other till you get to the hotel?" Gary grabbed Max's face and kissed him on his cheek, as he looked at Misty.

"I can't help it if I find your brother irresistible, can I?" Sue now joined in the banter and they both teased them as they picked up their bags.

"Come on you two fairies, there is plenty of time for that when you get to the hotel. Let's get going", Sue shouted as she pulled them apart.

Once they had got the luggage, they found the coach that was waiting to take them to the hotel. This was one of the perks of the job, Gary told them. They had got a five star hotel and en suite bedrooms, for next to nothing he told them.

"Just stick with me girls and you will be laughing." Sue and Misty rolled their eyes as Sue put him in his place.

"You're so full of yourself you are. I wish I had your confidence. Mind you if I got the looks in our family I can't expect the confidence as well can I?" For once Gary was lost for words and Sue giggled at his defeat. The coach journey lasted about an hour and all the passengers sung holiday song to pass the time.

"Oh were all off to sunny Spain, a viva Espana". They sang at the top of their voices and the atmosphere was electric. As they entered the town where they were staying, they made several stops dropping passengers off at their hotels. The coach driver finally shouted out the name of their hotel and they left the coach to retrieve their luggage. Quite a few families got off at this stop and like cattle they headed to the hotels entrance.

The hotel was painted white outside and palm trees grew all up the walkway. As they walked to the reception Misty was gob smacked at the shine on the marble floors. Everything looked so clean and the smell was amazing. It smelt like coconuts. The receptionist took all their details and handed them the keys to their room. Sue held up the key and laughed at the size of the key ring. The key looked miniature compared to it. The key ring to their room looked like a small surf board had been attached to it.

"Well I don't think I'll lose my key do you?" Sue smiled. The receptionist also smiled and told her that many people take it off the key ring, she said she would have been amazed at how many keys were lost to rooms and even the oversized key ring attached to it didn't prevent it.

Misty and Sue decided they would share a room and they hurried to pick the best bed. As they ran to their room dragging their suitcases behind them Misty felt like a child again. Once the key was in the door they both fought at who was getting in first. Sue was the first in the room and dived on the bed she had chosen as Misty followed closely behind. The room was like something she had only seen in films. The lights were like glass chandeliers and sparkled as they turned them on. They opened the patio doors and could hear the music of the night, pumping its beat into the night air. It was too late for them to go out and plus they were both tired and needed sleep for the days that lay ahead. Misty decided she would un-pack her clothes, as Sue threw her body onto the bed watching Misty.

"Aren't you so organized". Sue laughed. "I don't even un-pack I live out of my suitcase. I just grab it as I need it". Misty was so used to having things neat and tidy, that the thought of leaving her clothes in the suitcase for the week terrified her and perhaps the time she spent with Gordon had rubbed off on her. He had always wanted everything neat and tidy and old habits die hard she told Sue. Misty started to tell Sue some of Gordon's rules whilst she was with him. Sue listened with interest and her heart went out to her new friend, as she knew exactly what she had been through and identified with it herself.

They chatted late into the night and told of their life stories. Misty had said she wished she could help other women who were stuck in violent relationships as she knew what they were going through, as did Sue. It was such a shame that all these young girls thought there was no one to turn to and no one who understood what they were going through. It was only now when Misty looked back and she could see where she had made her mistakes in her relationship and she could have kicked herself for being such a fool. Sue agreed with her and throughout the night they put the world to rights and solved everyone's problems in a roundabout way.

Both girls fell asleep and slept like new born babies. The holiday laughter of small children playing woke Misty first as she looked at the sunshine glaring through the window. She lay for a few moments and realised where she was.

"Sue, wake up. Look at the glorious sunshine we're missing" Sue pulled the sheets over her head and tried to go back to sleep. Misty shouted her once more and started to pull the blanket from her head. "Get up lazy bones. Sun sea and sex awaits us. Come on get up". Sue stretched her bones and like a bolt of lightning dived out of her bed.

"Oh I can't believe we are here. I can feel the heat already". Sue opened the patio doors and stretched her neck over the balcony, trying to view the neighbours but couldn't see anything. Looking out across to the swimming pool she could see people pulling out the sun loungers and placing towels on them.

"Wonder whether the lads are up yet. Should we knock on their door on the way past to breakfast to check?" Misty agreed and they both started to get ready.

Sue was ready in a flash. She looked fantastic in her red bikini and silver sarong but Misty was struggling as she looked at her body in the mirror, her bikini looked great but no matter how much she tried, her stretch marks could not be covered. Misty was about to give up on the bikini as Sue pushed the door open.

"Come on what an earth are you doing". As she looked at Misty she could see something was wrong. "What's wrong love?" Misty felt her face blush as she looked at her stomach.

"It's my stretch marks. How can I wear a bikini with these?" Sue's eyes met her stomach and she bend down to take a closer look. At first she was surprised as Misty had a great figure and she wondered how she had got stretch marks in the first place but she felt too nosey to ask. Sue could tell she was distraught and told her to wait right there. When she came back, she was waving a multi coloured sarong in her hands. "Here, try this round your waist. It hides a multitude of sins. Why do you think I wear one?" Sue placed the sarong round her waist and tied it on the side.

"See nobody would know what you're hiding. You look great". Sue was right as she looked in the mirror. All her stretch marks were covered and she was ready to leave. She thanked her and they both headed to knock on the lads door. As they reached their room the door was already opened. Misty shouted Max and she could hear his voice from the bedroom.

"One minute girls we are just getting ready". A few minutes later they both walked out of the bedroom in the brightest shorts anyone had ever seen.

"Fuckin' hell Misty, put your glasses on. The colour from their shorts is blinding my eyes". Sue shouted. They giggled as Max and Gary danced round the room shaking their bums in the super tight shorts they were wearing.

"You're just jealous girls, that's all. You know we look great". Misty and Sue watched as they gathered their belonging together and put them into a large beach bag. Once they had finished they headed down for breakfast, before hitting the beach for a day of sun worshipping.

Breakfast was great and they all ate like Kings... and Queens. Everyone was eager to get to the beach, so as soon as they finished their coffee that's where they went. The beach was about five minutes walk from the hotel and as they approached the view was breath-taking. Misty had only seen pictures like this on postcards. The sky was so blue and there wasn't a cloud in sight. Fellow holiday makers were all scattered round the beach and it took them about five minutes to find a spot to sit. Once they had all put their beach towels on the golden sand they took the position for a day of sunbathing. Creams and oils were pulled out of everyone's bags as they compared which ones they intended to use. Gary had brought carrot oil and swore it would give the best tan ever and looking at his tanned skin they knew he had lots of experience in sun bathing, so without any more hesitation they all rubbed carrot oil all over each other's body. Misty still felt conscious about her body but once she had a good look round all her fears subsided. Every shape and size of women was on the beach and some of the ladies were covered in stretch marks and didn't have a care in the world.

Lots of women were topless and Sue laughed as she spotted the biggest pair of breasts she had ever seen. She nudged Misty in the side and whispered. "Don't get many of them to a pound do you?" Misty looked to where the lady was sat and agreed, the breasts were massive. The women on the beach sat proud as peacocks, displaying their bodies to all passers-by without a care in the world. The boys were too busy rubbing oil all over their bodies to care about breasts, they were more interested in getting a bronzed body than a saggy pair of tits and didn't take a second look.

The sun blazed down on them all day and they all told stories about their lives. Everybody had stories to tell about parties they had attended and holidays they had experienced with their friends, all but Misty, her life had been so boring.

She had spent most of her youth locked away in her house being a skivvy for Gordon and didn't have one interesting story to tell. Sue's life wasn't much better but at least she had lived a little. Max and Gary went for a swim in the sea and left the girls alone. Once they were out of sight, Sue started to ask more about Misty's life, as she knew there was a lot more to her than met the eye.

"So what was sex like with your ex boyfriend then, because I can tell you now my ex wasn't very good. He thought his penis was the bee's knees and I didn't have the heart to tell him that sex with him was crap. I think you just have to make a few noises during sex to let men think they are sex gods and get it over with don't you?"

Misty smiled and giggled as she spoke of Gordon. "My ex was like an animal during sex and he grunted like a pig when he was coming". Both girls held their bellies as they laughed and the conversation didn't stop there.

"I want someone with a massive willy to show me what it's all about", Sue joked. "I think all the time I spent in my relationship has been wasted. I will tell you now this holiday is going to be the start of the new me. What do you say? Shall we make a pact? Out with the old and in with the new?" Both girls shook hands and sealed the deal. Somehow they had met each other at a time in both their lives when they needed a shoulder to cry on and they would be each other's tonic for a fresh start in life. The rest of the day was spent telling each other of the life they had led and Misty confided in Sue why she had stretch marks. When she had told Sue she had lost a baby, she hugged her and told her she must be a strong person to have coped with all that grief.

In the distance shouting could be heard and as they looked closer Max was carrying Gary back across the sand. Max was also screaming as he tried to run.

"The sand is burning my feet. Please pour some water on

them", he shouted as they reached them. Max threw Gary to the floor and dived onto his beach towel to save his feet from burning anymore. "Next time it's your turn to carry me. My feet are on fire. Girls go and try it if you don't believe me. We have been stood at the water's edge for ten minutes planning to get back". They all laughed as Sue's eyes focused on the lads who had just sat themselves in front of them.

The men had bodies like Greek gods. Every muscle was oiled to the extreme and they looked amazing, even Max and Gary were aroused at the sight of them. "Hallelujah! At last a bit of eye candy for us" Sue shouted as one of the men turned round and smiled at her comment. "This holiday just gets better by the minute" she laughed as she sucked her belly in and lay down. Misty smiled at one of the men then became too embarrassed to keep eye contact and joined her friend on the floor giggling as she did. The sun beamed down on all four of them all day and by the end of the day they were bronzed beauties. As they walked back to the hotel they compared their tans. Gary pulled down the back of his shorts to reveal the before and after stage of his tan, closely followed by the rest of them.

After tea they all made the decision to go out clubbing and everyone was excited. Sue had already told Misty she had plans to try out a new hairstyle on her and if she was lucky she would do her makeup as well. Misty was excited at the thought of going out and loved the thought of some pampering from her new friend. The girls sorted out the clothes they were wearing and Sue helped accessorise Misty's outfit. Now the challenge of Misty's make up began. Sue placed a headband round her hairline and pulled out the biggest box of makeup she had ever seen. The box had a sea of colour in it. Every colour she could think of was present. Sue had quite a serious face as she began to transform her. The whole transformation took about ten minutes. All that needed to be done now was her hair. Misty had tried to look in the mirror but Sue dragged her back, as she wanted her to see the full effects when she had finished. Sue used a comb and backcombed Misty's hair, as she moaned for her to hurry up.

Taking clips from her box she started to pin locks of hair up in different directions. She must have used at least a can of hair spray but when she had finished she stepped back and looked at Misty in amazement.

"You look stunning girl. You don't look like you, if you know what I mean. Go and put your clothes on first before you look at yourself and you will be surprised". Sue passed Misty her clothes and she got ready, still unaware of her new look. Once Sue put the final touches to her she was then ready to look in the mirror. Slowly she turned to face the mirror and her eyes focused on the women that looked back at her. She moved closer and checked again. The women she saw was beautiful and reminded her of the Misty she knew so long ago.

"Oh thanks Sue. I look incredible, don't I?" Misty twisted and turned in the mirror and loved her new look. Once Sue was ready, they were ready for the night that lay ahead. They headed to meet the boys in the hotel bar and all eyes focused on them both as they walked in. Max couldn't believe his sister's new look and was gob smacked as he examined her.

"You look great sis. The men better beware tonight, because you look hot". Gary complimented them both and Max kissed Sue on her cheek and thanked her for her help. This was just what Misty needed and by the way she walked to the bar, her confidence was definitely back on the up.

The four of them drank and drank and by the time they entered the night club they were pissed as farts. Both Sue and Misty hit the dance floor straight away and the men flocked round them. Sue and Misty teased the men as they danced near them, doing some Lambada dance that Sue had shown her. The men's mouth drooled as they watched them dance and both of them could have had any man they set their eyes on that night. Misty's feet were throbbing by the end of the night and her feet felt like they were on fire. When they joined Max and Gary, Misty pulled her shoes off and rubbed her feet. Within minutes she had stretched her feet over to where Max had sat and shoved them towards his face.

"Please rub my feet, they're on fire. I just need ya to cool them down". Max pushed her feet away and laughed calling her toe nails hooves.

"Orr please", she pleaded. I just need someone to rub them".

"I will", a voice shouted from behind her. Max's face lit up as he saw the person who had shouted. He knew he was on holiday in Spain and had secretly prayed they would see him and his prayers had been answered as he watched his sister's face with delight. Max didn't speak as Misty turned to the voice behind her. At first she didn't recognise the handsome man in front of her but as she looked closer her heart skipped a beat.

"Dominic!" she gasped. "What are doing here?" Dominic smiled and replied in a calm voice.

"I'm on holiday. Why else would I be here?" he laughed. Max now stood and shook Dominic's hand. As he held his hand, he could see the love in his eyes for his sister, as at that moment he couldn't take his eyes off her. Max asked him to join them and he shouted the rest of Dominic's friends to come and join them too. Sue immediately spotted one of his friends and knew he would be going home with her tonight as he was absolutely gorgeous and she wasn't letting him get away, not at any cost. Dominic sat himself right next to Misty and kissed her on the cheek, with a cheeky grin on his face.

"Long time no see ay", he spoke in his deep masculine

voice. Misty was still in shock and couldn't find the words at
the moment to speak.

Dominic looked Misty up and down and he knew at
that moment he still loved her. He'd had strings of girlfriends
in the past but none of them had ever taken her place in
his heart. He wondered why she was away on holiday with
Max and the question that was on his lips, was where was
her nobhead of a boyfriend Gordon? He couldn't hold the
question any longer and out it came like leaping fire balls
from his mouth.

"So where's Gordon, hasn't he come out tonight?" Misty's
face changed and he could see he'd hit a nerve. He watched
her fidget about before she finally answered.

"Gordon's not here with me and I would prefer it if you
didn't mention his name again. I'm no longer with him
and don't want to talk about the life wrecking bastard". This
was music to Dominic's ears and he felt his heart beat in his
mouth, as he knew now he might stand a chance with her
once again.

"You look great Misty. You haven't changed one little bit,
you're still gorgeous. Mind you, you were always gorgeous
in my eyes". Misty felt tingling sensations run through her
body as he spoke. He still had that effect on her even after all
the years that had passed. She felt the room spinning and the
effect of the alcohol started to make her feel sick.

"I need to get some fresh air. I feel sick" she yelled as
the music pumped down her ears. She stood up and placed
her shoes back on her feet and headed for the exit closely
followed by Dominic. Sue didn't even see her go as she had
taken the dance floor with Dominic's friend and was having a
great time. Max watched her closely as they left and knew she
was in safe hands and carried on whispering sweet nothings
into Gary's ear.

Once the fresh air hit Misty's face she moved to the side

street and began to vomit. Dominic stood behind her and held her hair back and laughed at the sight that stood in front of him. When she had finished she picked her head up and wiped her mouth.

"Not very lady like am I. I've not seen you for years and look at me spewing up in front of you. You must think I am a right scruff?" Dominic laughed and helped her regain her balance, before he spoke.

"Misty Sullivan. You will always be a lady to me". She smiled at him and began to walk along the sea front. The night sky shone brightly and the stars seemed to twinkle like never before. The sea breeze hit their faces as they walked and Dominic held Misty in his arms like she was a precious gem. As they walked a bit further they took a seat on a bench and began to talk about what they had done since they split. Misty felt so at ease with him, it seemed like they had never been apart. Dominic was unsure of how she still felt about him and started to fish to find out.

"So Misty Sullivan. What do you think of me after all these years? Do I still rock your world or what?" He laughed and tried to make it into a joke but he waited eagerly for any feedback. Misty felt mixed up. Half of her wanted to jump on him and tell him she still loved him but the other half was quite confused and scared of where it might lead if she told him the truth.

"You will always rock my world you know that don't you", she spoke with a giggle in her voice. They both laughed and huddled together but as they did their eyes met, they both felt the love between them. Dominic slowly moved his lips to hers and she accepted his kiss and responded passionately. His lips felt like velvet and she enjoyed every moment of the kiss they shared.

Misty broke the kiss and pulled away as her body was shaking with the cold of the night and wanted to head back to the hotel. "Will you walk me home", she whispered. Dominic stood and helped her up. An invitation like that could not be missed he thought and any time he could spend with her was a bonus at the moment. Misty had already decided as they walked back to the hotel that she was going to have sex with him. He had made her heart leap about in her chest like never before and she didn't want to let the chance pass them by, like it had all those years ago. She decided she was going to relish any time she had with him because she knew once the holiday was over she would have to go home and face the problems that lay ahead.

Back at the hotel, they could hear Sue laughing in the bedroom with Dominic's friend. They must have left the bar shortly after they did. It was obvious she was keeping to her word because the sounds coming from the bedroom told Misty she was enjoying every minute fully.

Dominic pulled Misty to the settee and stroked her hair from her face. His emotions were on fire and he wanted her so much. His penis throbbed in his pants and he knew she wanted him too. He now pulled her towards him and kissed her ravenously, he kissed every inch of her body as he peeled off her clothes. Misty was so caught up in the moment she forgot about her stretch marks on her stomach and even let him kiss them. As he climbed on top of her, she held his masculine body and dragged him towards her. The feeling inside her she had never felt before and she had never wanted anything so much in her life. Slowly he pulled her knickers down and kissed her thighs and slid his tongue up and down her legs. Misty felt moist between her legs and knew she was about to explode with pleasure. He slowly slid himself inside her and she groaned with pleasure wanting every inch of him inside her. She had never experienced an orgasm with Gordon and had only read of this moment in books. Dominic caressed her and each touch felt like heaven. Looking into each other's eyes they both felt the explosion of their bodies together. She screamed with pleasure as his rhythm changed and the moment she had only seen on films finally took over her body. It started in her toes and like a wave of pleasure travelled to the top of her head.

"Oh Dominic", she shouted and he knew he couldn't control himself anymore as he listened to her shout. He too reached orgasm and thrust deep inside her as he held her body. They both lay there after they had reached orgasm and Dominic kissed her softly. He felt like the piece of a jigsaw he had lost so many years ago had now been recovered. He never wanted to let her go again, he had lost her once before and was never losing her again. He knew Gordon would never let her go either but he was a man himself now and not a child as he was before. He would fight to the death if need be because he knew now she was the girl of his dreams.

They lay in each other's arms for hours after and Misty felt so safe. She knew now there was no turning back and her life had changed forever. They both spoke of the years that had passed and filled the gaps they had missed about each other lives. Misty spoke openly about her violent relationship and felt rather silly for putting up with all she had over the years. Some of the things she spoke about made his skin crawl and he felt anger inside as she spoke. As he looked at her, he knew he had to declare his love, as time wasn't on his side as he was due to fly home in a couple of days. So without a moment to spare, he sat up and leant towards her face.

"Misty I still love you. Even though the years have passed, you have never been far from my thoughts. I don't know how you feel but I know if I don't tell you now, I will regret it for the rest of my life". Dominic paused and waited for a response but Misty was trying to make sense of what he had just said and delayed speaking for the moment. She had known from the moment she saw him she still loved him and she too regretted ever letting him go. This was her chance of happiness and she didn't want it to pass her by, so without delay she took hold of his firm hand and kissed it softly.

"Dominic, I still love you too. I didn't really know how much, till I saw you tonight. All my old feelings came flooding back and I'm sorry for ever hurting you". She pulled him towards her and kissed him. This was a moment she would remember forever and she knew for sure he was the man who still held her heart hostage, even after all these years. Both of them fell asleep in each other's arms and she felt like a princess lying next to him, he truly was her knight in shining armour. The sound of Sue opening the fridge caused Misty to open her eyes. Both girls looked at each other and smiled.

"Come to the bathroom" Sue whispered as she wanted to talk about the night's events. Misty slowly removed Dominic's hand from round her and wrapped a towel round her body. Once in the bathroom both girls giggled quietly.

"You go first" Misty whispered and Sue told her of her wild night of sex. "Never mind me. Max told me of the history between you two. I can't believe it. It's fate. You are meant to be together. The whole situation is so weird. It's like something that could only happen in a fuckin' fairy tale. Do you still love him?" Misty rubbed her hands together with excitement and told her all the ins and outs of the night.

"He told me he still loves me. Even after all these years and do you know what Sue, I still love him too. I just didn't realise it till now". Sue looked shocked but she held her friend and told her to grab any happiness that comes her way with both hands.

"Misty I'm so made up for you. Just be careful and be sure before you jump feet first into another relationship". Misty thanked her and they both laughed as they walked out of the bathroom.

"Right I'm going back to bed Misty," Sue laughed. "I can

feel a morning of hot steamy sex coming my way and I don't want to miss it. So see you later" she giggled as she walked back to the bedroom, cheekily showing Misty her bum cheeks as she did. Dominic opened his eyes, as she sneaked back beside him. He cuddled her in his big strong arms and kissed the top of her head and they too had a morning of hot steamy sex and then spent the rest of the day together on the beach. Max finally caught up with them later that day, as did Sue and her new love John. Max was over the moon to see Dominic and his sister back together, they looked so happy. He also knew that when she got home that was another story, as she would have the fight of her life on her hands to rid herself of Gordon. He just hoped she was strong enough. This time Max had decided he would stand right by his sister and help rid her of the man who almost broke her in two.

The days flew by and before she knew it Dominic was due to go home. Both she and Sue were gutted the day he left with his friend. Promises had been made between Sue and John and they agreed to see each other when they got home. Sue had said she had found her soul mate in John and had loved every minute she had spent with him. Dominic and Misty's goodbye had been heartbreaking to watch. None of them wanted to say goodbye and they held onto each other until the last minute. They had arranged to meet up as soon as she got home and planned their future together.

The plane left and took both of the girl's hearts home with it. The rest of the holiday was still fun but both girls were eager to get home to be with the loves of their lives and they counted the hours until they could be home again.

Finally that day came and both girls packed up their belongings and headed for the airport. Everybody else's faces looked miserable at the thought of going home but not these two, they were happy and singing as if there holiday was just beginning. Max and Gary were still hung over as they boarded the plane and couldn't wait to have a sleep on the journey home. Sue and Misty swapped phone numbers and promised that they would keep in touch. They didn't live far from each other so they could see each other any time they wanted to. It was funny that Misty had lost her boyfriend and best friend before this holiday and yet she was going home with a new best friend and a new boyfriend. Its right what they say she thought as she quoted the saying in her mind. What doesn't kill you, cures you. She felt like a new woman and her strength and self belief had both returned. She felt like she was ready to fight anyone or anything that stood in her way of happiness, she deserved it so much and wasn't going to be a doormat anymore. It was time to stand up and be counted she thought as she boarded the plane. As they took off, she said goodbye to the place where she had found happiness and thanked it for saving her in more ways than one.

CHAPTER SIXTEEN

GORDON WAS COUNTING the days until Misty's return. Francesca had found out from a friend of Lisa's that she had taken herself off to Spain. He was livid at the news and hadn't slept properly since she'd been gone. He had planned his pay back so many times over and over in his head and it was just a matter of time until he got his hands on her. Gordon's mates had deserted him now, they knew he was nothing but a ticking bomb. They couldn't take the chance of him being arrested through his domestic problems, so they left him well alone. Wayne had been to see him and wanted the shot guns back as soon as possible but when he had told him they were locked in the house, where he no longer had a key, he was furious. He told him he had a week to get them back to him otherwise he would be feeling his fist and Gordon knew he meant business by the look in his eyes and feared for the first time in his life for his own safety.

Drugs were Gordon and Francesca lives now. They had loaned money all over the place on the strength of what he had in the sports bag. His drug habit was bigger than ever now and he had to not only supply himself but Francesca as well. He was finding her very annoying at the moment and wished he had never met her. She was a leech to him, every second of the day she wanted to know where he was and with whom. His fist had met her face on more than one occasion and she had become his new punch bag. She found him aggressive and moody most of the time and knew Misty was the cause of it but she also knew she wouldn't get away with leaving him that easily and feared of what he would do to her when he finally got a grip of her.

The journey home was filled with anticipation for the two girls and when they finally landed in Manchester they hugged one another tightly. Misty hated goodbyes and didn't know where to start but luckily Sue made it quite an easy.

"Don't forget to ring me later. We'll arrange to meet up soon". Misty agreed and waved her off and started to look for Lisa, who was waiting to pick her and Max up. The crowds of people leaving the airport could have been compared to a boxing day sale in town and she and Max were finding it difficult to move. Finally they could see the smiling face of Lisa, as she waved frantically to try and get their attention. After a short time they reached her and she looked so happy to see them.

"You two look great. Look at your tans, did you have a good time?" Misty and Max smiled at her and began to tell her every detail about the holiday but Misty didn't mention Dominic yet, she wanted to keep the best story till last. As they walked to the car Misty told her mum she had met someone on holiday and she was going to carry on seeing him now she was home. Lisa never guessed in a million years the identity of her new love and they both watched her face as she revealed his name.

"It's Dominic mam. I couldn't believe it either when I saw him. We spent most of the holiday together". Misty didn't stop for breath till she told her mum all the details and Lisa could tell by the twinkle in her eyes that she was smitten. Lisa listened to all their news but didn't want to tell them how poorly their dad was till they got home. She also needed to tell Misty about Gordon antics and the endless phone calls she had received from him demanding to know when she was home. Lisa knew Gordon was very angry and now Misty was home she really feared for her safety.

As they walked in Lisa's back door, Butch came flying to greet her. He jumped up so high you could tell he had really missed her. She too had missed him and grabbed him in her arms making a big fuss of him. Misty and Max both flung their bodies onto the chairs and kicked their shoes off, waiting for Lisa to join them. A few hours passed and both Max and Misty were eager to get to the hospital to see their father. Lisa had told them he had contracted pneumonia in the last couple of days and he wasn't a well man, so without wasting a moment more they set off to the hospital to be by his side.

As they looked for Ken on the ward, he wasn't in his usual bed, so they asked the nurse on duty where he had been moved to.

"Come with me love", she answered, "he's been moved to a side ward where it is nice and quiet. Mr. Sullivan isn't well at the moment and I would appreciate it if you didn't stay long as he needs rest". They both agreed and slowly they walked into a dimly lit room. Lots of pipes and tubes were across Ken's face and they were horrified as they looked at him. They both whispered at his bedside and tried not to wake him. On hearing their voices Ken slowly opened his eyes and smiled.

"Told you I would be here when you got back didn't I. Only just though, I'm in quite a bad way at the moment. I just can't seem to shake it off". Ken struggled to breathe and pulled the oxygen mask to his face. Watching him was heartbreaking and they knew the days left with him were few.

Misty and Max never left their father's side for the next couple of days and finally on the third day Ken lost his battle for life. The day he had died had been very peculiar, as he seemed to be getting a lot better. He had spoken constantly about his love for them all and how much he had regretted his mistakes. Before he died he had sat up in his bed and looked at an empty seat next to his bedside. Misty and Max had both looked at each other as he began to speak to the empty chair.

"It's my dad come to see me Misty. Come and say hello to him. He hasn't seen you since you have been born, he died when you were a baby". Misty skin shivered as she watched him have a conversation with the empty chair. "I can't come yet dad. I'm not ready yet, he spoke to the empty chair. "You'll have to come back later. I haven't said goodbye yet". He looked like he was now getting quite angry and Misty tried to comfort him but as she looked she could see him holding his arms out to the chair. Ken looked like he had been given something precious to hold and he held it with great care before he spoke.

"Misty he looks so much like you. My first grandson" he spoke proudly. Misty's spine shivered at the thought of her lost child being there in her father's arm and looked at Max, who was now white with fear. Ken reached his arm out to the empty chair and looked like he was taking hold of someone's hands. His face now changed and he had the most beautiful smile she had ever seen, he looked so peaceful. At this moment they both knew their dad had left this world and they felt so helpless as Misty shouted at him to try and wake up. Max knew he would never wake up again and went to get the nurse as Misty screamed.

"Dad, Dad please wake up". She sobbed on his chest trying to hear his heart beat. She knew deep down, he had gone to a better place and he suffered no more but she still wanted him back.

Ken was surrounded by the doctors and eventually he was pronounced dead at eleven minutes past seven that Friday evening. No amount of tears would ever bring him back and once the doctors left they both said their last goodbyes.

The funeral was a small family gathering and the ceremony was so final. Ken had always sung a song when they were growing up and Misty played it as they laid him to rest. The words of the song began and Misty remembered her father's face as he once sang it to them as small children.

"There's a place for us. Somewhere a place for us. Time together and time to share. Hold my hand I will take you there. Somewhere, Somehow." The words from the song from 'West Side Story' touched everyone's heart, as they placed soil onto his coffin and the two smaller children even sung along as they left his grave side with only memories of their father to take away with them. Misty listened to the words of the song as she placed a red rose on top of his coffin. The words had so much meaning to her and she knew somewhere and somehow they would all be together again, it was just a matter of time.

"Goodbye dad", she said as her rose landed on his coffin. "We'll always love you". The words stuck in her throat as she walked away and almost immediately her family was by her side.

Everyone went back to Lisa's house after the service and she made everyone a cup of tea. Some of the older people had a glass of sherry and told stories of Ken in his younger days. Dominic and Sue had been in close contact with Misty all the way through her loss and helped her through this sad time. Dominic had been to see her every night whilst she stayed at her mother's house. He was like her rock helping her through.

Misty hadn't been home to her own house yet, as too much had happened since she had got home and she wanted to be round her family in their time of need.

Two days passed after the funeral and Misty felt she was

ready to go home. She had told Dominic she didn't want him to stay with her just yet, as she knew she had one last demon to face and she knew she had to do it alone. Lisa helped Misty carry all her bags inside the house, as Butch ran round her feet. As they opened the door to the house she could see the fear in Misty's face. This was the place where so much had gone wrong in her life and held so many bad memories. Butch ran straight to the dog hatch and made his way into the garden. She had meant to get a smaller dog hatch, as the one that was in the door was much too big but jobs like that had always got forgotten and pushed to the back of her mind as at the moment she didn't see it as important.

Lisa left Misty in her home and without her knowing, she called at a neighbour's house and told her to keep her eyes out for Misty. She told her all the details about Gordon and told her to phone the police if she suspected anything was going on. She then left and headed home, feeling slightly better knowing someone nearby was watching out for Misty as well.

Misty cleaned the house from top to bottom that day and felt surprisingly calm. The house phone had rang a couple of times but when she answered it the line was dead and she thought it must have been someone with the wrong number.

The first night she slept in her own home felt quite weird but with the company of Butch by her side she got through it alright. Each noise she heard in the night made her jump and she was up and down all night making sure her home was safe. Dominic had spent hours talking to her at night and for the first week of her being home he phoned her constantly. Misty had thought it strange she had not seen sight or sound of Gordon and prayed he was finally leaving her alone and getting on with his own life.

Friday night came and Sue and John went out with

Dominic and Misty to a nearby pub. Little did she know that once she had left her home that night Gordon set about his cunning plan to seek revenge.

Dominic had planned this night for weeks unknown to Misty. This was the night he had decided to ask her to be his wife and with the help of Lisa he had arranged for all her family to be waiting there for them when they arrived in the pub. He himself would act surprised to see them all when he first walked in the pub, just to keep Misty clueless as to what was happening. Lisa had already had her story at the ready, just in case Misty questioned her. She was going to tell her it was Rob's birthday and they were all out celebrating it now instead of the Wednesday the following week.

They all walked into the pub and the place looked packed. Misty immediately noticed different members of her family and commented to Dominic. "It looks like one of my family parties in here, nearly all my relations are in". Then she suddenly noticed her mother and walked straight towards her with an open mouth. "What are ya doing in here? You never go out unless it's a family party". Lisa thought quickly and had her reply ready.

"Its Rob's birthday so we all thought we would go out for a couple of drinks. It was only me and Rob at first, then Denise said her and her husband would come and before you knew it we were all out". Misty looked annoyed and went into a bit of a strop.

"Well thanks for asking me. I would have definitely come if I would have been asked". Lisa didn't want to get into an argument and apologised telling her it was all last minute. Misty smiled and accepted her excuse and went to see Rob to wish him happy birthday. Dominic whispered to Lisa how nervous he was and she calmed him down, telling him everything would be alright. The night got into full swing as the DJ played some cheesy dance songs. When the song had finished Dominic took the microphone off the DJ and coughed loudly into it, to get everyone's attention. He now called for Misty to come and join him on stage. Once she was by his side, the words he had been practicing all week began to leave his lips.

"Misty Sullivan, I have known you for many years now and think you're a wonderful person. You have changed my life since the very first time I set eyes on you. I love you with all my heart. I lost you once Misty a long, long time ago and never ever want to lose you again. You're my world, my life and my everlasting love and for that reason you would make me the proudest man on earth, if you would agree to be my wife". He knelt on the floor and pulled out a box containing an incredible looking diamond ring. "Will you marry me Misty?"

All eyes looked at her as she stood by him in silence. Tears filled her eyes and she truly believed she was the happiest women in the world. She now choked her emotions before she answered.

"Of course I will", she cried. "I love you so much and want to spend the rest of my life with you. You are my true love and it would be an honour to be your wife". Everybody cheered as he placed the diamond ring on her finger. Lisa was crying tears of happiness as she watched them both, as Rob held her. Lisa had always wanted Misty to be happy and the way she looked at this moment her wish had most definitely come true.

"It's about time Misty had some luck isn't it Rob, Dominic is such a lovely man, I know he will treat her like a princess and never hurt her". Rob agreed and they both went to congratulate them both on their engagement.

When Misty found out the truth about all her family being in on the surprise, she laughed and couldn't believe Dominic had gone to so much trouble to propose to her. Sue nearly pissed herself with excitement as she walked to see Misty, she grabbed her tightly and hugged her so tight.

"See dreams do come true, if you never stop believing. I wish you both all the happiness in the world, God knows you deserve it". The words that Sue had just been spoken would stick with Misty forever, as she knew everybody had dreams and sometimes that's all that kept people going in life. Everybody needs a dream she thought as without dreams we would all lead pretty unfulfilled lives.

The days she had spent with Gordon, had always been filled with dreams but never once had they came true. She hadn't ever expected to find her dream with Dominic but somehow fate had brought them together and made them complete .It just goes to show every cloud has a silver lining she thought. Misty squeezed Sue's arm.

"Thanks Sue. You're such a good friend, without you none of this would have probably happened. You gave me back my confidence and for that I will be forever in your debt. Whenever you need me I'll never be far away". Sue's face told her she was speechless for the moment and the words she had spoke had hit her heart with a bang.

"Fuckin' Hell Misty stop it .You'll have me crying in a minute. We both saved each other in one way or another and we were in the right place at the right time, that's all. I just feel sorry for all those girls who never get a second chance like us and end up in a dead relationship all their life. We are the lucky ones Misty. I thank you too from the bottom of my heart for helping me find my new love John. I love him so much". Her eyes now looked at John who was sat talking to Dominic and you could tell by her face she had found happiness too.

The music played loudly and all the family and friends celebrated the news of Misty's and Dominic engagement. Misty and Dominic danced to an old song they once sung together when they were younger, as Dominic pulled her closer to speak.

"This is the happiest moment in my life Misty. Fate has brought us together. I knew one day we would meet up again but how this has all happened is so, so weird". Misty held him close, as he swayed her round the dance floor. She knew then she would love this man till her dying breath. Dominic wanted her to move in his home with him straight away till they got their own place. His home was an up market apartment set on the outskirts of the town centre and it was decided she would move in with him at the end of the month and start their new lives together.

Meanwhile back at Misty's home Gordon had started his plan for revenge. When night had fallen, he watched Misty leave the house and began to carry out his plan. He climbed down from the tall oak tree situated at the back of the house and climbed the back fence into the garden. Then as quiet as a mouse he pulled his small knife from his pocket and started to make the dog hatch in the back door a lot bigger. The task took at least an hour before he could finally squeeze his whole body through. As his body squeezed through the hatch, Butch barked furiously at him and tried biting his head as he came through. He knew he had to silence the dog before he brought attention to the house and as soon as he squeezed his arms through he pulled out his knife and plunged it straight into Butch's throat to silence him once and for all. He hadn't wanted to kill the dog but as he entered the house he could see there was no movement from him.

Once he was through he ran to turn the alarm off .He just hoped Misty hadn't changed the number. Frantically he keyed in the number and watched the alarm disarm. He then walked back into the kitchen and bent to where Butch lay. He shook Butch's lifeless body and knew he was dead. He had to think quickly as his plan had to be perfect for when

Misty arrived home, because if she noticed the dog missing his plan would be most definitely foiled. He knew he wouldn't have long from the moment she walked through the door to capture her in his grip, because she would definitely shout for Butch as soon as she walked in and if he wasn't there she would start to worry of he's whereabouts.

Gordon now searched the cloakroom for the sport bag containing his money. At first he had to rethink whether he had moved it or not but after a few minutes he knew it had been moved. Rage filled his body at the thought of Misty having his money and most of all she would now know about the two shotguns inside it. His forehead sweated and his palms felt like they were on fire. Gordon quickly carried Butch upstairs with him and placed him in the laundry basket, he knew he would go undetected in there for now. His next move was to wipe up all of the blood from Butch's neck that had leaked all over the kitchen floor. The job took him all of five minutes to complete and he continued his plan to capture Misty.

Once the alarm was reset, he ran back upstairs and opened the wardrobe. He positioned himself inside, so he could see every angle of her bedroom. All he had to do now was to sit patiently till she returned and he knew then that the moment he had waited for so long would begin. Resting his head on some clothes in the bottom of the wardrobe he began his wait like a soldier waiting for war to begin. The hours passed and Gordon was becoming restless sat in the wardrobe. It was only when he started to move his aching body that he heard a car's engine drive close to the house. As he listened closely he could hear Misty shouting Goodbye to whoever she was with. His heart thumped inside his chest and he knew his wait was finally over.

Misty waved to Dominic and blew him kisses as he left. She was so happy and things couldn't have been better.

Searching through her bag she found her key and opened the door. As she went in the door she couldn't stop singing the song herself and Dominic had danced to. Once the alarm was turned off, her eyes focused on the ring Dominic had placed on her finger and she held it close to her heart and sighed a deep breath. The night had taken it out of Misty and she felt so tired, so she started to make sure everything was secure before she went up to bed. She shouted Butch's name and waited for him to come running. After a few minutes she decided she would go to bed, after all Butch was probably fast asleep lay on her bed. Still singing under her breath she entered her bedroom but didn't notice the absence of Butch. Kicking her shoes off, she now pulled her dress over her head and collapsed onto the bed. Her thoughts were solely about Dominic and the new life they were going to spend together. As she drifted off to sleep she was unaware of the eyes that watched her every move through the small gap in the wardrobe door.

Gordon was as quiet as a mouse when he slowly opened the wardrobe door. His heart was beating rapidly as he crept to the end of her bed. Slowly he pulled back the bed sheets and lay slowly next to her. Once he was positioned near her face he started to blow his breath softly on her cheeks. At first her face just turned and she moved her hand up, to move whatever it was that was bothering her.

"Wakey, wakey" he whispered into her ears and slowly but surely her eyes started to open. At first she thought she was dreaming and was in some kind of nightmare but as his face came closer to her she realised it was oh so real. "Hello my little princess. Who's been a naughty little girl then?" At this point she tried to move away from him but as usual he's strength was too much for her. He now continued in a stern voice.

"Did you have a nice holiday? You cheeky little bitch?

Well let's have a look at your tan then". Gordon ripped the blankets back and poked her bronzed body

"Looking quite sexy aren't you. Do ya want a shag for old time's sake then? I think that's what you've been missing haven't ya?" He now slowly undid the button on his jeans and pulled them over his arse cheeks. Misty wriggled as he mounted her and placed his hands over her mouth to drown out the sounds of her screams. As she tried to scream he squeezed her face to silence her.

"Shut it, bitch. It's what you want. You know it is, you dirty little slag". He now kissed her neck and bit her body as he entered her. He knew she didn't want sex with him and knew he would have to be quick, as her strength returned.

"You love it don't you? Say you love it" he demanded. His warm breath was on her face as he spoke and she could tell by his eyes how excited he was. "I've missed you so much, even though you have been a naughty girl. Have ya missed me?" Misty made no response as his pace quicken and then like a pig in a fit he ejaculated deep inside her. She tried with all her might to break free and nearly did at one stage, till he grabbed her hair and pulled her back onto the bed. Her hands raised to try and hit him but he was too quick for her to make contact. He held her arms tightly and laughed in her face in an evil kind of way. The smile soon disappeared from his face as he noticed from the corner of his eye the shine of the diamond ring sitting on her finger.

"Oh I see ya have been treating yourself with my money. You cheeky little slag". He could tell by her face that the ring meant something more to her as she tried to pull her hand away from his grip. His faced changed now and she could tell he wanted to know more about the ring.

"Where's the ring from? He asked in a jealous voice. "Is it from one of ya fancy fellas? Mind you, who would go anywhere near you. You're just a dirty little slut". Misty wanted to remain quiet but the years of torment from him couldn't let her remain quiet any longer. She wanted him to know that someone else really loved her, despite what he thought and he had loved her with all his heart. So with no fear in her voice she answered him and watched his face change with temper.

"It's an engagement ring. I've met someone else. Someone who loves me and doesn't treat me like a twat". His fist now flew into the side of her face and knocked her to the floor. He now stood over her and repeatedly kicked her. She screamed but this made no difference to him, he didn't look like he was ever going to stop. Suddenly he must have thought about his money and pulled her to her feet. Her body collapsed back to the floor but he still dragged her up and threw her onto the bed.

"You'll never ever get away from me. If I can't have ya nobody else will. I'll fucking kill ya first". Sitting on the edge of the bed he now lit a cigarette to calm his nerves. He watched her closely and made sure she didn't try to escape. He thought about the words she'd just spoken and tears filled his eyes, as he pleaded with her.

"Tell me ya lying Misty", he whispered as he moved towards her face. "Please tell me it's not true. I still love ya, always have and always will. Francesca was a big mistake and I promise I'll never hurt ya again." The lies rolled off his tongue as he tried to win her back but he could tell it was pointless. Gordon finished his cigarette and remembered the sports bag containing his cash.

Little did he know that the neighbour had heard all the commotion and phoned the police to report the screams through the walls of her bedroom fearing for Misty's safety. He now stood up and walked to the bedroom door.

"I'm only going to ask you once and if you start telling me shit, I'm gonna kill ya here and now". Misty knew what the question was he was about to ask and trembled inside but she also knew she had placed one of the shot guns under her bed and at this moment there was no way she could reach it. She knew she needed to play for time to reach the gun, unless her own little plan would be foiled and he would win again.

"Where's my fuckin' money bitch". he shouted. His voice was fierce and she shook with terror as she knew he meant business. He walked out of the bedroom and came back carrying a small parcel covered by a towel. As she looked at him, his eyes danced with madness and she knew he was on a short fuse. He repeated the question and moved toward her holding the small bundle. Misty still remained silent and tried to push past him but he pushed her flying back onto the bed and threw the bundle at her telling her he hoped this would jog her memory of the whereabouts of the money. She scanned the bundle lying next to her and spotted traces of blood on the white towel he had wrapped it in.

"Open it bitch" he shouted. She slowly peeled the corner away from the wrapped bundle as he watched eagerly. As she continued she could see fur covered in blood and her heart stopped as she realised what it was wrapped in the towel.

"Butch!" She cried. She quickly unwrapped him and held him close to her trying to revive him. The blood from his throat was smeared all over his little body and she knew it was too late to save him. She screamed at Gordon like she had never screamed before.

"You fucking bastard. You're a fuckin' mental bastard. You deserve everything that's coming to you. Is that all you want, your fucking money?" Gordon now looked pleased that he had hurt her like she had hurt him and felt like he was winning again.

"Yes, all I want is ma money and I'll be gone from ya life forever". Misty stood still and he could tell she was debating whether she should give it him or not.

"Just give me my money and I'll be gone out of your life forever" he repeated. "I never loved you anyway. I just felt sorry for you. Francesca is the woman I love, she gives me everything I need. She's not fucking frigid like you are. It's like shagging a corpse when I'm shagging you. Whoever you have met will find out sooner or later and he will be off leaving your sorry arse too and don't think you can come running back to me when it all goes pear shaped". His voice now laughed with madness as he watched her scrambling under the bed. He really thought she was getting his money and felt quite proud he had scared the living day lights out of her. Once she had given him the money, he would then leave her for dead. The thought of her with another man made his skin crawl and he could never let that happen and for that reason her fate was minutes away.

Misty climbed under the bed and saw the gun wrapped in the plastic bag . The moment she had waited for, for so long had finally come and she could rid herself of the bastard who had wrecked her life. She felt terrified inside but the thought of another day with the fear of him in her life had been greater and her choice was made. She pulled the gun from the bag and slowly started to pull her body from underneath the bed as Gordon continued to hurl insults at her.

Misty now stood tall and pointed the gun at him as her body shook from head to toe. His face soon changed when he noticed what she was holding. Her words were slow and clear as she started to speak. She had rehearsed this moment millions of time in her mind and now reality had took over there was no going back.

"Do ya feel scared Gordon? I hope you do, because your life is going to end. I know I'll go to prison but the sentence there will be easier than the sentence of living with you a moment more". Gordon now felt uneasy and laughed at her telling her to put the gun down and stop being a daft twat.

He knew it was loaded and he knew she could end his life any moment now.

"There's bullets inside the gun. So stop it before one of us gets hurt". He watched her closely and wasn't quite sure whether she would finish what she had started. He now prompted her to hand over the money and put the gun down. "Just give me the fucking money and I'll be gone. I promise you. What's the point in going to prison, when all you have to do is give me the money . Think about it". He now slowly moved towards her telling her to put the gun down. Her mind was racing as she tried to hold the gun steady. He noticed her hesitate and ceased his chance to grab the gun. They both rolled on the floor as she held the gun above her head but as he banged her head on the wardrobe door she lost her grip and he immediately grabbed the gun taking control of the situation once more.

"My, how things change," he boasted as he now stood with the gun pointing at her head. "Get me the fuckin' money now. No more games". He moved his body and stood with his back to the door. But at precisely that moment the door came flying open and several policemen come flying in.

They wrestled Gordon to the floor and took the shot gun out of his hands. A policewoman made her way straight to Misty who was now shaking like a scared animal in the corner. Seeing her state, she pulled a blanket from the bed and placed it onto her shaking body.

"Come on love. It's over now, he can't hurt you any more". Misty teeth chattered together, as her nerves fell to pieces and she felt like she was going to pass out.

The bedroom was filled with shouting policemen, telling Gordon to remain still while they tried to place the handcuffs on his jerking body. As she watched she could see four policemen struggling frantically on the floor trying to restrain him. The policewoman tried to find Misty some clothes, as all she wearing was her bra and a torn pair of knickers. It was quite obvious to the policewoman that girl in front of her had just been raped and her heart went out to her as she tried to console her. Finally Misty was ready to leave the room and the policewomen held her as she walked past the raging Gordon.

"Please tell em Misty. It's all a big mistake isn't it?" He pleaded. "Please tell em". Misty looked at the beast lay powerless on the floor and knelt to where his face was before she spoke.

"You dirty no good bastard. I hope they lock you up and throw away the key. Rot in hell for all I care. Good riddance to bad rubbish. That's all I can say". Before Misty stood to her feet, she spat right into his face and watched as he tried to break free trying to grab her. The policewoman took hold of her arm and now pulled her away, as Gordon screamed her name at the top of his voice.

No tears left her eyes as she walked down the stairs. She felt like she was floating on a cloud and her mind was spinning. It was only the sound of her mother's hysterical voice that brought her back to the reality.

"Misty are you alright love," she cried "Oh look at you. What has he done to you?" Her mother took her arm from the policewoman and took her into the front room examining every cut and bruise she had on her body followed closely by the officer. Lisa cried as she held her daughter in her arms.

"It was a good job I told the neighbour to listen out for you otherwise he would have killed you wouldn't he?" Misty never replied and sat without a word passing her lips as everyone round her watched the police drag Gordon into the awaiting police van situated outside. Lisa now went to the front door and shouted abuse at Gordon as they struggled to put him in the van. All the neighbours were at their windows and watched as the van drove away with a screaming Gordon in the back.

The officer sat with Misty and tried to take a statement but she could tell she wasn't in a fit state and left her alone for a few minutes. Lisa had phoned Dominic and he was on his way as soon as he knew what had happened. He had cried down the phone to Lisa, saying he should have never have left her alone and blamed himself for the night's events. Misty felt so strange. She felt like a weight had been lifted off her shoulders and for once in her life she could see the light at the end of the tunnel. Tears fell from her eyes but this time they were tears of relief and not sadness. Happiness was just a breath away she thought and she longed for the days with Gordon to be nothing but a distant memory.

All statements were taken as Misty lay in the arms of Dominic. When she told the policewoman Gordon had raped her, Dominic had broke down and cried as he listened to the gruesome details. Finally the statement was taken and the only thing left was for Misty to go to the hospital to be checked over by the doctor. The police also needed a record from the hospital of Misty's injuries, so they could keep Gordon in custody and once they had proof he had also raped her they knew he would be in a prison for a long time the officer told them.

The shotgun was taken by the police and Misty had told them Gordon had brought it to the house to shoot her. There was no mention of any money, so Misty kept quiet about it. All she wanted to do now was to get in the bath and wash the scent of Gordon off her body. His smell on her body was making her sick and she needed to wash it away as soon as possible.

The next few days passed quickly and Misty started to feel herself once again. The police had been right. Gordon was to be kept in custody until his case came to court. He was to be charged with a string of other offences. Rape and firearms were carrying the biggest sentences and the police were hoping he would spend at least ten years in prison for his crimes.

Misty moved out of Rob's house and finally moved in with Dominic. He had promised never to let anyone hurt her ever again in his life and she could tell by his face he would be her knight in shining amour till the day she died.

Everything fitted together like a jigsaw when Misty and Dominic were living together and she loved her new life. Recently though, she had felt quite tired and blamed it on the incident with Gordon. The ugly truth only reared its head as she held her head down the toilet one Friday morning. She vomited like she had never before and thought she had eaten something that had disagreed with her. As she wiped her mouth she looked in the mirror and the truth hit her right in the face. She had only ever looked like this once before and that was many years ago when she had been pregnant. She would never forget how she looked back then as everyone had said she looked grey and as she looked into the mirror the colour grey was right before her eyes, like grey clouds had landed on her face.

Misty sat on the toilet and tried to remember her last period. She and Dominic had used protection so she knew there couldn't be a chance she was pregnant. Then like a firework exploding in her mind, she remembered the rape.

"Oh please no. Please, please don't let me be pregnant". Misty couldn't stand the not knowing and ran to the chemist. Dominic was at work already and she knew she wanted to be sure before she informed him of her news. Misty ran in the chemist like a stampeding bull. Once she had got the pregnancy test she ran straight back to the house and cried as she opened it. She read all the instructions and carried out the test correctly. The test would take three minutes to reveal the result and it felt more like three hours as Misty waited. Once the time was up she hesitated looking at the results. Misty prayed as she reached for it hoping it would be negative but her prayers were not answered as she stared at the test window. She grabbed the test and looked at it closer. Her heart stopped as she read the words for a third time and knew it was true.

"I can't cope with this", she screamed as her body curled on the bathroom floor. "Why me. I knew it was too fucking good to be true. Fancy me Misty Sullivan thinking I could be completely happy. What a fuckin' fool I am". She was in tears as she left the bathroom and started to pack her belongings. Dominic would not want her for sure now, knowing she was carrying Gordon's child.

Gordon had planted his seed inside her and somehow she knew he had had the last laugh as always. She cried as she opened the suitcase and started to fill it with her clothes. She had thought about having an abortion but her morals would never have allowed this and after all the baby inside her was still a part of her as well.

As she started to phone Dominic, the front door slammed shut. She stood to face her grinning fiancé.

"I've thrown a sickie today. I pretended I was ill but the truth of it was that I wanted to spend a day lay in bed with the woman of my dreams". Misty broke down in tears as she rushed to his side.

"Oh Dominic I love you so much but it can never be between us now. He's ruined everything just like he said he would". Dominic's face looked shocked as he tried to calm her down but her tears choked her every word and he was unable to understand what she was trying to say.

"Misty calm down. What the hell has happened please tell me". He looked round at the packed suitcases and knew it was something serious. His body felt weak at the thought of losing her yet again.

"I'm pregnant Dominic. I've taken the test and it's positive". At first he smiled and felt proud she was carrying his child but as he watched her face he knew there was something more. He now gripped her and held her close.

"It's not the end of the world Misty. I'm quite happy to be a father". As the words left his mouth he realised they had always used protection and he knew now he wasn't going to be a dad. Misty held him and tried to explain what had happened.

"It's the end of the world for us Dominic, because Gordon is the father. He raped me and that's the only time I could have got pregnant. I've gone over it a thousand times in my mind and I know he's the father. I love you so much Dominic but I know my only option is to leave. I would never ask you to bring up another man's child, it just wouldn't be fair".

Dominic felt like a hundred knives had been stabbed into his heart and he fell to the ground with his hands holding his head. He couldn't lose her all over again but what other choice did he have? He tried to get his head round it and find a solution. Misty came to where he was lay and cradled him in her arms and they both sobbed together. He had mentioned an abortion to her but knew that wasn't an option. Dominic searched deep into his heart. He knew it was a big decision but it was the only way he could see of keeping them together. He looked deep into her eyes as he knelt before her and with an open heart he began to speak.

"Misty, I'll bring up the baby as my own child. No one would ever know. I love you that much that I know I could do it. This child is a part of you and I know I would love it with all my heart". Misty looked at him and her love grew for him even more knowing he would do this for her.

"Don't be silly Dominic. How could I ever expect you to do that. To bring up another man's child. It just wouldn't be fair."

Dominic now spoke firmly as he tried to convince Misty that his plan would be work but they both had to make sure the truth never got out. He begged her to think about it and the more she thought about it the more she believed it could work. They spoke for hours going through every scenario that could happen and at the end of it they both agreed that Dominic would father Gordon's child and nobody would ever know the truth, not even their families.

CHAPTER SEVENTEEN

THE CHURCH WAS full as Misty Sullivan walked down the aisle at St Patrick's in Collyhurst. Max walked down the aisle, like a proud soldier as he delivered his sister to her awaiting husband. She looked truly amazing as she stood next to him. She could only be compared to a fairytale princess bride and he knew he was a lucky man to have the chance to have this woman as his wife.

Lisa cried tears of happiness as she watched them both promise to love each other forever more. She knew she wouldn't have to worry about her daughter again. Dominic was a man who would cherish her for the rest of her days and always make sure she was happy. As Misty spoke her vows, she looked directly into Dominic's eyes and meant every word she had spoken. Sue stood at the side of her and calmed her as she spoke. She was her bridesmaid and looked stunning. Sue had also been lucky in love, as John had proposed to her and they also had set a date for the following year. The vows were completed and the priest said the words Misty's had only dreamed about since she was a small child.

"I now pronounce you man and wife. You may now kiss the bride." Everybody cheered as Dominic softly kissed the love of his life. When he had finished he whispered into her ears.

"Love conquers all. No matter what we face, as long as we love each other everything will always be fine". She squeezed his body tightly as they left the church arm in arm and she knew he was right. Dominic was a very wise man and she loved him with all her heart and she knew whilst he was by her side nothing was impossible.

Months passed and Mr. and Mrs. Casey were the happiest couple alive. The baby inside her had started to show and everybody congratulated them on their news. Misty had told Dominic about the money she had stolen from Gordon and at the last count it amounted to twenty three thousand pounds. At first Misty had wanted to hand it in to the police but then she had a fantastic idea, that was supported by Dominic. All she needed now was the help of her best friend and a few hardworking men to make it work.

Misty had called Sue round and wanted to discuss her new idea with her. If this plan was to work, Misty thought, she would need Sue by her side, as she knew she would give heart and soul to it like she would. Misty watched her friend's face as she ran the idea by her and she could tell by her reaction that she would be one hundred percent on board.

Misty and Sue finally opened the refuge for women three months later and it was like a dream come true when they finally opened its doors. The money Gordon had stolen had gone towards helping women all round the city to get away from domestic violence and demanding husbands. Misty and Sue wanted to try and help them rebuild a new life. They helped young mums especially, as she knew exactly where they were coming from and knew how hard it was to make the choice to leave a violent partner.

Dominic was the one who had made all this possible, as he and his friends had spent many longs night trying to renovate the building they had bought. All in all there were ten family rooms inside the building and enough space to keep everyone happy. Misty and Sue went on quite a lot of college courses to help gain all the skills they needed to open the centre and within weeks of them opening they helped three women on the road to recovery to rebuild new lives without an abusive partner. The doors of the refuge were open to anyone and nobody would be turned away.

Misty was now eight months pregnant and was excited about the birth of her child. This was going to be her last night in the refuge, before she went off on maternity leave. Sue was constantly worrying about Misty throughout the pregnancy as she knew what had happened last time she was pregnant.

The late hours arrived in the refuge as both Misty and Sue sipped a hot cup of tea. They chatted about the girls they were helping and how they could improve in their support toward them. As they spoke, the sound of the front door knocking frantically broke their conversation. Misty tried to stand to attend to the door but due to her large lump fell back to her seat and Sue told her to remain sat, as she would go.

The sound of a woman in tears could be heard as Misty sat on her chair rubbing her belly and she knew it was a women who needed their help. As she stood up Sue was stood at the door facing her.

"Oh this ones in a bad way. She looks like death warmed up. We can put her in the side room till the morning and sort her out then". Misty placed her cup on the table and made her way to the reception room. As her eyes met the troubled women's face she felt faint. How could this be, she thought. It wasn't possible. Before she could speak Sue sat by the women and relayed her situation to Misty.

"This is Francesca and she is eight months pregnant. Her boyfriend has escaped from prison when he was making a court visit and has been making her life hell ever since. I've told her she is completely safe here and we will help her as much as we can wont we Misty?"

Misty and Francesca's eyes met and they both looked

shocked. Francesca's eyes focused on Misty stomach area as did Misty on hers and they both looked at each other wondering if what they thought in their heads were true. Misty left the room and held her body against the wall to steady herself. She felt sick, as she knew that Francesca was also carrying Gordon's child. The truth was Francesca was carrying the brother or sister of the child she carried inside her. Taking deep breaths she returned to the reception room and offered Francesca a cup of tea. As Francesca set eyes on her she stood and cried into her arms.

"Misty, I'm so sorry for all that happened. Can you ever forgive me for the way I treated you?" Sue looked at them both and wondered what on earth was going on, as she watched Francesca throw her arms round Misty's neck.

Misty had forgiven Francesca a long time ago and felt sorry for the choices her friend had made but the only thing that mattered now was keeping her safe and keeping her away from Gordon. They both had secrets that somehow joined them together once more. Misty knew if her own secret was ever to be uncovered her nightmare would begin all over again and she just hoped and prayed the truth would never come out.

Like the old saying goes, 'the past always comes back to haunt you' and as far as Misty was concerned she just hoped it wasn't true, because if Gordon ever found out she had his child, he would surely make her life hell once more.

THE END

THE SEQUEL

BLACK TEARS

WILL BE OUT SOON

FOR MORE DETAILS VISIT:
WWW.EMPIRE-UK.COM